October's Son

The London Vampire Diaries

John Michaelson

Burton Mayers Books

Copyright © 2009, 2014 John Michaelson

Content edited by Richard Mayers of Burton Mayers Books.

First published by Burton Mayers Books 2014. Revised
November 2014.   2

A CIP catalogue record for this book is available from the
British Library

ISBN-13: 978-0957338739

Typeset in Palatino Linotype

In memory of Michael.
I am ready.

CONTENTS

ACKNOWLEDGMENTS

I could not have got to where I am without the help of Michael. I hope that one day he will read this book and give it his nod of approval. He was both my deliverer and mentor, and at one point in my life I considered him a friend and father figure.

I also owe a great deal to some of my strongest supporters (those that remain) – the people who encouraged me to complete my work, or offered me the support to spread the message through print and electronic media. You know who you are.

I have no family members remaining that I know of to consecrate this book to, and there are no witty anecdotes to be shared about the moment I finished this manuscript and held a soiree in a graveyard to celebrate its completion.
My sincere thanks go Richard and John of Burton Mayers Books for their patience and maturity; Tamsin, Edwin, Anne and The Donor – you are also the resilient few…

"The great enemy of truth is very often not the lie--deliberate, contrived and dishonest--but the myth--persistent, persuasive and unrealistic. Too often we hold fast to the clichés of our forebears. We subject all facts to a prefabricated set of interpretations. We enjoy the comfort of opinion without the discomfort of thought."

John F Kennedy
[*Commencement Address at Yale University, June 11 1962*]

AUTHOR'S NOTE

This is not a book about vampires.

If you're after a novel where the infected sparkle in the sunlight, or where a character's sexual catharsis results in him or her biting someone in the neck, then please return this book and search for a title from the young adult section instead; if you don't know what they look like, they usually have lots of black on the front covers, some red writing and a one word title like 'Yearning' or something else irritatingly pubescent.

If you've done your research properly, then you'll have already figured it out: the whole vampirism thing is just a fad, a dangerous myth disguised as the truth. Vampirism has lost its intended malice. The moralistic intentions of ancient tribal leaders, to prohibit breeding between different nations and races, have failed. Vampirism became diluted as the world strived for multiculturalism and moved forward, with the internet spawning several 'vamp' subcultures in today's global village. Vampirism has become engrained in popular culture, personified through Goths, Emos and fans of the Twighlight saga to name but a few.

This book does not talk in detail about Slavic folklore, endogenous viruses, occult rituals and Norse gods, nor does it feature a highly sexualized, yet flawed, anti-hero trying to find his place in society (you may disagree).

There is another thing you should know: I did not want to write this book. Admittedly, and ashamedly so, I tried a few years ago after the events originally occurred and were fresh in my mind. I rushed when I should have taken my time. I approached one of the few online friends I had at the period, consulting him on the best way to get published. He said I should present my journey as a story, a hyperbolic third person account aimed at the mainstream, so that when people read it they would see that it was not like other vampire novels and a mass audience comparable to that of The Vampire Diaries would follow, all of them wearing 'Team John' t-shirts as I soldiered on with my battle against the Ants. And so I did. But I soon found myself going heavy with the superlatives and trying to build tension when there was none; it had no happy climax, and there was no long-lasting love interest (will they, won't they?), and so on . . . even I began to question what I wrote. I couldn't do it, so I gave up. I recognized that what I was doing was disguising the plain reality, that life was pretty awful, and all because of a dangerous group, an organization that is hard to define and even harder to expose.

I should have stopped there, but instead I turned my attention and efforts to social media in an attempt to 'connect' with people to warn them about the dangers within London's boundaries. But I was laughed at, scorned for going against such popularised ideas, and ridiculed by trolls because my evidence was flimsy. And because I didn't have enough hard proof to go in tough, or the learned understanding to make a serious stand, I backed off, which is exactly what they must have known would happen. You must also bear in mind, reader, that these series of unfortunate events occurred at a time when the West's obsession with the vampire sub-genre was at its peak; slick vampire films and TV series such as True Blood were lucrative and hugely popular, pulling in mass audiences worldwide.

I was a nobody, trying to subvert a fetish that audiences enjoyed. And what I'd written was another pitiful excuse for modern vampirism, adding to the hyper-reality of the vampire phenomenon. I was heading down the same sodden path as vampire slaying bishops and occultist sleuths who manifested themselves online, proclaiming an unseen war and recruiting non-believers to support their cause (donate now) or stay tuned for more BS. And in today's consumerist realm, a video of a child unwrapping a Kinder egg would get more views in an hour than I could hope for in a single month. And as for the website, I might as well have filled it with found images of stereotypical vampires, scantily clad women with fangs, upside down crosses, some blood, the names of overlords and ancient tribes with badly translated Latin mottos, yada yada, you've seen this all before, right? At times it felt like I was obsessing with science fiction rather than science fact, competing to get my name up the search rankings before I came up with anything credible, something real to pacify the impatient: What are vampires? Are vampires real? Do you drink blood?

Eventually I realised that the whole online movement seemed pointless. It was nothing but a distraction. And so I stopped, and focused on doing what I should have been doing all along - going deeper underground, trying to explain my condition and understand my predicament through first-hand knowledge: researching, reading, and remembering all the details, piecing the clues together from my encounters.

Two years later, by which time I was starting to make breakthroughs, a different acquaintance – one whom I had met along my journey - suggested that I should expand upon what I talked about on my website and recount the experience in the style of a journal. It made total sense, given I was taking most of my inspiration from first hand texts written by people like me, and so I have endeavoured to take her advice on board. But my real inspiration comes from Michael who, until his departure, gave me all the real-life accounts, debate and knowledge I needed to warn people about the extent of London's plight.

I have reflected intently on events and written down my thoughts about my experience leading up to and after the disruption in my life; ironically, I have tried to describe the experiences the best I can – through narrative. I do not mean to sound melodramatic, and I am no Bram Stoker; this book is not be peppered with telegrams or elaborate weather reports, although I may pay homage where it is due. I do not have a science degree and this book is intended for a lay audience. October's Son is my story and as much for me as it is for anyone who wants to learn about the organizations behind the façade of vampirism. The characters described in this book all played their part in my creation; locations, establishments and events are also real but, for legal reasons, my publishers have asked me to concede and allow for certain details to be edited.

And so, reader, do not see this as just another book about vampires, but as a guide about how you can protect yourself. This book should be used as a reference point, as insight into the life of an ordinary Londoner who became transformed by a prevalent yet unseen evil.

To you, dear reader, I reveal the truth.

I am October's Son.

NOVEMBER

I left my flat earlier than usual so that I could arrive in good time on my first day back at work. But as I crawled to a halt along Holloway Road, one of the main routes pumping life into the heart of London, and saw people loitering about on street corners, sheltering in bus stops, and opening up grocery stores – I knew that it wasn't just me that never slept.

I'd hoped to be the first to arrive at the agency so that I could settle my nerves, but Julian was already there. He was wearing a crisp Thomas Pink shirt, tailored fit of course, and looked up at me from his desk at the back of the office. He was quick to rise and greet me as I walked in.

'How are you, John?' he said, trying to sound genuine as he offered me his hand. I forgot all the golden rules of sales as I held it limply. Julian was irritatingly handsome and his thick curls were sheened with hair product. The smell was nauseating.

'It's weird to be back so soon,' I explained.

'It's fucking good to have you back,' he bellowed, patting me across my arms and shoulders energetically, but already I could sense that it was bullshit, that he was assessing my strength, to see if I was fit for work. I stared into those charming brown eyes of his and understood that any special treatment I was to receive would be short lived.

'Thanks,' I murmured. 'I didn't think anyone would be in so early.'

'I wanted to be here when you arrived,' he said, checking out the scar on my neck, that and weighing up my choice of shirt and tie; pastel colours did little to disguise my blotchy complexion.

'So where's my cup of tea and a kiss?' I remarked.

He slapped me firmly across the arm again. 'C'mon, let's nip to the cafe.'

Julian disappeared down the stairs to adorn himself with his cashmere scarf. As he did so, I checked out the desks and could see that some new people had started in my absence. I also noticed that someone had attempted to organise my desk. Some of the window displays had remained unchanged, still falsely advertising swanky Docklands apartments at a rate £100 below their actual weekly rental. But the strangest thing about being at work so early was seeing a single stream of sunlight fill the office; during normal working hours the office was overshadowed by a converted bank-come-apartment block and the only light came from harsh downlights. I took it as a sign that the outlook for my working life was good. Julian returned, jangling his prized car keys, and the sun seemed to disappear.

The café had the familiar urban stench of stale chip fat and fried bacon. I recognised the sounds of anaemic pork sizzling and coffee machines hissing whilst some heavy handed barista hammered out the old grind. The idea of eating a hearty breakfast initially seemed good at the time but when it came out it was swimming in oil, which infused everything on the plate with its stale aroma. It tasted bloody awful; a sloppy and bland mess. I was conscious that with each mouthful I forced down, my freshly pressed suit would soon reek of the same odour. But because Julian wouldn't stop talking, I didn't have time to listen to my taste buds complaining.

He was keen to tell me that he'd hired a new girl in response to Ed and myself being signed off for at least six weeks (I had only taken seven). Her name was Martina; she was Polish and was apparently very good at her job. More competition, he joked, to help us work harder and to meet our targets. Oh yeah, Julian was full of shit most of the time – it was all about the money.

Sipping on the dregs of warm coffee, we talked

about Ed. Apparently he was doing well but needed an extra couple of weeks in hospital due to complications, some sort of blood infection, and Julian had even mentioned that he had visited him. I found it funny how the South London crowd stuck together.

Towards the end of breakfast, Julian was fully operating in work mode and had briefed me on all the new flats he'd added to the books. He also disclosed that he would go easy on me that month in terms of hitting commission targets. I nodded without really considering his words, knowing full well I would have to sit through the same guff in our morning briefing with the rest of the team. I wish I'd stopped for coffee on my journey down. As he rambled on, my senses kept honing in on the obscure - like when all I could do was focus in on the sound of an offensive ringtone, or listen to a car radio blaring out grime music, or the bubbly thirty-something diner who started recounting the details of her one night stand to her best mate over a frothy latte; he made her cum twice.

'Did you drive in?'

'Yes.'

'Where did you park?'

I made a gesture with my thumb pointing up towards Aldgate and explained to him that returning back to the car park, where it all happened, was not the best way to start the day.

Julian noted my unease. So, to brighten up my morning, he revealed his master plan: I would spend the morning in the office with him while the other negotiators went on appointments, and then in the afternoon I was to visit some of the new flats that were being refurbished in Canary Wharf; Jackie, one of the company's most valued landlords, was going to be there and wanted some rental valuations, and since she liked me (even though we'd never physically met in person) Julian thought that I should turn up and show her that I was back, and to reassure her that we were still the best estate agents in East London.

Back at the office, I gazed out through the window and caught a glimpse of London waking up. I took comfort from seeing the cars grind to a standstill and noting the stern faces of workers striking a path across the cold pavement.

On my desk was an envelope. I opened it. Inside was one of those nostalgic, humorous cards that were popular at the end of the nineties. Inside, the message read 'Welcome Back' and was signed by everyone in the office, even Martina who I'd never even met before. As I tried to find somewhere other than the bin to place the card, Grace walked in through the door. I remember her running over to me, the sound of her delicate heels tapping against the cheap laminate. She was full of warmth and sincerity, something my girlfriend deprived me of. Grace had the soul of a ten year old trapped inside the body of a starved woman. She gave me one of those awkward hugs you get from people you really want to embrace but can't -

our shoulders kind of rubbed gently together – then she sat beside me and we chatted briefly. As she spoke in her delicate Irish accent, I wanted to grab her cheeks and rub the colour back into them - that and maybe more.

The rest of the morning went very quickly. The staff briefing was extended to welcome me back and I was formerly introduced to Martina, a cold looking woman with large breasts (Julian's prompt) and mousy brown hair; she was sat at the desk in front of me and I noted her technical efficiency as she answered each call by the second ring.

The reality of office confinement assured me that life was getting back to normal. I found myself switching between emails and phone calls, all the time monitored by Julian who sat clandestinely at his desk guarding the water filter; when I went to drink he would grin at me, reassuring me that I was safe in his pack and that he would be looking out for me.

I took an early lunch and walked towards Wapping, an area I liked to frequent. I found a spot near the harbour at St Katherine's Dock where I could sit, unseen, and admire the splendid views of powerful yachts and ogle at the hordes of well-dressed office workers as they marched to and fro. For me this was the best part of the job: time alone. I felt normal just being able to watch the suits and skirts clapping along the boardwalk whilst enjoying the midday sun, a rarity for the middle of

November.   The skeletal arms of trees stretched high into the sky, their shadows thrashing across people like whips. There was no such thing as stoppage time in the city.   Time was money.   I could already hear Julian in the back of my mind telling me to do some deals. I began to feel clammy and feverish, so I headed back to my car to begin the drive towards the Isle of Dogs.

It was a soothing drive - therapeutic one could say - because I was driving away from the city. There was also a lack of traffic at that point in the day and I was able to appreciate some of London's finest modern, restorative architecture alongside the Thames.   In particular, I enjoyed driving through the tunnels, listening to the roar of the engine in fourth gear, echoing in the darkness – my senses quickened.

Great Providence Wharf was a collection of swish new apartments, like so many others that had cleansed what was once a deserted brown-field site. The concierge signed me in and I took the lift. I quickly checked out the particulars of the properties I had come to scrutnise; many of the rooms looked boxy and enclosed, but others had access to patios, balconies, and even horizon pools if you were overpaid enough to afford the penthouse.   All flats promised a glimpse of the river.

Jackie and I had built up a good rapport over the phone in previous months. She was different from how I imagined her when she opened the door and welcomed me in. Instead of a mumsy looking busybody, who often sounded flustered when I spoke to her on the phone, I was greeted by a tall, well-dressed woman who looked as though she enjoyed money. Her husband worked for the site's developers and they had obviously been given first pick when it came to buying flats off plan, of which they had several. She led me out to the main balcony of her largest apartment, which enjoyed a southern aspect and panoramic view of the river as it wound round the Millennium Dome (O2 arena) opposite. The dome itself was, in my opinion, a monstrosity that blighted the landscape - a place where thousands nested together for one piteous night where the end of the world sadly never happened.

As I paced methodically through each flat, inspecting the ubiquitous granite work surface, real wood quadrants and bespoke limestone shower basins by Stonevale - not forgetting the walnut veneer sliding wardrobes by Frances Hunt – and laughed at all of Jackie's jokes, I had an epiphany: it didn't impress me anymore.

'How does it feel being back at work?' she asked.

'So-so,' I said.

'And how's Ed?' Ed was her real favourite.

'I think he's at home resting.' I lied, checking my watch. 'We were in different wards so I didn't get to see him much.'

The conversation dried up as quickly as her

lipstick. We talked rental figures on the terrace, or rather she told me what she wanted them marketed at. The weather changed. Cold wind grew in strength and forced us both inside. I exchanged pleasantries with Jackie and left the complex with her business card and a headache. Within an hour the glaring sun had been overcome by black clouds which spread across the sky like giant ink blots.

As I drove back towards the office, I thought about Ed. I felt bad for not ringing him. Even Claudia (my girlfriend) told me that I was strange for not wanting to speak to him after what we'd been through together.

When I emerged from the Limehouse tunnel heading westward, the rain was falling heavily.

The traffic lights near my office seemed to be permanently stuck on red. I waited uneasily. To my right, one of the rival estate agents looked busy. I could see negotiators smiling and laughing – business was obviously good. Next to them was a decrepit café called 'Hollywood', not very apt for an E1 postcode. And to my left I could see the start of the DLR railway curving reflexively towards Tower Gateway. Beneath it was the entrance to the car park, its plywood gates and pebble-dashed cabin erected around it like the start of some East London shanty town.

My eyes were transfixed on the entrance. I gazed deeper into the dark pits of the railway arches. My heart was beating so fast as snippets of that evening came thundering back into my mind.

All I could think about was those pale orange eyes.

An irate driver began thrashing his horn behind me. I remember snapping back into consciousness just as the lights were turning back to red again. I pushed my foot down and the car shot forward.

I pulled up on a street near the office and tried to control my breathing. Beads of sweat had already gathered at the base of my spine and my throat began to ache again, as though someone else had taken another slice at it. I loosened my tie and undid the top button.

Back in the workplace I grew even more agitated. The other negotiators were all out on viewings. It was just me and Julian left in the office, and all he could do was comment that I looked like shit under the fluorescent lights. Daylight had all but vanished as the dreary November darkness took hold.

A pair of young city workers, fresh from their daily grind and probably enrolled on some undergraduate programme, walked in off the street and enquired about a flat we had in the window. I sat them down and, after explaining that it had just gone recently (several months ago), I tried to take their details, recommend some alternatives (more expensive) and deliver the company sales pitch about why they should rent through us.

I was 'piss poor' Julian told me afterwards, and I couldn't agree more. After all, I ended up recommending that they choose a safer part of London to live in on a budget that they could afford, both of them things we couldn't offer. It was agreed by Julian that I should finish early to 'sort my shit out'.

Before I knew it I was back in my car queuing northbound on Commercial Street at the worst possible time of the day. Julian hadn't really done me a favour at all, all he'd done was make me think more about the accident and the shitty predicament my life was in.

As the traffic finally thinned out, the optimist in me saw it as a turning point, a time to rethink my future career prospects and perhaps move on.

HOME TRUTHS

Back then I lived in Finchley, North London, with my partner, Claudia. She had found the past several weeks hell. Our relationship was already strained before the attack. If anything, the incident gave us the much needed break we both sought, however, rather than her be seen as the bitch she was and leave me to suffer in hospital, she demonstrated rare maternal visits to my ward. I had hoped that the event might have made us stronger, allowed us to wipe the slate clean so that we could move on, but we both found it hard to forget the stage our relationship had reached before.

Claudia never liked my job; she said it had changed me and that I had lost my way, neglecting my dream of becoming some hotshot city economist. I had wooed her with my big career ambitions, she had said. Instead I left university with a Desmond and - like so many other graduates - was unable to find a job in my desired field. So I answered the call of the Guardian's back pages where so many adverts promised high earning potential and a 'fun working environment' within London's booming property market. I was sold - anything had to be better than media sales. However, it was at the cost of our relationship, and our sex life had hit several partition walls. I remember promising her that estate agency was a job with long term rewards, that it might lead to a house and the chance to property develop, but this did little to comfort her, especially when I would answer her calls to my mobile with the company salutation rather than 'Hi love'.

Claudia looked surprised when I arrived back an hour earlier than expected – but not in an overjoyed way. Her hair was pulled tightly into a bun enhancing her high cheek bones and delicate ears that seemed to fold into her long neck. She gave me a kiss on the cheek and said that she'd start preparing dinner. I thanked her and went into the study.

The computer was already on. Part of my browsing routine was to check the BBC news website. What Claudia didn't realise was that I always liked to check her browsing history - it usually gave me an indication of what type of mood she was in. However, Claudia had become quite tech savvy herself when she saw me deleting my browser history after an online porn session in the early days of our relationship. Today, however, she had been sloppy. Her Messenger window was still active and flashing at me. I read it:

Are you still there?

Normally I wouldn't have done anything, but I didn't recognise the name Blue_eyes

I typed: **Yeah, had to answer the door.**

There was a break in the message. Blue_eyes is typing...

Be good to see you again.

This is probably where I should have owned up and confessed that I wasn't Claudia.

Yeah, that would be good. Any preference?

I was expecting a reply about a bar or restaurant. All the while I could hear Claudia banging saucepans and plates together and fumbling with the grill pan.

My place ;) x

Let's just say that at this point I went a bit light headed and felt very stupid for opening a tin of unpleasant worms. I quickly logged Claudia off, closed the browsing window and moved myself into the living room where I sat down and turned on the TV. As I searched the news channels I tried to place a face to who Blue_eyes could be.

Claudia came to the doorway and checked on me a few minutes later. I could sense her glancing in at me and checking the screen on the computer in the adjacent study.

'Sorry, I logged you off,' I confessed. 'I can't stand that thing flashing at me all the time.'

'Okay,' she replied. 'Dinner's going to be about ten minutes. Where do you want to eat?'

'I'll come through to the kitchen when I'm ready.' I half smiled as I said it, and looking into her eyes I knew that she had been cheating on me. She walked off towards the kitchen.

I felt numb. I had been half expecting it, but just not so soon.

I tried to focus on the news headlines: Imminent Tube Strike, London MP Forced to Resign, and Fire at a Camden Sauna Kills Four.

Claudia had prepared a squid and chorizo salad for us both. The squid was perfectly griddled and professionally presented with rich, oily strips of Spanish sausage, and a fresh rocket salad held together with a sticky balsamic glaze. She poured a glass of chilled Chenin Blanc for us both, and a warm loaf of ciabatta rested on the table between us like a wooden club. I loved her food more than anything else, and I knew that I would miss that the most.

'So how was your first day back?' she asked.

'Oh, you know, a bit strange . . .' I'd forgotten all about it until she asked. I realised it was polite small talk as she looked through me, and I through her; we had been together two years and this was the height of our intellectual conversation.

'Have you had a good day?' I asked.

I watched her delicately pierce the tentacles with her fork and marry it with some Romano pepper before bringing it up to her lips. I sat and listened to her chomp the leaves and breathe through her nose, heightened by the awkward silence.

'Yeah, busy - same as always,' she said.

I took a sip of wine and ate some of the chorizo.

'Busy with blue eyes?'

She didn't say anything at first, just finished another mouthful of food whilst staring down at the table. Her hand rested on the base of the wine glass.

I started to make things up. 'He told me everything, thinking I was you. What he wants to do to you, when he wants to see you again. I guess it was quite nice, me being in hospital.'

Claudia threw her wine in my face and burst into tears. 'How dare you!' she screamed. I remember watching her shake. 'It's been going on longer than that,' she narrated in mild hysterics.

I sat there and listened, chilled wine soaking into my shirt. I felt humiliated that she had cheated on me yet smug at the same time for catching her at it. I composed myself, trying to pretend I wasn't bothered that she'd wasted a good glass of wine on me as she blabbered on about how hard life had been, but I had already figured it all out.

'I reckon this began last May, on your weekend away with Mary,' I interjected.

She looked at me for a moment and nodded, taken aback by my perception, surprised at how well I really knew her.

'It's your job,' she began. 'I hate it. I hardly see you – you leave early and arrive back home late.

And when we get together all you want to do is sleep.'

This wasn't totally true, I liked to watch TV and go to the cinema occasionally. Recently, however, I hadn't slept well at all and this had had a knock on effect with her. I tried to think of a comeback, but I decided there was no point. Our relationship was over and I'd known it for months, yet like many other things, I'd just plodded along with life in the hope that things would improve. Like the scar tissue around my neck, I knew it would eventually heal and that you wouldn't see it, but it would always be there; the real dangers lie under the surface, the things you can't see.

The confession had been short and bittersweet. I didn't say anything else because my food was getting cold, and so I began eating again and ignored her. Claudia stormed out of the room crying, complaining that I was shirking all the blame on her, that I was too proud, selfish and responsible for all the evils in the world. After a few minutes, I finished my food and went into the living room to watch some more TV. I could hear her rummaging around in her room for some belongings. I knew that she would leave me that night and I didn't try and stop her.

I saw that night as an early release from a long and painful prison sentence and felt mildly euphoric as I heard her walk down the stairs carrying a small case. Claudia left the house without saying another word to me.

I watched awful reality TV for the remainder of the night in the hope that it would send me to sleep, but it never came. And when I retired to the bedroom in the early hours, I found it harder to relax and let myself drift off. My body was so hot, but the sweat didn't want to leave my body, it just clung to my skin, slowly suffocating me. I tried opening the windows to let some brisk autumn air in, but it did little to help. The room was stifling and I could smell the dust from the radiator.

I listened to the sounds of night-time suburban London: someone loading mugs into a kitchen cupboard, a heavy footed man strolling down the street with his dog; a tenant from across the road lighting up a cigarette outside his front door. I could practically hear people breathing. And all the while my limbs burned and my head throbbed.

Claudia's scent still lingered on the pillows. All of her make-up and toiletries pervaded the bedroom and bathroom, especially dirty cotton wool pads she'd flung aside after removing her heavy eye make-up. I thought about tidying up to fight the insomnia, but the prospect of catching up on some DVDs seemed the best way to ease my frustration.

I was a bachelor once more it seemed.

REBIRTH

For the next few days I continued to arrive at work early. And each day, Julian would already be in. One morning I decided to take a slower route which added over twenty minutes to my journey, purely because I felt like a change from the mundane. Stepping through the door I was surprised not only to see Julian again, but Ed also.

Ed was about my age (late twenties at the time) with thick curly blonde hair that he managed to stick neatly to his scalp with some kind of styling wax. His skin was adolescent in its appearance; it would often be blotchy and there would be several shaving nicks and razor burn across his cheeks. That said, he carried himself well with thick, stocky shoulders and a smooth, silky voice that could charm holding deposits out of most of the clients he took on viewings - and the women seemed to love him. Julian described him openly as 'hot shit'.

We weren't best friends or anything but we'd been through a lot together.

'Ed,' I remarked, 'you're back earlier than I thought.'

'Yeah, the doctors signed me off early for good behaviour. How are you?'

I sensed him checking me over and staring at my neck. I told him I was fine, flashing a look at Julian. I could tell that Julian hadn't finished telling Ed the good news about a new two bedroomed apartment they'd taken on in the Aldgate triangle. 'We'll catch up at lunch,' I said.

I veered towards my desk, baffled at his return; Ed had been stabbed near-fatally in the chest and his injuries were much more severe than mine, and whilst I was pleased to see him back at work and looking so well, I couldn't understand how he had recovered so quickly; a few blemishes aside, he looked fresher than I did and was full of life.

Gary, another male lettings negotiator, came in through the door a few minutes later and staged a cheer, saying that 'the dream team' were back. I watched the three of them metaphorically suck each other's dicks whilst I thought about how I was going to quit my job.

My morning was awful. The phone would ring, and every time it did I was too slow to answer. Ed, Martina or Grace got there first; Gary was too hung over to even notice. By 11am the office was empty, everyone was out on a viewing except me. I had one appointment booked in for 4pm, some banker keen to look at an apartment above a sandwich shop. It was a long shot, but I had to book something in to avoid Julian's scornful looks.

'I've just forwarded you a good lead,' he would say as my inbox pinged.

'Thanks,' I would reply before reading the email and deleting it. Sometimes they were genuinely good, but most of the time it was Julian resending an old email from someone who enquired weeks before, and when I'd ring I would get some irate client telling me to take them off their database (which we never did) because they had found somewhere.

Ed didn't make it back for lunch, he had too many viewings booked in and had already taken a deposit on a flat at the Aldgate Triangle. I lingered in the office, praying for some walk-in trade to arrive. An insurance worker from the offices across the road came in and made some enquiries. All through my pitch, I was conscious of two things: the man looking at my mangled neck, and Julian listening to every word I said. The man thanked me and took my business card. Before Julian could give me feedback on my presentation skills, I took my lunch break at the kebab shop a few doors down.

The food was awful, so many spices and bone were ground into the kebab meat that I couldn't tell if I was eating lamb or beef, and the chilli sauce was sugary and congealed. My body craved something more satisfying. I washed it down with some fizzy orange and left feeling angry.

I kept thinking about Ed. It didn't make sense that he could be back at work so soon, although I wasn't one to talk - I was back a week earlier than I should've been. There were obviously some discrepancies about the extent of his injuries that I didn't know about. But I remember being there, seeing his body chill in a pool of his own blood whilst something lapped at the wound in his chest. The image made me shiver and I felt like I could vomit up my lunch at any minute, which probably wouldn't have been a bad thing.

I remember loitering outside the agency to try and cool myself down. I checked my mobile, just in case I had any important messages, or a text from Claudia saying 'sorry for being a bitch'. Looking at the window display, I contemplated where I would rent. There was no way I could afford to rent my current flat on my own, and that would mean having to ring my dad and ask for a favour, something I hated doing.

I went back inside for some more phone watching. Julian announced to the office that Ed had taken another holding deposit for the flat above the sandwich shop, which pretty much shafted my afternoon.

Later, when Ed arrived back at the office, I made some half-hearted small talk with him. 'Straight back in then?'

'Yeah, got my rent to pay and women to please,' he said cheerfully.

I laughed a little to massage his ego. 'Listen, I really need to talk about what happened that night.'

Ed shot me an icy look. 'Now's not a good time.'

I gave an uneasy nod and decided not to ask why. I checked my diary instead, and sighed when I saw that my appointments for the next morning had all been cancelled by Julian because my clients had found something already.

I left work that evening without success, and without answers.

That night I lay in bed unable to sleep. Bizarrely, I felt more awake than ever. My body was an incinerator producing endless amounts of energy and adrenaline; my heart beat didn't drop below 80 bpm, even lying down, and I was feverish. I was convinced that I had somehow become infected, that I had picked up a virus from hospital, one of those superbugs that remains dormant and then eats your flesh from within, or a type of blood infection. My mind was also over-active. Truth be told, I was pissed off with Ed and the way that he had reacted to me. Maybe he was angry that I wanted to remember - it wasn't like I was asking him to recount a fun holiday experience – after all, this was a near death experience, one which didn't involve white tunnels, only blackness. I decided that I should start the next day with an apology and place the ball firmly in his court. For my sanity, I just needed to know what he remembered

after the attack, because those bright orange eyes
had haunted me ever since.

ORANGE EYES

Every last Friday of the month, Julian would take the whole office out for a staff social. Most of the time we'd all have hit or exceeded our sales targets and drinks would be on him for the majority of the night.

It was just after 10pm when Ed and I left The Brown Bear, the favourite watering hole of our agency. Our cars were parked in the car park beneath the DLR track opposite the pub. Up to a certain point in the day it was patrolled, but by 8pm the car park was pretty much deserted. You had to move your car onto the street by midnight, otherwise you risked vandalism from kids; I'd seen them make light work of a £20,000 BMW once.

The night sky was overcast and there was a fine mist in the air. We were both probably over the limit at this point, and a little clumsy. The lighting wasn't great in the car park, just some large striplights beneath the deep arches. We walked in darkness until we could see our cars, and that's when I noticed a figure leaning against my vehicle.

Full of Dutch courage, I diplomatically shouted, 'Hey, that's my car!'

'Da fuck you say to me, man?' the figure replied. His voice was coarse, with a thick East London accent. He was young, possibly black or Asian; it was hard to tell exactly. I approached more cautiously and was about to explain my point when something solid struck against the back of my head and my legs gave way. I crashed to the ground, rolling myself in a batter of mud, stones and building sand. I looked up to see Ed getting the same treatment, and that was when I saw the other man who was holding a metal scaffold bar. Ed didn't crumple straight away and tried to parry some of the blows, but it didn't take long for one of the men to connect a fist cleanly with Ed's jaw, the sound echoing in the archway. I tried to scramble to my feet but felt myself being pulled up by the neck and pressed against the wall. I cursed myself for not moving my car earlier.

'I don't want any trouble,' I murmured. A thick black hand slapped me across the face, once . . . twice . . . and then grabbed my lower jaw and shook my head.

'Fuck you, white boy. I'm gonna teach you some manners, gonna cut your fuckin' face up.'

'Shank that bitch!' goaded the other man.

Ed was on his knees, looking for his car keys.

The other guy, an Asian man wearing a white baseball cap and a thick silver chain, ran over to him, snatched the keys out from his hand and kicked him cleanly in the chest.

Ed should've remained on the ground and given up, succumbed to the fact that his new Volkswagen Golf was two hours away from being a write off in Canning Town, but he didn't. He couldn't.

'Give me back my keys!' Ed protested.

'Tell that prick to pipe down or I'll cut his boyfriend's throat,' the man spat. It was only when he said these words that I noticed something cold and sharp was being pushed against my jugular. I was wide eyed. I could already feel a trickle of hot blood spilling down my neck from where he had nicked me. I looked into the man's eyes to plead with him, to search for an ounce of humanity, but this guy was either high on crack or adrenaline, and way past the negotiating stage.

'Just leave it Ed, you're insured!' I cried.

The men laughed. 'Yeah, Ed, listen to city boy here.'

But Ed did not listen. He lunged for the guy closest to him. And he did well, too, managing to push him to the ground and land a punch on the mugger's face. I should have seen this as an opportunity to fight back, and in hindsight I blame myself for the outcome of that night because of my slow reactions.

The man - who held me by the neck - looked me dead in the eyes with pure hatred and forcefully pushed the knife deep into my throat. I could feel the metal tearing through my flesh, the blade snagging on sinew and cartilage as he did so. I held his arm as I choked on my own blood, and whilst I did so I could feel the spittle from his lips spray on my face as he coolly called me a 'prick'. Falling in slow motion (this is all I can recall), hot blood spurted over my hands as I brought them to my neck to try and stem the blood flow. There was no pain at this point, even when I hit the ground, just a burning sensation, wild panic and the fear of knowing that my life-force was spilling everywhere onto compacted earth. I rolled over on to my back and tried to compress the bleeding. I saw Ed being pulled up and thrown against the car. Within a heartbeat the same man stabbed him twice in the chest and let Ed fall to the ground in a torrid heap.

The blood felt like it was thickening in my mouth, clotting as I tried to breathe air into my lungs. The two men started arguing about why he had 'shanked him' so hard, and at one point I thought they were going to turn on each other. But as they started Ed's car and wound the windows down, I could hear them both laughing.

They drove off, wheel spinning a cloud of dirt and debris in our direction.

I could see Ed's breath, faintly against the brake lights, and I knew that he was still alive, just. By this point I was stone cold, trembling and losing all strength of my limbs. I managed to roll onto my side so that I wouldn't choke to death, and watched

Ed's chest rising slower and slower with each breath.

'Stay with me Ed,' I rasped. Feeling for my phone, I was surprised that they hadn't stolen my possessions. Had things not panned out the way they did, with Ed trying to fight them, I'm sure they would have stripped us bare which might have been their original intention.

I dialed 999 and put the phone on speaker. A lady answered and asked me which service I required. I managed to mutter the words 'ambulance' and 'Royal Mint Street' - there might have been more conversation but I can't remember. As my body continued to chill, I found myself thinking about Claudia, my old uni friends, and times spent with my Dad as a child.

My eyes fixed on a small sodium lamp in the adjacent street as the noise of the city seemed to phase out into a hum like seashells had been pressed against my ears. But there was something else, something lurking in the darkness. That's when I knew that we were not alone, that something was watching us. I managed to rock my head to the side again and could see two small lights, no bigger than the reflectors on the pedal of a cycle, shimmering under the railway arches. But they were moving, swaying cautiously towards us.

These are the moments that continue to haunt me the most. Even as I write this, my hands are shaking and my heart beats painfully in my chest. The lights were not discs but eyes, bold menacing eyes glaring at me from the shadows. The creature approached, limbs caked in matted fur. At first I thought it was a fox, but this fiend seemed bigger, bolder and more menacing. It pitched from archway to archway, perfectly silhouetted. There was no other defining detail other than the eyes which burned and kept looking over at me. I could sense that it was wild, the size of a lurcher perhaps, with a heavy looking head. I attempted to make a shooing sound but it came out as a gargle - blood sprayed out of my mouth. Whatever it was, it seemed to be attracted to the blood.

Ed's body was closest. I watched as it began lapping the blood from his chest. Fox or dog, nothing should have behaved like this. I watched Ed flap his limbs briefly as if to fend the animal off, but all this did was cause the beast to growl deeply and nuzzle harder into the wound. My hand gripped a pile of stones and I tossed them in its direction. The beast stopped feeding and looked over at me, which was when I first noticed how disproportionate its head was to the body. It swaggered slowly over to where I lay, its eyes burning embers, and before I knew it the being was upon me, slopping, licking and then snapping at my neck. I could smell it, like putrid flesh amidst the stench of engine oil and damp earth, and I could hear its jaw bones clapping together as it snuffled and slavered frantically at my wound.

Like so many other nights, I woke from this nightmare with a shortness of breath and a rock hard feeling in my chest. My sheets were soaked through and the veins in my neck pounded violently. My mouth was bone dry and I could feel thick, gritty mucus clinging to my tonsils.

I rushed to the bathroom and switched on the light. The skin around my neck felt like it was on fire, and on closer examination in the mirror I could see that it was red and swollen. I wanted to scratch hard, claw wildly down to raw flesh in the hope that the scar would look neater, tidier than the strips of sinew it was, and cover up the tell-tale signs of stitches. I splashed cold water on my face and went into the kitchen.

The kitchen lights off, I stared out of the window. The only light source I could see was from the streetlamps along the main road. It wasn't much, but enough for me to see the rats run along the roof of a neighbour's chicken coop. I could just about make out a very faint reflection of myself in the glass, small amber embers for eyes and orange absorbing into the sweat and grease of my face. I remember feeling so tired at this point, the muscles in my eye lids were spasming, and my fucking war wound looked as fresh as ever - it always seemed worse at night.

I had made a point of this at the hospital, but the response was always the same: there was no medical evidence, in their opinion, to suggest that my knife wounds were aggravated further by an animal. On paper I had been stabbed badly with a three inch hunting blade which accounted for the tears in the muscle, the serrated edge helping to that effect. I had to resign myself to believing that there was no beast.

The counsellor added to my woes, and told me that this recurring dream was significant but was heightened by deep rooted anxiety; an episode of post-traumatic stress syndrome was not uncommon about a month after a patient's initial experience, and he told me that remission was most common amongst victims of knife crime. The image of a dog or fox was my mind's way of trying to make sense of moments where I lapsed in and out of consciousness.

That was the medical explanation given to me, but now I know this to be wrong.

Something preyed on us as we lay dying: fact.

DIAGNOSIS

I rang Julian the next morning and explained to him that I needed to see a doctor urgently. I remember the pregnant pause at the end of the line, and perhaps a little sigh; I imagined him swiveling in his chair, staring at the keys to his Porsche. He said he hoped the doctor could make me feel better, and then asked me to be in by lunch to commit to the viewings I had booked in for the day. I reluctantly agreed, but it did confirm all my suspicions about Julian being a cunt.

Looking at my scar from a good three feet away, and remaining seated, the doctor glanced at my notes on the screen in front of her before reaching for her GPs encyclopedia – the equivalent to a Hayes manual for doctors who couldn't diagnose more than a case of influenza and mild conjunctivitis. She said there was nothing to suggest anything other than a sharp serrated blade could have done the damage, and then reminded me that I was lucky to be alive. She read my notes at least. There were times where I cursed myself that my attacker hadn't pushed a little harder.

'It may have been the light in the bathroom,' she explained. 'There is no evidence of secondary scarring around the area or signs of an infection of any sort. It is natural for scar tissue to itch as the body repairs itself.'

In hindsight I couldn't blame her for being so dismissive. In natural light I found it hard to see anything other than the tidy sutures made by the surgeons.

'As for the nausea and dizziness,' she continued, 'coupled with swelling around the neck, I suggest you take it easy – perhaps ask for some time off. If you overdo it, you can get painful ulcers at the back of the throat.' She prescribed me a mouthwash to use three times a day and an anti-inflammatory spray. 'This explains the pain and burning sensation you get in the evening, especially if your tonsils become infected with pustules. Take ibuprofen to ease some of the discomfort.'

I remember the last line she said so vividly, that a shop-bought painkiller was the answer to all of my problems. I thanked her and left feeling deeply unhappy. To add insult to injury, she had prescribed me medicines which cost more on prescription than identical products I could have bought over the counter.

The traffic was clear on my way into the city. I had been rehearsing a conversation with Ed in my mind. I ran through several possible scenarios, outcomes and reactions that could occur if I managed to grab him for five minutes to discuss what happened that night. I also considered the idea of speaking to Julian about renegotiating my working hours, but the look he shot me as I walked through the door made me think otherwise; Julian would only listen to my demands if I could hit amazing sales targets.

The new girl, Martina, was sat at the desk in front of me. I began trawling through the morning's emails when she turned round to make polite conversation like she did most days.

'How are you?' she would say. I would look into her sleepy brown eyes as I tried to process her accent; she sounded more Russian than Polish and I wondered whether Julian had vetted her properly.

'I'm fine,' I would reply, not really bothering to keep the conversation going. After a couple of minutes I did return the small talk by asking her where Julian was heading out to. Apparently he was meeting a lady from an estate agent recruitment agency. I did a quick check of the properties that were on our list, and unless he was expecting to take on loads of new instructions (unlikely), there was no good reason to start hiring another lettings agent. The flats we had remaining on our books were in poor condition, hard to shift and overpriced. Julian had attracted a lot of landlords from rival agencies by giving discounted management fees and assuring them that he could get the price they wanted. For example, one of the flats was a penthouse apartment in the Docklands. We had put an asking price of £1200 a week for something that was built in the early 90s and needed serious renovation. Okay, so it had access to a helipad and its own private lift, but the living quarters were not worth the money; Julian had even confessed to overvaluing it by £400 a week, but that - like most of our other flats - some investment banker with a small dick would pay it just to say that he lived in a penthouse apartment that cost that much money. I kind of believed him.

Martina left the office to go on a viewing and I was left alone. I saw this as an excellent opportunity to browse Ed's desk for any tell-tale signs of trauma, including emails about his feelings sent to friends. If he walked in I would say that a client rang and that I was trying to find some info (as an estate agent, I had already lost most of my dignity and morals by this point). Besides, from looking at the diary I could tell that he was on viewings all afternoon.

I found nothing of interest, a few emails between him and an on-off girlfriend – nothing too risqué; client details, internal banter between him and Gary, and a few flagged emails from Julian and David. David was the other partner of the firm and was rarely in as he was setting up a new office in the Docklands, that and seeing to his wife who suffered from severe post-natal depression; when he was in, I often caught him looking at online porn in his office downstairs, but that's another story.

One of the emails caught my attention.

From:　　　Julian
CC:　　　David
Subject:　　Lunch
Message:

Ed, great to have you back and on good form. Keep lunch free on Friday – David and I have a proposition for you.
Julian.

I was going to read Ed's response when Julian and David walked through the door, laughing together. I played it cool.

'There are more subtle ways to steal Ed's clients,' remarked David, looking jolly after a couple of glasses of Lambrusco.

I ignored them both.

'You feeling better, mate?' Julian asked.

I nodded.

'Do some fucking deals then,' he said, whooping with laughter like some playground bully.

I got up and returned to my desk. I knew he was half joking, and banter was one of the only things that kept me going in the job. However, their little private invite confirmed my suspicions that I was no longer the 'flash in the pan' I had once been dubbed, and now sat outside of their intimate circle. I could only assume that they were prepping Ed for a senior role in the new office.

I managed to do a deal that afternoon. Two Korean students wanted to be close to Tower Bridge so that they could travel easily to university, so I talked them into renting a shitty two bed in a housing development in Bermondsey. It was a managed property, too, which meant better commission and would hopefully put Julian back in his cage. But it wouldn't be an easy deal, there would be lots of faxing and emailing to make the deal stick, and I would have to assure the landlady that South Koreans weren't communists.

Ed walked in later that afternoon with a certain prowess, seeming wide awake and full of energy – sapping away all of mine. Looking back at it now, it seemed hard to believe that he would be dead within six months. I quickly checked the diary and saw that he was free for the remainder of the evening. I called out to him, suggesting that we should grab a quick coffee.

He stood and looked over at me, his thick blonde eyebrows arching upwards. At first I thought he was going to react like he did the previous day, but I had perfected my poker face and expected nothing more than a yes, which is what I got.

The only coffee shop still open was some two bit

arrangement off a back alley nearby. Inside it had loads of neon lights and tacky Hollywood memorabilia from the fifties and sixties plastered across a tea stained wall.

I ordered a mocha and Ed opted for a shorter double espresso – he had given away his secret to staying so sharp.

'How are you doing?' I asked.

'Good,' he replied, 'but it's been really manic catching up with everything.'

I nodded and complemented him on how well he looked.

''You too,' he commented. 'Your scar's healing nicely.'

I was surprised to hear that. I ran my finger along it and mentioned that it had been giving me problems and that I had to get it checked out.

'Yeah, Julian mentioned it in the morning meeting,' he said casually.

I reflected for a moment. Why the fuck did Julian make it everyone's business during a morning sales meeting? 'Nice of him to do that.'

'You know what he's like - can be a real cunt sometimes.'

I laughed and nodded. This was a different Ed I was talking to. I couldn't imagine him talking like that at a private Friday lunch club. 'Let's see your scar then,' I said. 'You've come back guns blazing; I want to see what they've put inside of you.'

Ed gave me a small smirk before unbuttoning the top of his shirt to reveal a neat and tidy scar from where the knife went into his heart. I was amazed at how much it had healed, it looked more like a small appendix scar than the messy gash I had on my neck. Without thinking, I told Ed that he should be dead.

'I should,' he replied, 'but I'm not. And I'm still really fucking angry about it all.'

'You hide it well.'

He nodded. 'It was bad.'

'It was more than fucking bad - we both nearly lost our lives.'

'And they're no closer to making any sort of arrest?'

I shook my head. 'Doesn't look like it.'

We both took a large sip of our coffees. Ed nearly finished his in one go. I had to be quick. 'What do you remember?' I asked.

Ed stared at me long and hard, the whites of his eyes were perfectly clear, and his iris seemed to pulsate hypnotically. 'Not much,' he said, stalling. 'I remember them going for my car keys. And I remember seeing you fall to the ground, covered in blood.' He watched me shuffle as he spoke. 'I mean, they pinned me to the floor and whacked a bloody great knife in my chest.' He paused for a while and ran his fingers around his coffee cup. 'Then I remember waking up in Whitechapel Hospital, a gorgeous nurse telling me I'd survived heart surgery and that I was making excellent progress.'

I nodded. 'And that's it? You don't remember

lying there waiting for the ambulance to arrive.'

He shook his head.

'You were mouthing something, looking up towards the sky,' I said.

'What do you mean?'

'I remember what happened after the attack, and I really need to know if you can remember anything else.'

Ed stirred another sugar into the remainder of his coffee.

'Do you remember there being some kind of animal?'

He took the last of his coffee, sipping it slower this time. 'Can you be more specific?'

'I think it was a fox.'

'Why would I remember a fox?'

'Because it started drinking your blood!'

'Jesus!' Ed sat back and began to laugh out loud.

After a beat or two I started to laugh also. It sounded so macabre and stupid at the same time, especially my delivery, overdone and with too many pauses (I didn't want to sound stupid). But as the laughter ceased, I regained my poise. 'Seriously, I'm not joking. Something else attacked us both.'

'Maybe it was a pit bull,' he said, half-heartedly. 'These guys sometimes carry them around as trophy dogs and can train them to do crazy aggressive shit like that. But judging from the scarring around your neck, you're in a better position to know.'

I ran my fingers along the embossed scar tissue, tracing the stitch lines.

Ed remained cold. 'In truth, I can't remember there being any kind of wild animal. I just hope they catch the creatures that did this to us.' And with that, Ed buttoned up his shirt, stood up and left. 'Catch you back at the office.'

Like most of my loosely imagined role-play conversations, this had not been one of them. The point about the trophy pit bull was a good one, and I kicked myself for not coming up with that myself, but I was more intrigued by the fact they he could see the full extent of my scar. I'd hoped our conversation - albeit brief - would answer my initial question about what lurked in the car park, but to my frustration it only added more. My only hope was that I might have jogged Ed's memory and that he would come back to me on another day with some insight.

I sat and finished my coffee, staring at one of the movie posters in particular: Scarface; Tony Montana was pointing his little friend in my direction.

NARCISSUS

Back home I could do nothing but stare at my reflection. I detested what I saw and I grew deeply frustrated with events at work. I was stood in the bathroom for most of the evening, scrutinising my mirror image. Sure enough, I could see the outline of the scar on my neck protruding angrily as ever. I felt like checking myself into A & E and getting nurses to confirm that it was a bite, but I was firmly starting to believe that medical science could not explain its cause. I tried some of the inflammatory spray for my throat and took a few ibuprofens which did nothing but give me a stomach ache - probably not the best thing to have with a beer.

Claudia had been to the flat whilst I was out and had cleared out the majority of her stuff. She left me a note. It simply read:

I'm cancelling my standing order for the rent. Will collect the rest of my things in a couple of

weeks. Do what you want with the fridge. Claudia.

There was nothing to eat in the fridge so I decided to head out to the gym and eat there.

The best thing about the David Lloyd gym was the club bar. They served an excellent meaty steak which I enjoyed rare. It was glorious, and served with a healthy addition of fresh watercress and thick cut handmade chips. Afterwards I read the newspaper before sauntering into the changing room to embark on a trip to the pool. But I never got round to swimming, I sat in the Jacuzzi instead watching the swimmers in the water or subtly picking out the finer details of the people sharing the hot tub with me. I hoped that they would also adore me.

After a good soak, I would retire to the sauna in the gents changing room. It was a comforting place to rest; the heat seemed to hold me in a meditative state and my desires of craving human affection and the symptoms of sickness disappeared. For nearly half an hour I sat there. I thought about Julian, Ed, Claudia and anything else in my life that seemed to bug me at the time until my mind naturally vaporized each image.

I managed to get some sleep that evening, so I decided that a nightly excursion to the gym would become part of my routine to relieve stress.

MANNEQUINS

The next day I arrived late for work and missed the morning briefing. Julian was not impressed. I wasn't deterred, however, and went to my desk. I was going to get to the top of the sales ladder again. But I didn't factor in the arrival of Diana, a new negotiator. She was a bubbly, voluptuous Asian girl with a strong (too strong for my liking) Glaswegian accent.

Julian had a smirk across his face for the rest of the morning. I loathed him even more for employing Diana. It wasn't that she was getting all the leads, in fact it was quite the opposite - she was slow to answer the phone - but when she did pick up she talked loudly for ages and got appointments booked in because of her bubbly anecdotes about 'my first day' and 'I haven't seen that one . . . oh that looks nice doesn't it?'.

By lunchtime I was struggling to book in

appointments, spending most of my morning weeding the 'shit from the money' as Julian put it so eloquently. Of course, employing another negotiator will only turn me into a more aggressive, competitive sales machine.

Julian, David and Ed sauntered off for their secret lunch meeting. Diana was sat round the corner out of sight but I could still hear her; she was mildly obese and struggled to breathe clearly through her nose; when she talked, she had the combined volume of three ladies doing a boozy business lunch. I made a bogus appointment in the diary and popped out of the office to clear my head. I knew just the place.

I walked north up Leman Street towards Aldgate. I was disturbed by my behaviour when I passed women, leering at each one that I passed in the street. I put this down to not having a girlfriend anymore, to being a young sexually frustrated man again and not something more sinister. As I walked, images of Ed, Julian and Dan quaffing wine over a business lunch made me furious, hot and bothered. I could imagine Ed at the end of the meal ordering a double espresso and telling them that he met me for a coffee to discuss whether he can remember being licked by a dog; David erupts into a fit of laughter and then orders a Baileys.

Just off Commercial Street, I entered a building and crossed the foyer of the Aldgate Triangle complex. The security guards knew me well enough and I dangled a set of keys at them to show that I had a viewing.

In the lift I had a satisfying moment of calm as I made my way to the top floor, it felt like I was inside an incubator: enclosed, secure, warm and at peace; the vibrations were soothing and I felt like I was ascending to nirvana; I cleared my head of images of eroticism and violence, and when the lift stopped I exited and ascended the final few stairs up onto the roof terrace.

One of the main selling points of the whole complex was its roof garden with views across the city, especially since most of the balconies or terraces overlooked another block of flats. It was ironic that the whole terrace should be empty during the day whilst people were most likely caged in an office void of greenery, a habitat of artificial light and air-con instead.

The sun came out from behind the clouds. I relished the feeling of its warmth. I was no different to the other workers of London – trapped in an office and suppressed by a manager I grew to dislike more each day. I took long, deep breaths. Like a winged predator, I had a good view of the street below. I saw cars mainly, the odd flurry of human activity crossing at traffic lights, and blonde thirty something's with straight black pencil skirts and sometimes a laptop case in hand; lots of Pakistanis and Indians were strolling towards Brick Lane; and then there were lone figures – people who just seemed to be waiting for something to happen. This is common in London – check out any area with half a mile of a tube station and you'll always find people who seem to stop as if they've lost their direction or purpose. They hover with an uncertainty, block your path as they deliberate, and stare blankly at a phone waiting for it to ring. But most of the time they have simply fallen out of line, dropped out of sync with no-one to follow, waiting to be nudged or knocked back into action.

There were two such men like this on the road below. Their faces were obscured by black bowler hats. After some time it came to my attention that they appeared to be looking up at me, doing to me exactly what I was doing to them: staring. I pretended to look through and around them at first, but I grew uncomfortable very quickly. I scowled back at them, waving my arm primitively at them to make them turn away and then, one at a time, each of them raised their arm up in the air and just pointed it at me, their palms directed at me, like some evolution of the Nazi salute. Their faces, from what I could see, seemed blanched of all emotion: white-washed, down-turned mouths, cold eyes. My heart suddenly began to race and my mind was filled with vivid images: bright orange graffitied walls, oriental women performing sex acts, men fighting within a sea of flashing light-bulbs. I felt dizzy, confused. I stumbled back a few paces out of view feeling cold and sweaty. It was the same sensation I felt after waking from my recurring dream. I crouched to the floor and regained control of my breathing; my legs had pins and needles and my chest pounded. After a few beats I steadied myself and then plucked up the courage to look back over the edge again. Sure enough, they remained there staring at me with their fists held high. I felt angry. Violated. I wanted to leap off the building and land on them. I had no fear, only rage. I desperately looked for something to give me purchase to climb over the walls, started to grip the metal safety reals, and then I suddenly realised what I was doing. I fell backwards onto the ground and it knocked some sense into me. I was seconds away from jumping.

I wasn't safe on the roof.

Perhaps it was just a mad coincidence that I had felt those same symptoms, the same I had every night with that same dream, but I suddenly felt fraught and needed answers. I had to confront them.

I charged down the stairs which helped warm up my muscles in case I needed to engage in any sort of fight. My heart continued to beat furiously and I could feel the adrenaline pumping through my body. In my whole life I had never properly been in a fight - incident with Ed excluded - yet here I was preparing to attack two strangers for no reason other than that they gave me a strange salute.

By the time I got to the bottom of the stairs and into the foyer, I was sweating and out of breath.

The porter looked concerned. 'Traffic warden!' I remember saying. Emerging out onto the street I quickly scoured the area for signs of the two idle men. There was no trace of either of them. They were replaced by a staggering smack-head and a woman reading a newspaper.

I jogged over to each spot and hunted down each road with my eyes for any sign of them, for anyone wearing black bowler hats. There was no sign of these life sized Third Reich mannequins.

Exhausted, I slumped myself against a wall and cursed myself for taking the stairs, which probably gave them a few minutes extra time. I walked towards the nearest tube station in a last ditch search, but by this time the effects of adrenaline had worn off and I felt weak, cold and sweaty again.

On my way back to the office I stepped into a local pub and drank some lager to calm my nerves.

DESIRES

Julian approached my desk at the end of the day and asked if I was going for a drink. I had forgotten it was the last Friday of the month, a time for us all to pretend to be great mates and bundle into the Brown Bear. I hadn't been there since the night of the attack and was surprised that he had suggested it as a starting place, but I figured it was best to face your demons head on.

'Sure, you buying?' I asked.

'Do some fucking deals,' he barked.

During the last hour of the day (7-8pm on a Friday) I started checking through the emails, most of them internal. It had been a busy day for everyone: new girl Diana had taken an impressive holding deposit on a two bedroomed apartment, Ed the same, Grace a three bed maisonette, and Martina a studio flat. This left me and Gary with big fat zeroes for the day. I had an email from the tenant referencing agency we used to tell me that my two South Korean students would need a guarantor to pay the rent, which I knew meant devoting most of the following week to making international phone calls and sending faxes.

At this point of the day I realised just how bright the office lights were. My skin looked green and I felt sluggish and unmotivated to do anything. What I should have been doing was booking myself a holiday in the sun. I certainly wasn't in the mood for a staff social given the events of the past few weeks. But Claudia wasn't expecting me back so I looked on the bright side of being a bachelor again.

The Brown Bear had a certain charm about it – it was one of those small, traditional pubs where you could buy pork scratching and scampi fries from the back of the bar, like they were still advertised as a new product. Dusty bottles of mixers were packed onto each shelf (not even chilled) and the wooden bar counter had the familiar sticky film you get from years of neglect.

David bought the first round of drinks for us all. We occupied one corner of the pub, sitting at a few tables in our micro groups. I sat with Grace who tempered my heart with her wonderful Irish tones, sighs and gasps. We got talking about work as usual, then holidays, and finally about other members of the team.

I asked her casually about her thoughts on the new recruits.

'I think they're really nice,' she said. 'Julian and David are like two school boys giggling all the time.'

I nodded. 'How's Ed been? He sits in front of you.'

'Fine,' she shrugged. 'Really well, actually, he's got so much energy,'

'Depressing isn't it?'

'What is?'

I shook my head.

'Oh, you're brilliant,' she replied. 'My god, I'm still surprised to see you back so soon, and working again.'

'Perhaps I should have milked Julian and David a bit more before returning, or even have taken a holiday.'

'Oh, absolutely.'

Saying the words, I felt resentful that I hadn't been strong enough to do so. Ed had come off pretty good about the whole thing, like he had been on some weird kind of vacation of his own and completely recharged his batteries.

'What about you, Grace?'

'What do you mean?'

'What's going on in your life? Are you with somebody?'

She blushed slightly and flicked her golden locks to one side. 'Well, I've kind of finished it with Bernardo.' Bernardo was her on and off Italian exchange student/boyfriend. 'I'm just enjoying being single again,' she said firmly.

'Me too,' I announced.

Unexpectedly, she grabbed my arm and asked about me and Claudia. As I recounted the story all I could focus on were the murmurs in my heart, it was if the aorta had opened up and was being flushed clean of bitterness. Grace covered my hand with hers and I noted how her skin was unusually cold, and I tried to imagine if her breasts would feel as cool and supple.

In the weeks after Claudia's departure, I hadn't even thought about getting into another relationship. Yet, being touched by a female - albeit gently on the hand by someone warm and sincere - proved just how absent of affection I had been. I wanted to be touched again.

'I told her I had my eyes on this gorgeous girl at work,' I said.

She looked at me seriously for a moment and then started to laugh. 'Stop it.'

'It's true.' I placed my other hand on top of hers.

'You're such a bad liar,' she said, pulling her hand away.

We laughed together and I was starting to ease up when Julian called me over. 'Mate, come and join the men.'

What made it more frustrating was the fact that Grace seemed to be under Julian's finger.

'Can't you see we're courting?' I said.

He said nothing, merely opened up the circle and expected me to join the group. Martina, as if on cue, shuffled over to Grace and began making conversational small talk you'd find in a 'learn English' travel guide. I got up and rested a hand on Grace's shoulder. I felt her shoulder blade beneath the padded suit jacket and I was adamant I could feel her heart beating.

Julian and the other men stood like a group of feral football supporters in suits, every movement was overstretched and each laugh exaggerated, booming across the pub.

'We were wondering,' said David, giggling to himself, 'if you've had your teeth whitened.' The whole group erupted with laughter.

I would have laughed with them had it been like the good old days, but I was confused by his comment. 'What the hell are you talking about?'

'Look at them!' shrieked Gary. 'They're like fucking mirrors on a disco ball.'

The heckling did little to bring about a deep anxiety about my teeth, but I did suddenly think back to when I was a child and how sore my throat had been when my back teeth came through. Even then I recalled the rash on my cheeks and feeling of feverishness at night. I ran my finger along the back of my teeth and along my gums; they were solid, as though my teeth had hardened deep into the roots.

'We're heading up to Desires later. You're coming with us,' Julian stated.

Desires was a lap dancing club in Hackney; when the full moon was out, men seemed to flock to the place to spend their hard earned cash. 'Are you taking the girls as well?' I asked.

Julian shook his head; male bonding session, no girls allowed.

'It's been a while since I've seen any action,' I remarked.

'You not with the missus anymore?'

I shook my head.

'It'll do you good - I'll treat you!'

Coming from Julian, it was hard to resist such an offer. I looked back at Grace and weighed up the odds of her stripping off and dancing for me. I imagined it there and then, bony limbs with an awkward swaying of the hips as she oohed and aahed in her gentle Irish tones. She was pure, of that there was no doubt, and if I saw her naked it would take away the charm and innocence and everything else I loved about her, and probably ruin the fantasy. It was then that I realised how sexually starved I was – I needed a wild sex kitten to writhe in front of me. Grace looked up and smiled and I knew then that we would not go any further that evening.

We all hopped into a black cab. All except Ed, whose excuse was that he had to meet someone in the West End. We joked that he had joined some private gentlemen's club and I thought nothing of it at the time, although I would soon learn a much darker reason for his exploits around that part of the city.

Entry to Desires was a tenner. I could hear the

muffled sound of an old PA system beating in the basement. The odd flash of red light reflected off the mirrored walls of the staircase as we descended into the nest where all the chicks gathered. The establishment personified seediness. A spiral staircase was positioned in the centre of the club and tables were littered around it. Women danced at tables with their breasts on show for everyone to see, and on a stage the women wore nothing; they were watched by a swarm of agitated eyes eager to buy some personal contact time.

I had barely sat down when a woman with unnaturally blonde hair asked me if I wanted a dance. 'Let me have a drink first,' I said coolly. I looked round to see that Gary had already charged off to meet his favourite dancer – it later turned out that Desires was entirely his idea. David got a round of beers in at the bar. Julian sat beside me.

'Take your pick,' he said, sweeping his arm across the club like some Roman emperor offering me first pick of which servant I wanted to sodomise. I was shaking at the thought – I had never been in such an establishment. Maybe it was the fear of having my drink spiked or my credit card billed with large amounts of cash for services I didn't ask for, or didn't get.

'Let's just have a drink, enjoy the show a bit.'

Even now I remember how that evening summed up the office politics – women were second rate, and the men collectively shared derogatory views about them. I was going the same way. I'd caught David looking at swingers' sites twice; Julian referred to most female landladies as dizzy bints; Gary openly admitted to paying for sex, and Ed had a reputation for sleeping around with anything that had a pulse and three holes. I thought about Grace (the dizzy Irish blonde), Martina (the big-boobed European) and Diana (the giggly fat Asian). We were short of some feminists. David joked that they were ticking off all the boxes on the equal opportunities form so that they could apply for more investment to open more offices. I half believed him.

We sat - the three of us – drinking, watching and salivating. I felt less resentful towards Ed, knowing that I had been included in the evening's events. And after another beer I could feel the effects of the alcohol; I began to loosen up and the symptoms from the illness began to lapse.

Julian waved his hand excitedly at a brunette dancer who was scantily dressed in a glittery red number. She was beautiful with dark brown eyes and thick auburn hair. Julian spoke to her and gave her £20. She turned and looked at me, bent forward and whispered in my ear: 'I'm Marissa - I'd like to dance for you.'

Julian and David adjusted their seats to get a prime viewing angle and she slowly began to sway in time with the music in front of me to Love Will Tear Us Apart by INXS. All throughout the dance she never took her eyes off me; they flickered in the light, green and red, glistening as I became slowly hypnotised. The music muffled and everything dropped and went into slow motion. My heart purred smoothly in my chest. It felt magnificent.

Sadly, the dance ended as soon as it had begun. David and Julian clapped like idiots. She pulled her dress back up and leant forward again, asking if I wanted to go upstairs with her. I didn't question why because it sounded great. The optimist in me believed that I had pulled and that I had been invited back into her dressing room for some individual attention, in hindsight a natural male thought given the situation. She took me by the hand and led me up the winding stairs. I didn't even glance back at Julian or David. I wouldn't see them again.

We ascended into a more relaxed lounge area. There was a small oval bar with a solitary barman dressed in white overalls stood behind it, something reminiscent from a scene in The Shining. He smiled at me. To my right I saw Gary in a private booth; he was sat obediently whilst a curvaceous black woman, half wearing a metallic green dress, shook her booty in his face.

I glanced round at all the other sofas. 'So what's the deal?' I asked.

'It's fifty pounds for half an hour,' the man replied.

'Or ninety pounds for an hour,' Marissa chipped in. 'Would you like an hour?'

I wanted to ask what I got for my money, but my hopes of intimacy had faded when I saw where we were. 'Let's just go for half an hour,' I said, opening my wallet. 'Do you take cards?'

'Yes, but it's a seven pound charge,' he replied. 'Would you like a drink?'

'Why not,' I muttered, resigned to the fact I didn't have to part with the money physically. I ordered another beer and Marissa said she'd like a Baileys. Very smooth.

She led me to an unoccupied booth and we sat down together awkwardly. She had a smile on her face that made me feel pretty damn stupid and ashamed of what I'd just done. I felt duped. I tried polite small talk, the type Martina used in the office, and attempted to focus on her eyes rather than her body.

We got talking and it turned out that she was from Estonia and had been working at Desires for about six weeks. The conversation dried up quickly. I asked her what usually happened upstairs. She explained that I got two private dances, and that one of them would be in a special chair. I had to discipline myself to look and not touch – those were the rules.

During the first dance, she told me off for tapping her bum as she wiggled it inches away from my face. Throughout the routine, which was longer than the one downstairs, she tried her best to sexually arouse me; I focused on her eyes and the way that she ran her tongue across her lips. At one point I could have sworn that I saw fangs. I focused on my own teeth and what the men had said at the Brown Bear. My teeth felt hard like the rest of my body.

'You've got a great body,' I said afterwards, thinking of how I was going to drag another ten minutes out to get my money's worth – she had already finished her Baileys.

'How did you get that scar?' she asked, stroking herself across her neck playfully. The sight of her doing that made my heart race. Her hair seemed to flop over to one side so that I didn't notice the marks on her.

I felt like being crude, telling her that my ex had experienced such a strong orgasm that she tried to bite my neck in two. I didn't. Instead I lied and told her that I had been in an accident: a car crash. She seemed disappointed.

'Shall I dance for you in the special chair?' she asked after a minute's silence.

The special chair was a tatty leather armchair that vibrated as she performed her final dance on a mini stage, stripping completely down to her birthday suit. By this time, however, my appetite had waned; I didn't want her sexually anymore, I experienced a different type of yearning, and one I hadn't felt before.

Watching all of these beautiful creatures magnified by mirrors on the walls and ceilings increased my appetite.

At the end of the dance, Marissa asked me if I'd like another half an hour.

I declined. I was hungry.

On leaving, the bouncer told me I could get back in with the UV stamp they put on my hand. I looked down at it and could see the feint outline without holding it under a lamp.

I should've taken a taxi ride back to my house that night but I decided to go for a walk instead. I needed to walk off the anger and frustration that I felt after my disappointing investment of £50 in the hope that my raging hard-on would slowly disappear.

I walked back through Bethnal Green, Brick Lane and Aldgate – that way I could stay seen and in sight. At one point along Sclater Street I was adamant I could hear voices calling my name from below. When I passed the food outlets, my body didn't yearn for any of it, even the salt beef bagels.

As I neared Leman Street, I thought about what London would have been like in the Victorian times and I found myself thinking about Jack the Ripper – how he must have ventured out in the early hours, hungry for young women to butcher. But more enigmatically, I wondered about how many occasions Jack went out and didn't come back with blood on his hands. How many near misses had there been? I was probably walking the very same path, yet rather than be hustled by street prostitutes; I had paid to hustle them in a protective cage. The image of Marissa was still inside my head, her mouth half open in a gasp, her legs slowly opening wide as she palmed her hands across her thighs and breasts. I didn't like how things had ended at Desires.

My car was parked outside the office. The kebab shop was shut and there was little activity. About 50 yards away were the railway arches. Despite my intrinsic fear, I felt captivated to venture towards them to see if some red furred beast lurked beneath the archway. But I decided to exercise caution and face my demons another time.

I got in the car and drove off.

THE THIRST

I don't know what compelled me to travel to Crouch End that evening. I'd never visited in the day and had only eaten there once before with Claudia about a year before. Something drew me in, took me away from my usual path home. Perhaps it was the spontaneity of it all, taking a blind road and seeing where it would take me, or the ferocity of the torrential rain that made me want to take a more tree lined route. Maybe it was because I knew that I was driving over the limit and wanted to take smaller, quieter roads home. I'll never know. I'll never understand my actions.

The rain continued to beat fiercely on the windscreen and there was a rich blackness about the night. There was little activity around The Broadway, only a hazy amber glow from bars and shop windows. There was the odd man running through the rain, his jacket collar pulled tight against his neck. The suburbs were definitely asleep.

I had pulled up along a side street, not really knowing what I was looking for. All I could hear was the gentle sound of water collecting and trickling along the roads, running towards the drains. But then I saw it, simpering on the corner of a street with its crooked, weathered sign and dull, yellow light: sauna.

Maybe it was psychological, or some deep-down motivation fuelled by my lap dancing experience from hours before, a catalyst that led me to that spot; that or I craved companionship and intimacy, something I hadn't felt for months.

I sat in the car in complete darkness and composed myself. This would be a first for me. My heart didn't feel right; it was gnawing at my chest, trying to eat its way out. The windows had begun to steam up and I felt as though the car was closing in on me. Eventually there was a break in the rain and I opened the window. I watched another lone figure run past me on the street, a lank newspaper acted as protection from the rain as he dodged the many puddles which lapped across the pavement.

I took one final look at myself in the mirror. My eyes were wide but lacked warmth and sincerity, qualities I took for granted; instead, cold and hard grey eyes stared back at me with flecks of orange from the streetlamps hitting my cornea.

I got out of the car and walked briskly. I nearly

missed the entrance because it was so subtle, and yet so blatant; a poorly varnished door with a peep hole, a metal buzzer with a well pressed button, a thin strip of light above it, and a small CCTV camera in the corner. Hardly a warm welcome but it offered the level of seediness I desired.

The door buzzed open and I entered. A young Thai girl dressed in a loose beige t-shirt greeted me inaudibly through a glass booth. Behind her I saw women, lots of them, standing and sitting in what looked like a waiting room, all of them dressed in white nylon outfits like nurses. I caught my breath and looked down at my hands. I asked her how much it would be.

'Ten pound entry. Forty pound to the girl,' she replied bluntly. I reached into my wallet and dissected its contents. Two twenties, a five, and as I rummaged through my pockets I realised I had just enough loose change to grant entry. I must have looked pretty desperate, pathetic even, as I slipped the fiver and loose change through the bottom of the bars. The girl counted it all carefully, got up off her seat and unlocked the second door, letting me into the cage.

The girl muttered to me something about 'choosing' one of the girls, and so I stood quietly, hands in my pocket, searching the room. I felt ashamed. My skin was beginning to burn, my throat became parched. I should have left. To the girls, I must have seemed like most regulars, dressed in work clothes, shy and stagnant, half-drunk and lingering with filthy intent. My eyes hunted across the room at the therapists before me: a buxom, harsh looking blonde stared back at me with piercing blue eyes, but she looked sad and was overweight; my eyes crept to a skinnier brunette who stared down at her slender legs which were tightly folded from the bottom of her uniform down to her scuffed, brown sandals; my attention then focused to a group of women stood with their backs to me, smoking cigarettes. From their shape I could tell that they were Asian; their thin, straight brown hair hung down their backs and contrasted against their starched white outfits. And then I saw her - as the group accidentally parted - peering at me through the sloped hips of two girls. They parted again and I saw a woman of dark complexion smiling back at me. My eyes flashed around for a second or two at the other women, but none of them showed any interest. She was the only one who smiled and nodded at me subtly.

My arm felt heavy as I raised it up and pointed at her with limp wrists. A couple of the other girls seemed to snap out of their morose thoughts and watch her walk towards me. I smiled modestly at my choice; she was well proportioned with muscular thighs, radiant skin and auburn hair which framed her deep brown eyes.

'Hello darling,' she said softly. She muttered something to the girl behind the counter in Thai then turned to me again. 'Please, we pay the money now,' she said. I handed her the two twenty pound notes and she quickly checked them before delving in her handbag and handing over ten pounds to the cashier. 'Okay, this way please.'

She took my arm and led me up the stairs. Yellowy orange wallpaper clung to the landing walls and the brown carpet was well worn. As we took a second flight of stairs, a door opened and an elderly man and a young, British looking girl emerged and surreptitiously slid past us both.

I followed closely behind the woman. I could detect the scent of jasmine. The soles of her shoes were worn and the straps on her bag looked chewed. She turned to me again and smiled as she led me into a large open room. The light was dull and repressive, contrasting horridly with the high ceilings and tatty wallpaper. In one corner was a thin, black massage table with long strips of tissue covering it, the other a wooden chair; and next to that a bathtub shielded with cheap pine cladding. The windows were boarded from within; only a slit of glass protruded above the bare shutter and tired beige curtains which might have once been white.

'My name is Cha-Cha,' she said, shutting the door.

'John,' I replied, holding her hand awkwardly. She gestured towards the chair, telling me to undress, and started sorting through her bag by the windowsill. I stepped timidly over and began to remove my clothes, hanging them neatly on the chair. Undressed, she pointed at the small massage table and told me to lay on my front. I did so and waited for her instruction. I turned my head and watched her remove her clothes in one swift movement. There was no eroticism about her actions, she was mechanical almost, yet I found her assertion arousing. Cha-Cha smiled when she caught me peering at her voluptuous body. Her hands disappeared behind her back and she unclicked her bra revealing large firm breasts that seemed to shimmer in the light. From her handbag she removed a condom, some talcum powder and a small plastic bottle of oil.

'What would you like?' She asked. I nodded towards the talc.

She stood next to me and began rubbing my skin with her strong hands. 'You're very hot,' she said, applying gentle pressure across my shoulders.

I gave a cliché reply. Not much more was said. I focused on trying to relax but I was anxious that I was about to break into a fever and she would ask me if I was ill, or stop massaging, or worse still, refuse to continue. Surely the talc would absorb any excess moisture, I thought to myself. I tried desperately to relax but my muscles felt primed to spring into action at any moment. Slowly I grew firm.

She asked me to turn on my back. She patted more talc into my body and around my groin before Cha-Cha began stroking my balls. I surveyed her, noticing how soft and smooth her skin looked. She caught me looking. 'It's okay. You can touch.'

I stroked and caressed her naked flesh as she followed through the rest of the ritual and began to perform fellatio. I could tell she was experienced and gave deep pleasurable sighs. For a moment I thought about nothing, just savoured the closeness of it all, but then I kept noticing little things about the room: on the walls were dried patches of semen, there were budget cleaning products next to the bath, and I could hear a light knocking sound permeate through the ceiling. My body continued to burn up.

She instructed me to sit up, then Cha-Cha lay back on the narrow table and hooked her legs around my ribs and pulled me inside of her. As she directed me in, our eyes fastened and she began to breathe and sigh heavily, part of the performance; her lips pouted at me as she exhaled and I thought about Marissa licking her lips and the tips of her fangs. I didn't know where to look – it felt wrong. I stopped and then announced that I wanted to try things differently. She laughed.

'Whatever you want, darling,' were her last words as she positioned herself on all fours.

My heart accelerated. It felt like I was taking part in high intensity physical activity. I focused on my hands which tightly grasped her hips like talons, the tips pushing into her fleshy thighs as my muscles tensed further. My breathing intensified and I felt sweat dripping off my brow. She moaned as I thrust in and out, and the hairs on my back flicked up in a singular motion and I began to chant.

She was unaware, almost passively enjoying the steady rocking motion and the sound of flesh pounding against flesh, when it suddenly happened. Nearing climax, I grabbed her hair and pulled her towards me, tilting her head up towards the ceiling at a canted angle. With my other hand I cupped her mouth and drew her neck towards me. I felt my teeth flex, my tongue fork and my jaw unclick as I fixed my mouth purposefully around her jugular and sucked hard to create a seal. I remained inside of her and felt her life-force drain hopelessly into mine, her arms flapping hopelessly. I couldn't stop myself. My skin was on fire. Sweat poured off me with each pulsing heartbeat. I knew I was feeding from her but there was no taste, just a sensation of crimson fire shooting through my body as air flared in and out of my nostrils in sharp bursts.

After a while her stifled moans stopped and she went limp. Satisfied, I broke the seal and slavered at her neck and breast, kissing and sucking the liquid that began to weep slowly from what looked like a large burn mark.

Her body slumped forward. I withdrew and focused on the scorch mark on her neck. It wasn't the clichéd fang pricks I had expected to see, more of a severe love bite. I ran my hand across my neck to feel a sticky yellow discharge around the scar tissue. Initially the feeling had been one of glory as my body shook with vigour, but now that feeling had quickly descended into agitation, guilt and despair as the light in the room seemed to brighten and the blurred lines and shadows suddenly came back into focus.

I touched her skin. It was still warm and elastic, bronze almost in the fuzzy glow of the room. The light fitting seemed to shake slightly as the knocking sound from above grew louder. I understood that other men were satisfying their animal instincts in the rooms about me, but in different fashions.

I tried standing but my legs were weak, tensed to the point where blood hadn't been able to flow properly in the angle that I fed; they were numb like I had stepped on some electrical cable. I fell to the floor and thought about my actions. Murderer, I thought to myself. Cha-Cha's head was turned towards me; she had a glazed expression and lips that still seemed moist. I rolled over and saw the bath, crawled over to it, pulled myself up and ran the taps whilst the feeling came back into my legs. Hot water spilled out and steam quickly filled the room. By this point I was more conscious of my actions. I felt remorse and began to panic. Fixing my watch around my wrist, I knew that forty pounds probably bought me half an hour max, with most girls bouncing their clients to a climax in about half that time. I needed to hurry. As the bath filled up I thought about what to do.

I turned off the taps and looked over at Cha-

Cha's body. There was enough water for me to lower her body in. The colour had already faded from her tender mocha skin to an Earl Grey complexion. I stroked her hair and closed her eyes, whispering how sorry I was, and then gently lifted her from the bed. I noticed that a few droplets of blood had shot across the tissue paper base and walls, adding to the bodily fluid artwork already congealed around the table. I carried her over to the bath, lowered her in and watched the water envelop her. To my surprise, she didn't float.

The sound of a lone motor vehicle swooshing through water tracks outside brought me to my senses. I peered through the window and could see that it had started raining again. I dressed myself and checked I had all my possessions, did one last sweep of the room (gathering the paper towel in my pocket) and then exited the door, shutting it behind me.

The cage seemed busy, like some of the more popular ladies were back in the room making small talk in their mother tongue, smoking Marlboro Reds. I kept my head down and tapped at the door to be let out. The door buzzed and I pulled it open, shuffling past a group of men - regulars perhaps - who were at the kiosk, counting their entry money in high spirits. One of them looked up at me as he removed his hood. I stared back at him until he looked away and then I stepped out into the night, a free man.

The night air was cool and refreshing. I undid

my coat and shirt and took deep breaths before running back to my car.

I got in and gazed at my eyes but I did not recognise the person staring back at me. The crease of a smile momentarily dug into one side of my face as I remembered the intimacy, the presentation of her body, and minutes later the violent resolution and her end.

It makes me shudder just to remember that night. The calmness I felt as I drove away.

I was no better than old Jack the Ripper himself.

REMORSE

On arriving back home, feelings of intense jubilation and deep satisfaction had switched to those of worry, panic and fear of reprisal. I immediately ran into the bathroom, flicked the light on and stared at myself in the mirror. My eyes no longer shimmered and sparkled but were heavily bloodshot and watery. I ran my fingers along my teeth, and I could taste jasmine oil on my skin. A milky secretion came from one of the fingers above the cuticle, and between my gums and roof of the mouth I felt like I had an ulcer or an abscess of some sort that seemed to weep; it tasted salty and bitter.

I began to wonder if I had fed at all, round my mouth and on my neck there was no trace of blood. One thing that did stand out, however, was the scar on my neck - it protruded in such a way that Fibonacci would be proud. I couldn't help but feel

I had been marked like cattle.

In the kitchen I drank pints of water mixed with really sweet orange squash to get rid of the taste. My body craved sugar and I was ravenous for more food, frantically finishing off leftovers from the fridge and kitchen cupboards. All the while, I had flashes of her lifeless body in my head, slowly sinking in the water, her arms folded across her breasts. They would have found her by now, I thought to myself, and surely the police would have arrived on the scene. Why I had committed this heinous act was beyond me, beyond logic, beyond the science that I understood at the time. I imagined a grainy CCTV image of my face being circulated across police stations and news channels, and that flashing blue lights would appear outside my flat at any moment. Then I would start receiving obscene text messages from family and friends asking if that was really me. Because of this deep dread, I spent the remainder of the night awake, sitting in fear with the lights turned off.

I imagined criminal psychologists putting together a profile of a man, a killer sat in an air conditioned office of an estate agency somewhere in east London. The detective leading the case asks what motivates this type of man to do something like this. The newspaper story is already printed in my head: male, late 20s, visits lap dancing clubs, recently split from partner, possible post-traumatic stress from an injury or attack where he lost a lot of blood. And I feel shame. My head is fuzzy from the thoughts. I have news channels switched on and local radio stations turned up, waiting for any mention of a murder, but then the chatter of reports seemed to merge into one continuous noise. I am even Googling local news websites with 'prostitute killed' or 'brothel murder', but I find nothing but a string of past murders by depraved loners.

At day break there was still nothing. Each news tab was regularly refreshed and I hopped from news channel to news channel to see if my horrific actions had made the headlines. Nothing was reported.

By midday there had still been no reports of such a crime. Surely with a business that traded through the night they would have noticed a dead worker? Maybe people pay for that? Eventually my eyes grew heavy and I fell asleep.

When I woke it was dark again. I felt invigorated at first but when I acknowledged that the radio and TV were still on, I knew that this was my reality. I refreshed every web page, even popped round to the corner shop to check the papers. Maybe the life of a prostitute doesn't make for good news coverage anymore, I thought, like it had back in the day of old John Pizer. Then I considered that I had imagined the whole thing or that Cha-Cha had played along with my game and pretended to be dead. Perhaps I was drunker than I thought, or worse still I had had my drink spiked. The only way I could get to the truth was to ring the sauna in question.

I found the number on the internet and then left the house to find a payphone two bus stops away, somewhere out of sight.

I stood within a glass coffin along the high street in Golders Green, fed fifty pence into the slot and dialed the number.

A woman's voice answered. 'Hello?'

I said nothing at first, I just stood there with the phone pressed to my ear and listened to the road noise. I confirmed I had the right number and then asked if they were open. I recognised the voice, it was the same girl I spoke to before, and she confirmed that they were open. The girl asked if I was still there. I apologised and then asked if Cha-Cha was working that night.

'One moment please . . .' The line went quiet. I imagined that there were police on the premises, armed with tape recorders and a tracing device. A moment later she returned. 'Sorry, she's sick and not working today, but we have many other new girls to choose from.'

I wanted to ask more, about the details of her illness, whether they'd even checked the room we had been in, or even emptied the bath!

I thanked her and hung up. A wave of relief came over me and I nearly crumpled to the floor as I believed that the night before had been nothing but some acid induced dream. My suspicions immediately rested with Gary, purely because he'd boasted about taking LSD and ecstasy on big nights out; perhaps I'd picked up his drink by mistake or it had been his gift to me.

I contemplated other explanations as I walked home in the rain, dazed. It was the longest two mile walk home. I felt like a man who had just been acquitted of a scandalous crime, escaping a life sentence of misery and regret.

Back home, I began switching off all the radios and refreshed all the web pages once more before logging off. As I did so, a news report caught my eye: a woman had been violently attacked in her flat in West London. The news didn't have any images, but she was believed to have been a worker from the city – a PA. The detective interviewed said it was one of the most violent attacks they had ever seen and that the motive was unknown.

Later, I rang Julian. I rarely did this outside of work unless we'd fucked up a deal and had to appease a landlord. He answered the phone with his usual faux cockney tone. "Ello mate' I remember him saying. I could hear his young kids bleating in the background. 'How are you feeling?'

'My head's a mess,' I replied.

He explained that David had been sick for most of the weekend from food poisoning and that he suffered from a hellish hangover the next day.

In that moment I decided I would research the physical symptoms of food poisoning and the psychological effects of a trip. I kept the call short to avoid the small talk about work.

I stayed in that night watching an undercover documentary about fraud within the property trade. I soon drifted off into a deep sleep again, however, the night brought with it the most vivid and twisted images in my head.

I dreamt about being with a woman, she was laughing and pulling me by the hand, leading me into her apartment late at night. I could see no mirrors, not even in the elevator, only my hands, except they weren't my hands. The woman was playful and flirtatious, flicking her long blonde hair over her shoulder. In her apartment I remember surveying the layout: kitchen, bathroom and bedroom. I followed her into the kitchen and began touching her all over and trying to kiss her neck and caress her breasts. She laughed some more, pulled away and began removing her cardigan. I poured myself a glass of wine and then looked at my hands again. They were shaking. The nails seemed to elongate as she left the kitchen. I followed her into the hall. My breathing was laboured. My muscles tensed. My vision turned hazy.

She turned to me once more and then froze – the face of a playful temptress suddenly switched to that of damsel in distress. She screamed. I begged her not to at first, holding my hands out defensively, and that's when I noticed my hands were crooked. When she kept screaming at me I became enraged and leapt forward, striking her across the face. My nails caught her cheek and she fell to the floor, stunned and bleeding over beech laminate. My hands were talons ready to shred her to pieces. I grabbed her by the ankle and pulled her across the floor towards the bedroom. She began to stir again and shook her leg, wailing in terror. By now her skin was pale white, porcelain almost with crimson spots splattered across one side. In the bedroom I reached down, picked her up and threw her across the room like some rag doll. She smacked bluntly against the wall and slumped awkwardly face down on to the bed. A patch of blood and cracked plaster was left on the wall. Before she could stir I was upon her, tearing her clothes off frantically like some rabid, deprived soul, preparing for a feast.

I woke at this point, unable to breath. I could taste blood in my mouth. It felt like I had been chewing the inside of my cheeks. I ran to the bathroom and threw up. Blood came spewing out, and not just a little bit; long strands of sticky, glutinous clots seemed to separate and sit around the pan like rotten albumen. My skin was hot steel, glistening, and my neck itched like crazy along the right side. I saw that same horrific expression in the mirror staring back at me. Whilst I slowly realised that the dream was just that, the blood was definitely real. I stood shivering, debating whether I should take myself to hospital but grew paranoid at the thought. I returned back to my bedroom and I could see that there were pull marks on the sheets and covers from where I had thrashed wildly; somehow I had managed to tear right through.

THE EARLY BIRD

It was nearly 5am. I decided to get dressed and take an early trip into work. It would earn me a few brownie points from Julian, I thought.

I took the quickest route I could, yet despite being out and about at such hours, others had already started their daily commute. I pondered their job roles, where they were going and where they had come from, and how many, if any, had time to dream between shifts and deadlines.

I parked my car outside the office and was taken aback to see that someone else was already in. The security shutters were up and there was a light coming from the bottom of the stairs. I cursed my luck; how could Julian be in before me again? The office had a toilet and running water, but there was nowhere to settle for a kip or take a shower, and no-one sold or let properties at that time of day. I unlocked the door and approached with caution, just in case I was about to have a run-in with an early morning thief; we did, after all, border the deprived estates of Shadwell and Tower Hill where drugs and prostitution were still rife.

I was silent, shuffling across the laminate floor, listening for signs of life down below. I heard movement, like that of someone stirring from a light sleep, and stopped in my tracks, my heart in my mouth. I debated whether I should say 'hello, who's there?' like a proper pleb or just continue to hover aimlessly at the top of the stairs.

Ed's voice called up. 'Julian, is that you?'

I called back down: 'Ed, what are you doing in so early?'

I heard more rustling, bags being emptied, furniture being moved, and then footsteps. Ed appeared at the top of the stairs looking ruffled and with a heavily creased shirt, the same from Friday night.

'Don't tell me, your missus chucked you out?' I said.

He smirked. 'I've been in Bristol all weekend. When I came back late last night I realised that I only had my office keys, and my flat mate was away until Monday, so I had no other option.'

It was a well-rehearsed explanation – I'm sure Julian would have bought it.

He asked why I was in and I gave him a story about not being able to sleep. Seeing him agitated me and I now felt obliged to entertain him. I told him to go back to sleep but he declined.

'How about we catch some breakfast when

Leman's opens in an hour?' he suggested.

I accepted his offer. I thought perhaps that he had remembered details of that night and wanted to share them with me.

I sat at my desk and logged on to the PC, and that was when I noticed that the bins were full of takeaway boxes and chocolate wrappers. Ed's story of a dirty weekend in Bristol seemed a bit lame, especially as the cleaners always came in on a Saturday afternoon.

I heard Ed rustling around downstairs and visit the bathroom on several occasions. As I tried to focus and catch up on work, I grew distracted by the questions I was so desperate to ask him, so I jotted them down on post it notes and tried to learn them in the hope of a mid-breakfast interrogation.

Phil, the friendly fryer at Lemans, was surprised to see us arrive so early but welcomed the business. We sat ourselves in a booth drinking hot coffee. I honestly felt the tables had turned this time and that I had the upper hand over Ed; he looked tired and anxious and kept stressing that he needed some real food to sort himself out. I played along at first, but halfway through our fry-up I began my interview:

'Who did you see in Bristol?'

His story started with the usual 'I've been seeing this girl I used to go to uni with' and elaborated how he'd been texting on a Saturday night to his 'friend' when things got a bit explicit . . . in the end, he spontaneously got a cab from London to Bristol so that he could 'top up his minutes' – that was the weak pun he used.

Even now, it makes me laugh to think that I almost believed him.

Ed sat forward and turned the questions on me. 'You say you couldn't sleep. Was it anything to do with what happened?'

I shook my head coolly. We looked at each other and acknowledged that we were both being mendacious.

I took a mouthful of greasy eggs and fried bread before asking him for more details. 'What was this club like, the one you went to on Friday night?'

He explained that it was more of a private members club his friend was part of, and that he couldn't remember the name since it had a discrete entrance, but it was somewhere in The Strand.

I asked him what the clientele were like. He described it as a rich mix of city bankers, lawyers and restaurateurs. As he spoke I couldn't help but gaze at his eyes and notice the way in which they kept darting off to the side. And when he spoke, his voice often trailed off and I knew his mind was on other things, and so was mine.

'That's what I like about London,' I said. 'The fact that it's so big, that you can always walk past a street and discover something new; millions of possibilities presented to us on our doorstop each day, a new route to work, a new place to eat, a person to kill.'

Ed fixed his eyes on me. 'What are you talking

about?'

'Nothing, I was just checking you're awake.'

He laughed and rubbed his face briskly.

We got back to the office and Julian whooped with delight when he saw us walk in. In the morning meeting, Julian mocked us both; Ed for going on a dirty weekend in Bristol (which he had recounted downstairs to them all before debriefing) and me for my personal session with a lap dancer at Desires.

Grace said nothing as the rest of the office laughed and joked. She simply looked away.

BALANCE

I struggled through the rest of the day. Flashes of my dream haunted me. I thought nothing of it though, reassuring myself that it was coincidence and the result of a bad trip.

I spent the next couple of hours researching dreams and hallucinations, psychosis, bipolar disorder, and delusions. I began reading up about stories of people who were so convinced that their own dreams were real that they had handed themselves into the police. It made for disturbing reading. So that I could gain closure on the matter of Cha-Cha, I diagnosed myself as someone who had brief reactive psychosis.

I could sense that Julian was looking over at me so I had to keep minimising my tabs, and when he knew that I was not browsing through client lists, he got a little irate and swore at me to stop dreaming and do some deals.

I went through the property archive and reflected on the flat above our offices that was recently rented out. There had been an incident a few months back where two American students, both in their late teens, had been followed home and raped by an Indian man. The police came in and interviewed us all because the office held a set of keys. Finger prints were taken of all the staff. Naturally, the woman moved out shortly after the attack. They never caught the guy. Desperate to get some more tenants in and put a 'let by' sign in clear view of everyone, Julian allowed the apartment to be rented out again to another couple of young girls. Did we tell them what happened? Even when they asked what the area was like at weekends? Ask Ed, he let and tied that one.

Seeing that my appointment diary was empty, Julian hovered around me all afternoon. He asked me if I was busy, and whether I'd like to accompany him to a valuation. I agreed.

We walked together towards St Katherine's Dock, trailing along the streets enjoying the November sun, the last patch of good weather before winter properly took hold. Julian was uncomfortably quiet for a change and I could tell that his mind was ticking away frantically.

'Is everything okay?' I asked.

'Yeah, sound mate.' He then confided that Molly (his daughter) has been teething and keeping him up a lot at night.

'How about you?' he asked. 'We haven't really

had time to chat about what's going on.'

'I'm okay.'

'You still living on your own?'

I nodded. 'I haven't really planned my next move.' Which was true, I had been procrastinating in my flat and hadn't even tidied or cleaned for weeks.

'Are you happy at work?' he asked. There was a hint of sincerity in his voice, like he genuinely cared about me when he asked this.

I looked at our surroundings to judge whether it was a good time to tell him the truth or not. I could hear birdsong and a break from the traffic. 'No.'

There was an awkward silence. 'Can you . . . why is that?'

'I'm tired. And I'm finding it hard to keep up the pace like I did when I first began. I'm tired of driving two hours a day, if not more, in rush hour traffic. Don't get me wrong, I like working with you guys (lie), but I'm starting to question my commitment to the company.'

I might as well have just quit on the spot, this was a pretty damming confession yet painfully accurate.

Julian was taken aback. He was probably only making polite conversation and didn't expect much of a response. 'Shit,' he said reflectively.

We kept walking – all the while I could hear the cogs in his brain turning and grinding to a halt. My performance was poor at present, but it hadn't always been, and on an excel spreadsheet I was sure that I still looked shit hot. Julian and I knew that - despite my flaws and terrible punctuality record - I was one of his strongest negotiators. He knew that, I told myself - he must know that.

'I don't know what to say. I'm sorry you feel like that. I appreciate you've been through quite a bit lately (lie) . . . if you need more time off, just say so.'

For once it seemed like I had the upper hand over Julian. I continued to confess. 'I don't know what it is. I've changed. I can't remember the person I was.' That was God's honest truth.

I mentioned to you, reader, that I had morals and a good sense of character, even a high opinion of myself at one point in my life. Claudia used to say she was attracted to me because of my confidence, sociability and consideration of others, but it had all been eroded in the pursuit of a sale, the pursuit of wealth. The accident, if you can call it that, had done me a favour and was moving me away from that life; to what exactly was still unclear to me at the time. The path I had taken had led to some kind of moral erosion. Claudia saw me as a man with no depth, that's why she left me; and I let her go, because I'd neglected her needs also. In my epiphany, I concluded that you either do a job compliantly or you don't do it at all. There is no happy in-between. I thought of Grace and how she had limited aspirations and yet was happy just to work and live her life – perhaps a commission or a bonus here and there. That just wasn't me.

We arrived at the valuation appointment. A young trader, about my age, had made his first investment purchase: an ex-council flat situated close to St Katherine's Dock. He'd done the usual: new kitchen, wood floor treatment, Ikea furniture, and now he wanted us to tell him it wasn't highly overrated and that he'd get the rent he wanted. I watched Julian respond like a machine; his sales pitch so polished and in tune with his body that I could predict every eyebrow twitch, hand gesture and pitch shift of his voice. The man nodded, looked at his watch a few times, and after his questions were answered he asked for our terms of business to look through and waved us both out of the house.

Julian didn't broach the subject with me again after that. If anything he seemed upbeat, jokey even, trying to do impressions from Channel Four comedy shows – really badly – in the hope that I would laugh out loud. I went along with it, realising that there was no way I could revoke my confession. In the back of my mind I was anxious about being cut loose back into the world.

I couldn't sleep that night. My mind was over-analysing every decision that I'd made and every word I'd spoken to people that day; I was worried that I'd been too hasty, not thinking things through properly, rash, naïve. It was inevitable that I would be unemployed by the end of the week, and I'd failed to grasp the full consequences of my conversation with Julian. Claudia no longer lived with me and the prospect of paying over £1400 a month in rent on my own whilst having no income coming into my account was not a settling thought – my credit cards were also maxed and I lived in my overdraft. I hated being dependent on a job, especially since all I was doing was aspiring for a lifestyle full of luxuriance: meals out, drinks at exclusive cocktail bars, gigs (even though I hate crowds), and nice holidays. This would have to end.

It rained all through the night, the patter magnified in volume as each heavy droplet struck the concrete courtyard. The couple in the flat below were having sex, moaning and whimpering, and it felt as though they were in the same room as me. I could hear youths around the corner, the tininess of their MP3 players as they slurred youth speak at each other.

I was the city-suburb insomniac, probably one of many. I thought about the incident at the Aldgate Triangle complex days before. What troubled me more was that I had seemingly forgotten all about that incident so quickly. Convenient amnesia, I thought - surely another symptom of psychosis.

After shaving in the bathroom, I stared at my reflection in the mirror. Like some tribal looking motif, my scar was still prominent as ever. It seemed to protrude more at night that in the day – perhaps because I could feel the blood pumping more heavily around my body at night or because the light cast tiny shadows in the creases. I considered that I was changing; my memory at the time was lapsing. I forgot the name of the prostitute in the sauna. Like any dream, details continued to fade days after the event.

I carried a glass of red wine back into the living room and paced back and forth. I'd left the curtains open (Claudia hated me doing that) and was looking out onto the street. Everything seemed normal. Beneath the glow of a lamppost, the rain looked like little sparks of hot iron; a couple of other lights were on in houses along the road like tired embers, home to fellow insomniacs like me. But then I noticed a figure, about fifty yards away dressed in a long navy raincoat and an old fashioned Victorian style cap; he or she was tucked away in the shadows, standing firm. I had to squint at first and push my face to the window to get a better look, but there, sure enough, was a body and head angled in my direction. What troubled me the most was the fact that I couldn't see this person's eyes, but I could feel that they were staring right at me. I remained still, watching, waiting for something to happen, but nothing did. Slowly, that same feeling of anger grew from within. Was this person a thief, looking for an opportunity? Or a stoner who had forgotten what time of day it was? My brain fired back to Aldgate and the people watching me on the roof. Just then the figure raised his arm, in that same mechanical way they had done at Aldgate, and my head started to feel fuzzy. I gritted my teeth and began to swear under my breath, and in that instant I wanted to run out of my front door, give chase and confront this entity - but at 3am? Outer London or inner-London, confronting strangers was never a good idea.

I ran down the stairs to check that my door was locked. The chain was secure and everything seemed normal apart from a small square of paper that lay on the door mat. It was wet, and looked as though it had only been recently pushed through the letterbox. I bent down, took it and returned upstairs to the window.

I looked back out onto the street but the figure had disappeared, so I read the note. **Finish the job** was written in fine black ink. I was bemused. Finish what job? And who the heck was passing cryptic notes through my door?

At work the next day I was tired, irate and still baffled by the message. At about eleven, whilst I was daydreaming somewhat, Julian and David came up the stairs together.

'Can we have a word?' David asked. I nodded and they beckoned me outside.

December had finally brought with it a biting chill and a strong gust of wind forced us to retreat around the corner outside of the locksmiths. I felt like I was back at school, about to get a good kicking from the school bullies.

'Julian mentioned to me that you aren't' happy,'

David started.

I didn't deny it and nodded at him.

'That puts us in a bit of a difficult situation,' he continued.

'What do you mean?'

'Usually, when a neg stops performing, there's no point in keeping them on.'

I explained that I understood the situation, that my choice to leave was a hard one (lie) and that I really enjoyed working with them (lie), but I asked them to give me until the end of the week to get my head together before being cast out into the world of unemployment; I explained that there was admin that needed sorting, and that I had two South Korean's to move in to a flat. Julian didn't say a word, he just looked right through me - maybe he was sad at losing me? They both looked at each other and, having made a good case, they agreed to preserve some of my dignity by allowing me to stay until Friday. We shook hands on it, a strange formality at a sacking/resignation, but I was glad it was like that.

My estranged father didn't talk to me much, but the best piece of advice he ever gave me was that I should never burn my bridges.

Now I needed to ring him for support and more guidance.

FAMILY

There's nothing wrong with the relationship I have with my dad. He was always around when I was growing up; he just liked to keep his distance - thinking time, he would call it. My mum died at childbirth and I don't think he ever got over it. Deep down I believe that I reminded him of her death. Perhaps he felt let down by a system that should have prevented this; after all, it was the early 80s and not the 1800s. He was always passing me between child-carers, nannies and nurseries, after school clubs, holiday clubs, etc. And since I was the only child, I had no one else to discuss my situation or feelings with. Claudia casually referred to him as a social retard, and joked (I think) that I had inherited most of his genes. He kept himself to himself and never liked to talk much, so when - as an adult - I moved out, nothing really changed. Each year we would have a nice meal to mark mum's birthday, or his, or even mine, and occasionally I'd get an email letting me know his intentions, i.e. a golfing holiday in Portugal or a weekend mountain trekking in the Brecon Beacons. He visited me in hospital, once or twice, and told me to let him know if I needed anything.

I remember the phone call from that night:

'Dad?'

'Hello son.'

'You okay?'

'I'm okay. How's your neck?'

'Much better, thanks. I need to ask a favour.'

'Could you not just email me?'

'I thought it would be better to ring. Claudia walked out on me and I've lost my job.'

There was a long pause. 'Sorry to hear that. I liked Claudia.'

'I need a place to stay.'

'Do you want me to get your room ready?'

'It won't be until the weekend.'

'E-mail me the details.'

'Thanks.'

It is hard to write objectively about your own father, but if I'm honest with you, I felt closer to some of the tenants I moved into properties.

When I arrived back at home I checked the mail for any other handwritten notes. There was nothing. I had no food left, so I decided to visit the gym. I should have really begun packing my apartment up, but I felt lured by the comforting warmth of a real sauna.

Over the next couple of days I was spending an average of three hours going between the pool, Jacuzzi and sauna each evening. And by the end of the week I knew everyone else's patterns and habits. One woman wore a wetsuit into the Jacuzzi, just to hold it all in. Perhaps this was for religious reasons? Either way, I knew she'd only last a maximum of ten minutes. Then there was a hairy Arabic looking male with dimples across most of his face that spent almost as much time in the Jacuzzi as me. The list could go on, including the attractive blonde who made two appearances in one evening. I freely admit to perving over the bodies of other women, whatever shape, age or size, after all, we were all at the gym to be looked at or adored, if not by ourselves then by others; anonymous voyeurs who carried out a silent etiquette.

During Thursday's staff meeting, Julian announced that I was leaving the company and that Friday would be my last day. I felt sad, like I had somehow held the office together with my sarcasm and humour. Grace looked upset.

The rest of the day was spent going through admin, ringing my prospective tenants to inform them that Grace or Ed or Martina or loud, gobby Diana would help them find a place to live. And there were moments when I reflected on the slip of paper pushed through my door, and how it had arrived a few days too late.

During my lunch break, which I had at my desk,

I contemplated searching for jobs but decided to check my private emails instead. My dad had messaged me to tell me that he would be away at the weekend and would leave the key in its usual place for me to find.

Later that afternoon, the two South Koreans came to pay their monies and I gave them the keys to their flat. They stared at me blankly, said thank you and bowed at me. I wished them luck and told them to ring Julian if they ran into any problems.

One benefit of renting a fully furnished flat is that moving should be easier, that you only have to carry your essentials with you. Back home, I finally got round to packing some of my possessions. The fridge was already emptied, apart from jars of pickles and smoked cheese, so I booked myself another table at the gym and asked for a table by the window overlooking the river. The receptionist didn't get my humour and put me on hold for five minutes to find out if there was actually a river besides the bar.

All my friends were there at the poolside – the lady in the bathing suit, the hairy Arab, and some middle aged businessmen, both having a conversation about their divorce for all to hear. I noticed a cute brunette that I'd seen a few nights before and she acknowledged me with a smile. In the sauna there was one man, heavily built and with sharp, angular facial features, who outdid my personal best of forty-two minutes in the sauna.

I thought nothing of it at the time, it just made me more competitive and I vowed that I would last for forty-five minutes the following day.

LOOSE ENDS

I'd like to say that my last day at work was the best ever, that I enjoyed every minute: the messages of goodwill from colleagues and clients, novelty gifts, and good weather, all surrounded by happy faces. But there was none of that. There was a brief gift presentation ceremony that afternoon where Julian and David presented me with a bottle of Crème-de-Menthe liquor (some kind of private joke that they found funny), and I got a card signed by everyone in the office. It was agreed that there'd be drinks in the Brown Bear afterwards. Grace said she was looking forward to a chat – she'd even put some lipstick on.

My desk drawer was filled with parking receipts, petrol receipts and old pens, packs of gum and business cards. It didn't take me long to ditch most of the rubbish and file all the necessary expenses receipts, wipe down my desk and pass all my admin onto David. I knew I'd get some commission in next month's pay due to late move-ins, and this was a nice thought to leave on.

I read some of the old emails as I deleted them. There were some personal ones from Claudia, thank you emails from clients and tenants, comedic web links from Gary, and a couple of emails from old uni friends I no longer kept in contact with. There were two unopened emails in my deleted items. They were from Julian to the whole office, the date of one was after the stabbing and the other was sent the day before I came back to work.

They read: As you can imagine, we're all in shock about what's happened to Ed and John. Both are in a serious but stable condition at The Royal in Whitechapel. David and I will be visiting them both when we get the all clear – and there will be a collection for flowers and fruit. Speak to us if you want to know more.

Nothing unusual there, I thought, except I can't remember there being any fruit. I followed the thread and saw that a couple of days later, another group email was sent: As you can imagine, there's been quite a lot of press interest about this incident. Police are still operating around the area which can make parking tricky, so if you're going to take prospective tenants out on viewings, might I suggest that you park elsewhere. And please be careful who you speak to. In particular, a red-haired journalist posing as a tenant managed to coax Ed's details from Martina. Thankfully she didn't get hold of John's details. I hope you appreciate the sensitivity of this email.

The email sent the day before my return to work:

Subject: John is returning tomorrow.

Obviously we're thrilled to have him back much sooner than anticipated. Please avoid asking him questions or mentioning journalist's names to him. The more ways we can help him settle back into work the better. Ed is expected to return at the end of the week, so please ensure that the above applies to both. Julian.

At the time I found it ironic that I should stumble upon this on my last day at work. And I can't deny that I was intrigued – why delete these emails? And who was the journalist? I hadn't even thought about asking whether there had been much interest in my attack, probably because I wanted to put the ugly incident behind me. I was actually relieved and very grateful that my details weren't given out – and I can thank Claudia's sensitive nature for not wanting the attention as the grieving girlfriend.

I looked up to see Ed working at his PC. I had an empty diary for the next hour, as did he.

'Ed, fancy one last kebab for old times' sake?'

He shuffled in his seat and then agreed it would be best to grab a coffee.

Ed bought me a double espresso; it would be as short and bitter as our conversation. He asked me about my plans and I told him that I was moving house and would probably take a holiday. I fired back the same question and he said that he'd been approached about a different job in the city. I made the assumption that it was through his private member's clubs, but he didn't react well to that.

'I thought Julian and Dan were approaching you about a promotion?'

'What makes you say that?'

'You were all sneaking off for working lunches a couple of weeks ago.'

Ed took a sip of his coffee and added two sugars. 'It's not really any of your business. We get on well, you've got to appreciate that I've been here since the start.' I nodded. 'I'm sorry about what happened to us, really I am. But you've got to move on.'

'I am.'

'It's good that you're going – I think I'll be more . . . relaxed.'

I just sat there and stared at him, dumbfounded. Ed's eyes weren't quite right; behind a yellowy film I could detect aggression. He squinted back at me.

'I told Julian that you weren't happy in your job, that you'd been affected by the attack more than me,' he mentioned.

'Why would you do that?'

'To get ahead. That night made me realise that you only get one crack in life, so I'm trying to get ahead. I felt that you were trying to pull me back, stay in the past, that you weren't prepared to move forward. Hell, I think I did you a favour because you just haven't been performing.'

His comment about dragging him back really hit a nerve and I sat there waiting for an appropriate comeback, but it never came. Probably because I knew he was right; Ed had really changed and I had stagnated.

'Don't take it personally,' he added, swilling his espresso around in his cup. 'But it is good to see you move on.' With that he stood up and returned to the office. That was to be the last time I would see Ed for months.

I sipped my last dregs of coffee slowly, even the gritty bit at the bottom with sugar that hadn't dissolved. Fired up, there was nothing else for me to do but go and visit the arches where it all happened. Ed had pitched his argument, accusing me that I was unable to face my demons and let go of what happened that night. I had to prove him wrong.

The car park was unattended, which was a bit of a joke considering you paid for peace of mind that someone patrolled it. I strolled right in, past the Audis, VWs, Julian's Porsche and a selection of other city cars. Ed's car was still there. I walked to where I used to park my car. My heartbeat was erratic at this point. I stood at the spot where I fell and reflected in silence. The sound of London was as clear here as anywhere else in the city. The arches were still shrouded in darkness - no light and no sound came from it. I continued walking, checking the fences for any gaps or secret tunnels, small enough for a large dog or fox perhaps. There was none. At the very end of the car park was a large sewer pipe, nearly four feet square, but it was sealed and locked. Where it led to I did not know, and that for me summarised London: a city of mystery.

I wondered what the area had been like before the rail link was even built, imagining that work yards, alleyways and passages to the unknown were probably common place. Then I pictured Ed venturing towards The Strand and finding a small alleyway that took him to the Backstabber's Gentlemen's Club.

It was my last day working in East London and rather than feel relief at being set free, I was worked up and annoyed by the way that Ed had declared himself better than me and that I had been somewhat in his shadow. What annoyed me even more was feeling like a failure, considering the fact that maybe I was nearing my lowest point but with a grim realisation that the worst was still to come.

Leaving the car park, I imagined coming across two black youths leaning against a car of their choice, watching, waiting and laughing. What would I do different this time – fight back or freeze? Stupid city boy, I thought, they should've shanked me a bit deeper, and then perhaps this dream would have ended peacefully.

Back at the office, Julian was sat at the back, buttering up a difficult landlord on the phone who was unsatisfied that his tenants wanted to leave after two months of moving in. It was hardly surprising since the flat in question was situated directly above a late night café where members of East London's finest youth would gather to eat noisily and smoke joints. The rest of the office was empty. I just sat at my desk looking at my screen blankly. The striplights gave me a headache and my throat felt sore again. It began to rain outside.

Eventually, Julian called time and said we should (those still in the office) go to the Brown Bear for one last drink. He announced that Ed had called in to offer his apologies because he was showing a young couple of lawyers a string of apartments in the Docklands. I was glad, because I could focus my attention on Grace. She looked sultry; her hair had been delicately swept back revealing the fine lines of her jaw and neck, her lips were also pink and looked moist. This was the type of memory I wanted to recall again and again, that of beauty captured.

At the pub, we managed to grab some time to chat, and we both felt relaxed in each other's company. Julian and David said their goodbyes and left after one drink, wishing me well, and the rest of the negotiators had all made other plans. It was the type of send-off I wanted – low key. Grace and I were finally alone. I asked her if she'd eaten and whether she'd like to join me for dinner. She agreed.

We walked into Wapping together and tried our

luck at a popular Italian restaurant. It was busy, with a vibrant buzz; generous looking portions of food were being carried diligently and spun from table to table by experienced waiters. Even though we hadn't booked, we managed to get a table because of a last minute cancellation.

We must have looked very much the couple as we sat down and ordered wine. We talked about silly things, made each other laugh and drank lots. She ordered a warm artichoke salad for starters; I had scallops, pan seared with Italian sausage and garnished with rocket. We got through another bottle of wine, and two courses later we were sharing a tiramisu and were feeding each other like all of the other couples. I started to believe that leaving the job was the best decision I had ever made. Did I mention that we held hands across the table for most of the night? In six months I had never felt so alive, and my heart felt warm with affection for her. I told her often that I loved her spirit, and that it was nice to be friends with a genuine, good-natured girl. In return, she gushed about how she'd miss my silly emails, our late morning banter, watching me arrive late, and how nice it was to hear me repel Julian's flippant comments like water off a duck's back.

I wanted to tell her that I loved her.

I settled the bill in true gentlemanly fashion and we left the restaurant together. The air was damp and the streets glistened with the light from all the converted warehouses. It was almost like stepping back into Dickensian London when we crossed cobbled streets. I half expected someone to be selling chestnuts on the street corner. We huddled together for warmth.

She looked at me and I could see the streetlamp flickering in her eye. 'My flat's just around the corner,' she said.

My heart stepped up a gear. To decline her invite would have surely ended the night and I would have saved some good memories: her smiling face, physical contact, no strings relaxation. In fact, I had experienced enough intimacy in one night that I could have gone home and masturbated without complicating things. My mind erred on the side of caution – had I so easily forgotten what happened in Crouch End? Without thinking, I stepped away from her.

'I mean, if you want to go, that's fine,' she said dejectedly.

I didn't want to upset her. 'That would be lovely,' I said, and I took her hand and we walked together.

Our footsteps seemed to echo across the empty streets and I could hear water trickling into old drains and sewerways as we walked. As we approached her flat I found myself counting the rhythm of my heart beat. It was almost like there was an extra reflex of the muscle: three beats. I'd never felt that before.

We stepped into the lift of her apartment. It felt familiar. She was flirtatious, flicking her hair playfully. I gazed at her longingly. The lift stopped, the doors opened and I followed her out. My feet barely made a sound on the tiled floor. The door opened up and we stepped in. The apartment had a homely smell of freshly brewed coffee and the aroma of vanilla scented candles; her abode was small, almost classifiable as a self-contained studio, but it was warm and cosy.

'Can I get you a drink?'

'Whatever you're having,' I replied, surveying her pad. I hung my coat on the hall pegs and looked at all her photo murals of friends and families on the wall. All the while, my heart pumped wildly inside. Bam-bum-bum, bam-bum-bum. I watched her kneel to get some mugs out of the dishwasher and bump her head on the work surface as she did so. She giggled to herself. I laughed with her.

I sat in the lounge and waited for her. Grace came in holding two mugs of coffee, placed them on the table, sat next to me and rested her hand on my shoulder, hey eyes gazing right at me.

'Oh my god!' she said. 'You've got the most amazing eyes.' There was a pause and then laughter between us as we realised how corny that sounded, then we locked eyes again, leant in and kissed. She pulled back. 'Sorry,' she said steadying herself. I didn't say anything. She looked around nervously, got up and grabbed two glasses from a small cabinet in the corner of the room, and with it a bottle of Baileys. I got up to follow her, to pull her back and tease her lips back to mine, when suddenly my joints stiffened and I began to shiver wildly - it was as though I had trapped a nerve at the base of my spine and I was temporarily paralysed. Sweat poured down my back and my hands were contorted into a tight fist; my fingertips were numb from the pressure and they looked grey, felt cold, and there was fresh blood slowly seeping along the cuticles.

I watched Grace crouch next to the sofa and look through her CD collection, oblivious to my predicament. I felt my skin tighten and my throat ached and burned - like I'd just smoked a whole box of cigarettes in seconds; my gums felt swollen and I had an acrid taste in my mouth, and my tongue felt puffy like I was about to go into anaphylactic shock.

It's happening, I thought, it's happening again like in the dream. Every sound in the room was magnified in volume as I struggled to breathe. Beads of sweat collected on my forehead as I thought about what to do. I panicked. I couldn't do this to Grace, not her. Run, I told myself, run to the door and leave – but what if someone else saw me? I managed to angle my body and stagger towards Grace's bathroom. I couldn't let her see me like this, if she did she would scream and I would surely kill her. I didn't want her to die.

I pulled the bathroom light cord and managed to slide the lock across with my crooked hands. My nails looked like tiny white razor blades and the skin across my knuckles seemed to crackle from being pulled so tightly, all I could see was the ivory peaks of bone. I looked at my face in the mirror. The whites of my eyes were bloodshot and covered in a yellow film, my pupils were dilating and my cornea looked like shiny black onyx; my face was drawn and all I could see were the veins around my temple pumping furiously.

Grace called to me from the hall asking if I was okay. I tried to call back but couldn't find my voice. I wanted desperately to warn her to stay away, but the pressure around my throat was such that I thought I was going to black out. I began to retch. Grace's hands tap lightly against the door. I retched again until a stream of sticky yellow liquid came out and stuck to the side of the sink. Saliva followed, lots of it, as though a gland in the roof of my mouth was free-pouring.

'Are you okay?' she asked.

Thick globules of spit collected in pools around my mouth and I spat them out. They were like mini clots the size of pomegranate seeds and rich in colour. I managed to cry out in pain.

'Oh my god, are you okay in there?'

Tears ran down my face. I examined myself and noted how my lower jaw seemed to hang loose. My gums had receded and there was black, putrid jelly at the base of each canine. I must feed, that was what my body told me. But I was transfixed, staring back at this drooling monster.

'shhick,' I managed to garble.

'What?'

'Sick,' I growled. 'I'm sick!'

'Oh God, was it the scallops?'

I paused, reflecting on her words, and moaned in frustration, almost gargling as I pushed my fist hard against the wall to balance myself. My hair was a lustrous black and my hands no longer felt like they were ridden with arthritis as I started to regulate my breathing. My fingertips were numb, the nails sharp and ready to tear at human flesh, and I wanted to do exactly that to her for asking such a daft question.

Grace asked through the door if I wanted a cup of nettle tea to settle my stomach. I looked at the door, at the small lock that stood in the way between her living and dying – all it would have taken was a small flick across and she would have been mine. I noticed in my reflection that blood was seeping from the corner of my eyes and my jaw seemed to quiver; I felt the only way I could fix it back in place was to chomp down on something hard. Kill Grace, that's what my body wanted to do. But to kill Grace, feed off her and take advantage of such an innocent soul, would have been to kill the last ounces of humanity I had left in me. Then the beast within started to reason, and it made me realise that the kill would be a clumsy one, and certainly lead to my capture. Suddenly Grace was no longer a friend in need, but food; she was a bridge, and killing her would have determined how I would live the rest of my life. It was no dream, of that I was certain. On that very night, I realised that if I took her life that I would spend my days on the run, in the dark, become a ghost – no better than those who prey on the weak and elderly.

I heard Grace walking away to make tea. During that time the real me slowly began to resurface. Hunched over the sink, I gripped the cold white ceramic as I fought with my demon, writhing in agony as parts of my body seemed to click back into place along my ribs and shoulders. My skin loosened and I found that I could breathe more easily. And since I could no longer see these features I believed that everything was returning back to normal, to how it should be. My eyes, however, remained bloodshot, and my clothes were now saturated in sweat and saliva. I looked down at the sink, at the thick globules of bloody phlegm, and tried to wash them away. Eventually they slipped down the plughole, but not without time and effort. I splashed water over my face and my hair and took a cool flannel to the back of my neck.

Grace knocked on the door again to ask if I was okay.

'I'm fine,' I whispered. 'I've been a little bit sick, but I think I'm back to normal.'

'God, you worried me, I thought you were dying in there.'

'Me too,' I replied, and with a deep breath I unlocked the door and opened it. She was stood there, her eye make-up smudged as if she had been cupping and pulling her face in angst. Her shoulders seemed to protrude and I could see her bra straps clearly between the bony peaks.

'I'm sorry,' I said, grabbing hold of her arm. She came forward and embraced me and I pulled her head against my chest and rubbed her back gently, cradling her. I hadn't considered that she might get wet from my clothes. We just stood there for what seemed like minutes, and that's how I wanted to remember her – still and untouched. I believe that it was my hidden love and compassion for Grace that kept her alive that night.

'Your heartbeat is so strong,' she whispered. And it was, back to the normal two beat bam-bum. The monster had appeared magnificently and then disappeared almost as quickly as it had come. But I knew that if I stayed the night with Grace that there would still be a good chance that she might not live. I explained to her that I needed to leave.

'Thank you for a wonderful night,' I said.

'Will you be okay? You can kip on my sofa.'

'Thanks, but I need lots of fresh air. The walk will do me good.'

'Okay.' She seemed disheartened. 'Okay,' she said again.

We walked to the door and I turned and kissed her on the forehead, as though I had given her a blessing. She smiled. 'It'll be nice to see you again,' she said staring deep into my eyes. I could tell from her reaction that she saw what I had seen, that

I was not myself, and perhaps that made her feel relieved.

'Definitely,' I said. 'I've had fun. I'll pop by at work some time and take you for a coffee.' And with that I got into the lift and waved to her as the doors closed.

I breathed a sigh of relief as the lift descended and then I punched the metal wall in frustration, leaving a small indentation. My emotions were mixed, as I looked at my reflection I saw someone who was weak, unassertive and shy of the world. And then I imagined what my life could be like if I tamed this monster inside me; but I was vexed at having such a curse bestowed upon me, and fearful of the implications. In my whole life I'd never felt a danger to anyone, and neither in my job nor on a night out had I ever posed a threat to someone's life before until that evening.

As I began my walk back to North London from Wapping, I thought about the character of Jekyll and Hyde. Maybe Robert Louis Stevenson wrote from experience, warning others about the implications of seeking power in a world driven by money and greed; or perhaps he was foretelling what would happen if you put aside your morals and allowed the primeval spirit to flourish deep within.

SOLIDARITY IN THE CITY

Wapping is renowned for its poor travel connections to anywhere other than the city or docklands. Most people who lived there owned flash cars or paid for taxis. I needed to go north and the trains had stopped running. I was too drunk to drive and couldn't risk taking a bus in case I had another seizure in front of other late night revelers.

As I walked through Tower Bridge I remembered the girl in my dream. I knew I hadn't killed her in real life, but the physical transformation I felt during that vision was identical to how I had felt with Grace. I still felt guilty, and the nerves behind my eyes stung at the thought. I recalled the experience with the prostitute, whilst it seemingly was resolved and nothing but a product of my own disillusionment with life, a symptom of self-diagnosed psychosis, I began to doubt myself. It made no sense – did it happen or was I imagining things? I had a desire to walk towards Crouch End and go back in, but I couldn't, I wouldn't dare. What made it more frustrating was that I could not share this secret with anyone at that point in time.

Someone once told me that it's a relief to hit rock bottom, because then you can plan for better things; I didn't see how being a 'vampire' could bring better things to anyone. That's what I believed I was becoming at this point.

I'd never really considered exploring London by foot before. I guess it was because I'd found a job as soon as I moved back to the city and saw no need to venture beyond the areas I already knew. At the time of my early transformation, I was totally unaware of where the ant collective would gather. The city offers a wealth of protection, with networked tunnels, secret alleyways and much more, all usually within a couple hundred yards of each other. I figured that as each generation continued their lifecycle (work, breed, move out, retire), that people became inured to the wealth and grandeur that mocked them, that they stopped looking beyond the obvious differences in wealth and elite social classes and accepted their place in the food chain, an empirical caste system that no one talked about. Buildings became protected from the outside world; the city redesigned itself and became regenerated by invaders from other cultures, invaders with even more money to pour into London: Americans, Arabs and Russians to name but a few. In a way I'm glad that I made a discovery. And because of that I've changed. If you live in London and you're reading this, you're probably thinking big deal, I don't live near there, it doesn't matter, and I won't be affected. I suggest you take a friend on a late night walk around your area and look for evidence of what's going on beneath your feet. If you find a collection of foxes, chances are that you're near a hive entrance. Streetlights that don't work or remain off at certain times of the evening or during the week can often mean two things: that the light has stopped working, or that it's a signal that a safe house is nearby. This is no conspiracy, just a simple truth that you choose to ignore - you do not question what you don't know; what doesn't matter to your world, your own precious life, is not important.

Had I not changed I would be saying the same thing, but I cannot choose to ignore the obvious. My advice to you is to ignore my advice, to seek comfort and be reassured by your own instincts, accept what signs and plaques tell you about a place - never question what you are told.

I do not need to explain myself to anyone.

TRAILS

The route I took home was relatively busy. It was still Friday night to some; it was Saturday morning to me. Drunken partygoers were spilling out of Shoreditch and Brick Lane at a phenomenal rate and taxis seemed to have an endless stream of business around the Old Street area. There were moments of calm as I drifted through Canonbury, flanked by grand four storey town houses and empty garden squares where the only litter you could see was a mushy pile of autumn leaves. I checked my back regularly to see whether I was being followed; ever since my attack I'd been passing alleys and gangs of youth with more caution.

Holloway Road, a route I would no longer need to suffer on a daily basis, was still teeming with cars, vans and taxis. When I got to Archway, I was tempted to take the main road under 'Suicide

Bridge' but I chose to simper through Highgate, a sleepy village at that time of night.

By this time I was tired from walking and the soles of my feet burned. I passed the private schools, the park and then the cemetery. It was whilst passing the east side of the cemetery that I found myself stopping to massage the temple of my forehead. Maybe it was the cold air that had numbed my face to the point where my nose continuously ran. I rubbed my face vigorously to bring it back to life, but there was something not quite right that was causing my mind discomfort and I could feel my heart begin to beat irregularly again. I felt how I did during the night when a figure came to my door and posted the note through the letterbox – unsure and unsettled.

The road was still deserted. I checked my watch: 3am. I told myself to keep walking, that I was only another hour from home at best, but I couldn't, because I could hear whispers, a woman's soft voice moaning delicately, gasping with pleasure. Though faint, I wanted to trace it down, to hear more of these erotic harmonies, but I stopped and reflected on my situation. Three hours ago I'd nearly butchered a beautiful work colleague. And with my new guise, rummaging around graveyards at night searching for the source of voices didn't seem like a very good idea.

I snapped out of my trance and coaxed my legs to begin moving again and I carried on walking towards Highgate's summit. My attention now focused on the flickering street lamp up ahead which had two men stood beneath it. My head down, I told myself not to engage them in any way. But there was something awkward about the way in which they held themselves. They were like figurines stolen from the Nike store in London; their faces masked by large white hoods. I clenched my fists and raised my shoulders in a meagre attempt to look threatening; my steps also became heavier as I tried to show that I was a man who shouldn't be approached.

The irregular heartbeat, the three strong beats, returned and I feared the worst; I feared I was prepping my body for an attack. Them or me? Less than ten metres away, they remained motionless, wax mannequins of menace. The streetlights kept flickering. I held my breath as I passed them, anticipating anything, even the slightest movement would have triggered an explosion of energy on my part. I'm going to kill them, I thought. I was ready to lash out, bounding right past, my heels stamping into the ground, and then before I knew it I was ten metres ahead of them. I heard nothing, felt nothing, yet I could feel them watching me. Twenty metres, a good sprinting distance away from them now, enough for me to turn round to stare at them. They were gone. Worse still, the light had stopped flickering and the street was void of life again.

I got to the top of Highgate Hill and contemplated going straight to my dad's house; his email hinted that he might have already left the key out. But if I arrived unannounced and he was still in, I knew he would not be happy and it might damage the goodwill I needed from him; he might have also known that something was wrong with me, so I picked up the pace and broke into a gentle sprint, even though I was still a few miles from Finchley. I'm not cold at this point, but I do have a burning desire to get into bed and rest, even if it's just for an hour.

By 4am I had arrived outside my flat. My legs had pins and needles from all the walking and mix-match sprinting, my feet felt like they'd been dancing on hot coals, and I could already feel the blisters as I slid my shoe off.

One thing I am good at is trying to save on unnecessary waste, this includes electricity. I was good when it came to switching things off like appliances and lights, so imagine my surprise when I found all the lights to my flat had been left on. I grabbed the broom in the communal area and ventured in. The weight of the handle wouldn't be enough to kill anyone, but it would be enough to defend myself and perhaps buy me some precious seconds, just in case someone did ambush me.

The flat looked untouched. There was no sound of movement in the house and it looked how I had left it. I figured that Claudia may have made a surprise visit looking for something amongst her junk I had piled in one corner of the room, and then rushed out. The flat looked like any other bachelor pad with empty glasses and dirty mugs scattered around. The answerphone machine flashed at me intermittently. The message was from the estate agents who were trying to rent out my flat, informing me that they were bringing someone round that evening and that I should ring them back if this wasn't okay. Legally it wasn't but I was past caring.

I awoke at around midday, amazed at how well I had slept. Perhaps it was the fact that I no longer had to work at the godforsaken office. I sat in the living room and pieced together fragments of the previous night, and like before I managed to convince myself that nothing happened at Grace's apartment, that it was just another one of my funny turns. It seemed my body had developed a mechanism for blanking out these morbid memories completely.

I decided to ring Grace to find out what happened. She was working that day, a downside to the job, but the office was quiet and I was glad to hear her voice answer the phone. She was expecting a client to walk through the door so I made it quick, firstly by apologising for my rushed departure from her flat, and then by stressing that I'd really enjoyed myself in her company. She told me that she had fun, too, and that we should catch up again soon. I told her that I looked forward to that. I then quizzed her about my behaviour – all she said was that she heard me being sick and that she was sick shortly after I had left. She sounded different, like we hadn't been as close as I thought. I went to ask her more but her one O'clock came through the door and she seemed keen to get off the phone, so I left it at that. I had blown an opportunity to tell her how good she made me feel.

A few minutes later the phone rang again. It was my dad; he said his plans for the day had changed slightly and that he would be around for a while before meeting a friend at a wine bar in Covent Garden. I agreed to meet him at 4pm and began packing my clothes into black bags. Most of my important belongings only took minutes to pack away; the CDs, books and DVDs that I owned went into two cardboard boxes.

Before leaving I decided to take a shower to freshen myself up. It was an unrushed, hot and invigorating one which allowed me to reflect on a pretty harsh week. I was officially a bum again - jobless and single. On stepping out of the shower I looked at the mirror and I felt instantly cold. There, in the condensation on the mirror, was a message: finish the job. This was no coincidence, and there was no way that I would have written such a thing in big, scrawly writing. In that moment I concluded that someone had broken into my house and was playing some sick joke on me, messing with my mind. It made me angry, and scared at the same time, but most importantly it motivated me to pack my things and get the hell out.

HIGHGATE

My dad's house was probably worth in the region of 1.5 million at the time I wrote this, hidden in a quiet street not far from the main high street of Highgate. It had four bedrooms and the décor had remained unchanged in over twenty years. The school round the corner was where I was privately educated, and I think that's another reason why my dad seemed so disappointed with how I had turned out.

Dad had retired, although he did the odd bit of consultancy work, or so he said. Most of his time was now spent at private members clubs where I imagined him drinking single malts and reading the newspapers with a string of hot cappuccinos.

He stood at the front door as I walked up the steps of the front garden. For a moment I thought he was smiling, but on closer inspection it turned out to be more of an analytical squint. He shook my hand.

'Hi son, I'm running late. Here's the key, and you can use my computer to search for jobs.' And with that he walked out of the door straight towards his car. On reflection you could say that my dad is the main reason I became so emotionally hardened at such a young age; Claudia always said that I was unresponsive and that it was like talking to a brick wall when it came to discussing feelings. She was right.

The house was exactly how I remembered it. There was a minty mothball smell mixed in with that of stale scented candles; the living room had a nauseating aroma of fake Turkish delight. On a further sweep of the house, I found that the kitchen was the only room that had been modernised with lovely chrome fixtures and fittings, including a large granite work surface by Butlers and Morris, and a breakfast bar which had a lovely outlook onto the sun terrace. Leading out from the breakfast room were sliding doors to the patio area which had been kept in order. The living room was commanded by an original Victorian feature fireplace and an original Chesterfield suite complimented the original parquet flooring. There was a downstairs cloakroom and a large study, complete with broadband internet connection. The first floor had three bedrooms and a family bathroom with a whirlpool bath by Victoria Plumb; each room was a double, two of which had en-suites. The landing also led to a loft room which had eaves storage and a feature wall by Graham & Brown. My bedroom was the one that was most out of sight and tucked away.

I dumped my stuff and nosed around the rest of the house. The main bedroom, the room my dad slept in, was the only one kept in any sort of reasonable condition; the room had a sunny outlook with views over the front garden. I thought about how quiet it was compared to where I had lived previously. I was surprised to see pictures in frames; one was of him with old work colleagues, another of him on his own abroad which looked like it had been taken recently; finally I found one of me as a child and a picture of my mum. It was on the windowsill and remained badly faded, but it was good to know that my old man still had a heart, somewhere. Further exploration of the rooms revealed a wardrobe of old shirts and suits from Austin Reed - all neatly organised. I made a note of the book he was reading, something about travelling around Europe, and crouched down on the floor. Behind the side table of his drawers was a porno magazine called 'Office Slut' the contents of which contained various images of women being spanked and dominated by old men in suits. The date was recent, so I knew that not much had changed since I last lived with him.

It was easy to tell where he sat in the living room because of the dip in the sofa. The fireplace was ready to be lit, so I did the honour and settled down for a rest and helped myself to a glass or red wine, Chilean.

It was soon dark. I rustled together some basic food from the fridge and watched the London TV news. The feature story was about London's missing people and the efforts some organisations go to in order to trace them and reunite them with their families.

I must have dozed off momentarily, for when I came to I found myself running over to the patio doors and being violently sick outside. The vomit was dark in colour, tasted bitter and was made worse by heavy tannins from all the wine I had drunk. I felt like I had done the previous night, with Grace, and considered that my body was protesting at being intoxicated once again. I washed my hands and face in the downstairs toilet and decided to use the computer.

My dad's study felt more like a city office; everything was perfectly organised and streamlined with an abundance of technology, enough to run a small multinational company. The PC was on. He'd left a few internet tabs up, one of which was that of a lettings agent recruitment company. I quickly closed these down and opened up news websites. I also did some investigation on the UK Missing Persons Bureau website and was surprised to see - on average - about 50,000 people are reported missing in London annually. And whilst a large number are eventually located, over 300 bodies remain unidentified in London alone.

Typing in 'Highgate History' in to Google yielded a string of results, but none more popular than that of Highgate Cemetery. A website talked about the famous patriarchs who were buried there and how the cemetery had fallen into disarray; it was closed due to unpaid debts and was now run by a group of volunteers. I noted the opening and closing times and found a minefield of other links about Highgate cemetery, including the cemetery's eastern extension, and its darker past and associations with the occult. Deeper research led me to some old news sites detailing reported attacks on young women along Swains lane, and then there were claims that Highgate was at the confluence of several energy lines, whatever that meant.

I wanted to believe that vampires were real, that what was happening to me was somehow linked, and that I was in with a chance of finding some people suffering like me if I entered the graveyard at night. Being brought up in Highgate myself, I considered it my God-given right to parade in this area. It was a childish, stupid thought, and I was glad that I had enough sanity to rule out that idea. However, the history of the area intrigued me greatly and I took an unhealthy interest in my findings from the Highgate Vampire Society. It appeared to be nothing more than folklore at the heart of it, but nonetheless I had already planned to see the cemetery for myself the next day based on some of the writings.

The rest of the evening involved me sitting on the sofa watching TV, trying to convince myself that I was under a great deal of stress and that the symptoms I felt were trauma related and not a physical reckoning. That and I had a bout of food poisoning.

Dad strode in through the door at about midnight, stood in the living room and made a note of how much of his wine I had drunk, and then he asked me how I was. The conversation was brief and he was quick to say goodnight and retire to his room.

4am. My skin was saturated in sweat as I woke, my hand at my throat, gasping for air. Another dream, this time more vivid and grotesque than the previous vision; the woman was a leggy, pretty brunette who led me to an apartment block off Brick Lane where I proceeded to copulate with her before biting off a chunk of flesh from her shoulders as she lay face down on the bed screaming for me to stop. The dream lasted longer, but that was all I could remember – all I wanted to. It felt so real and I could taste blood in my mouth. I crept to the bathroom to check, and sure enough I found myself coughing up globules of blood coloured phlegm from deep within my lungs. I could hear my dad moving around in his bedroom below – he probably wasn't used to having company in the house, let alone a vampiric son shuffling about in the attic room. He called up to me to check I was okay. I explained that I had a fever and that I was very dehydrated, then I asked him where the soluble aspirins were. He dutifully left me some outside the bathroom and returned back to bed, but not before making some lame remark about me having night terrors as a child.

I took the aspirin. A few minutes later I felt my temperature drop. I looked at myself in the mirror again to see that my eyes were bloodshot, almost yellow in colour. I went back into my room and looked out at the full moon through my window.

What a coincidence.

CEMETERIES

By 8.30 I was downstairs eating breakfast. My dad had already been out and picked up a copy of the paper, and who should be on the front but a woman who looked like the one from my dream. She wasn't reported as being dead, however, or missing. She had committed suicide, thrown herself off a block of flats in South London.

'Terrible shame that,' dad remarked. 'She had her whole life ahead of her.'

I nodded.

The weather was excellent that morning, so I decided to go grave exploring. The main cemetery was not open until later in the week, because it was run by volunteers. I arrived promptly at the gates of Highgate East Cemetery just as they were about to open. One other man was there, an elderly gentleman who was smartly dressed in a long black coat; his hair was grey and neatly combed back and he carried with him the most interesting walking stick I had seen, if you can call it that; I would describe it more like a wizard's staff, wider at the top with a decorative silver hound, etched with Latin text, circles and triangles.

The entry fee was nothing considering it allowed me into a labyrinth of paths, old and new, each one lined with tombstones, head stones and giant concrete busts, including that of Karl Marx; his grave was impressive - not only did he have his face sculpted in stone but he also had one of the best aspects in the whole graveyard.

Soon other people trickled into the yard and dispersed like ants, foraging for information. I found myself deliberately wandering down dark overgrown paths in the hope of finding something out of the ordinary. There were so many names. I had read on the internet that the whole cemetery was practically run down at one point and used as an area for rituals by members of the occult. I'd never given it much thought, although there I was looking for evidence of vampires or a hidden entrance to a tomb.

It was amazing how quickly I arrived in darkened patches, shielded by overhanging branches and heavy mantles of stone. There was an eerie silence, foraging amongst the dead, stepping over death beds that had been covered by blankets of vegetation, but my thirst for answers kept me going.

As I lurked further, I stopped in my tracks. My

heart murmur returned, that same feeling I'd felt before. Someone or something was aware of my presence which had set off a trigger. I turned to see the elderly man from the gate watching me from afar. He put on a pair of black leather gloves, held my gaze and then turned and walked off.

My immediate instinct was to follow him, but I couldn't be sure that I was reacting to him, that it might be in some way linked to Highgate Cemetery and its 'energy lines' (I was beginning to buy into this idea). I continued looking but found nothing untoward and eventually gave up my search for a secret pit, or magical gate to the underworld, and made my way back into the open. I rejoined one of the main paths where I proceeded to scout for the elderly gentlemen. I did a full circuit of the cemetery twice but couldn't see him again, so I gave up my hunt and decided to call it a morning.

Strolling back through Highgate Village I remained in deep thought about the woman from the city who had committed suicide. The image the press had used showed her to be smiling; she was very pretty and glamourous. I felt sympathy for her family rather than guilt for a change. She had everything, even an amazing job it seemed, but sometimes the body yearns for more than worldly desires.

As I crossed the Broadway I caught a glimpse of the man from the cemetery. I noted the number of the bus he got on and thought nothing else of it.

As I approached home I began thinking about

Grace. I was incredibly disappointed that nothing happened between us given the amount of sexual tension we obviously both felt. I wanted to call her again, to show her that I was interested, and maybe even see her. And then it dawned on me: I was now unemployed and would soon run out of money. I needed to formulate an action plan.

Back home, time passed quickly. It was dark again before I knew it and I'd spent most of my evening researching famous people of Highgate rather than work on my CV and search for jobs. I delved a little deeper into the Highgate Vampire phenomenon - or hoax as others coined it - and decided that I would try my luck again with another visit. The image of the man from the graveyard stayed with me for most of the night

My phone rang and I automatically answered it using the company name I no longer worked for. It was Claudia. The exchange was brief, but there was a civil tone between us. She asked if I'd cleaned the flat as she said she wanted her share of the deposit back. I told her that I'd moved out because of a potential break in. She didn't seem concerned but did acknowledge my comment with a sigh, then she agreed to do a day's cleaning at the weekend if I had all the rubbish tidied out by the following Friday. Any of her belongings were to be placed in a box. I agreed to her plan. That was the last time I'd speak to her.

The next day, despite being a chillier morning,

Highgate Village was buzzing with activity. It felt good to have the freedom to walk and to shop without the constraints of a day job. I entered a small café, enjoyed a coffee by the window and watched cars and buses go by as I read the paper. I realised that I would have to go back to the flat at some point to continue packing, but I was still freaked out by the message left on the mirror and I wasn't in a rush to tidy, despite what I'd promised Claudia.

On finishing my drink I decided to go back to the East Cemetery. As I walked, I considered it only a mild coincidence that the elderly man was watching me, but all I could do was think about seeing him again so that I could satisfy my curiosity and study him more closely.

The graveyard was already open when I arrived. I paid my entry and exchanged pleasantries with the clerk. I cut through the many rows of stones to where I'd been before to see if I felt the same physical symptoms. I started buying into the idea of there being energy lines, and that our body's own energy signatures could be changed or moulded by external forces, but when I arrived in the same spot as the previous day there was nothing to see, and I felt nothing. I ventured a bit further into the undergrowth, exploring new areas that I didn't see the day before, even more dense and thick. Then there was a patch that seemed to open up.

Ivy and weeds choked many of the graves and

moss had infected many of the granite headstones, slowly eating away at them. It was impossible to read the effigies left by loved ones on many of the graves, and so they remained unmarked. Something rustled in the trees and I turned my head to see two squirrels fighting, or had something startled them? Nature was abundant, and I realised that there was probably a foxes den nearby because of the smell – there were some particularly large holes dug into the ground. I felt like being brave and crawling inside to take a look; it was certainly wide enough to enter, but it was probably the most stupid idea that I'd had that week. It would be a week for stupid ideas.

Eventually I found my way onto the main path again and - to my delight - I caught sight of the old man. He had an air of authority about him as he walked, and I was fascinated by the way in which he gripped and spun his staff, as though he were wielding it as a weapon. I remained unseen and watched him venture away. I decided to follow him, another one of my foolish ideas. As I did so I felt a crunch beneath my feet, not of leaves or twigs, but something manmade: a pair of women's glasses, new and in good condition, now cracked in two beneath my feet. I put it down to coincidence, but then wondered how a pair of glasses could get to where they were given that I had only visited the area the day before.

The man walked about fifty yards ahead of me. He was scouring the grounds as if looking for something – maybe he'd left the glasses, I thought. I wanted to approach him, like I'd originally intended to, and ask him a question, but something told me not to. Even though I'd say he was in his late sixties, he had the presence and frame of a man nearly half that age, the authority of my old House Master. And secretly I got a buzz out of stalking him for reasons I couldn't explain.

At times I felt as though he knew that he was being watched. When he turned to check, I was already out of sight, watching him from one of the many overgrown bushes or large gravestones.

Eventually he left the graveyard and I followed. Rather than tail him up the hill, which had few places for me to hide, I decided to make conversation with the ticket attendant. I mentioned the missing glasses, handed them in, and then asked about the elderly man and if he was a regular.

The attendant laughed. 'Yeah, he's a regular. Every month he comes for six days on the trot, always around the time when there's a full moon. You can guarantee he'll be here. Apparently he's been coming for years.'

I asked if she'd ever spoken to him. She confirmed that it was only to say 'good morning' or 'thank you' when she gave him a receipt; she described him as stern looking guy and not someone who you would typically make conversation with, although he would occasionally ask her if anyone else had been hanging around. I thanked her, but not before asking how many times he'd visited that month. That day was his fifth visit.

During my walk back home through the park, I began creating my own colourful backstory to the man. I imagined that he was a writer, or an expert in London's dark history, perhaps even a lecturer on the occult – I may have even read some of his work.

At home I thought about the email that was said in the office about journalists snooping around after the attack. I thought it might be a good idea to research how my attack was reported in the press, a gentle way of dealing with my demons. I searched online archives using my library card and gained access to records of what was happening in London during that day. The Evening Standard had the day off on the Saturday, and most of the other tabloids and broadsheets reported stories of a MPs gay expose. Not even the Metro mentioned anything about a 'city stabbing', probably because we had survived. I decided that I needed to track down this red headed journalist, out of intrigue more than anything.

I lay in bed that night with a raging temperature. Internally I was convinced that my bones were melting together to form plates of armour in my chest and down my spine. I took a cocktail of ibuprofen, codeine and paracetamol to control the fever - it did little to halt my overactive mind.

MICHAEL

The next day was wet, cold and windy. Gusts of icy cold air swept through the streets of Highgate and forced pedestrians to clump together in shop doorways and pile into all of the coffee shops. It wasn't all bad, I'd tried to disguise myself that day by choosing the largest hooded jacket I could find in my dad's wardrobe, and I carried a large black umbrella – I blended in perfectly.

I made it down to the cemetery for around the opening time: 10am. I entered and quickly took up a strategic position on a bench behind a miniature mausoleum.

A few minutes later I caught sight of the man entering the graveyard, dressed exactly as the previous two days. He marched along the main path like a centurion. There was something about the thrill of covertly mirroring his every movement; I got an inexplicable obsession from watching his behaviour.

From nearly 100 yards or so I observed him disappear into the undergrowth, the same patch I had rummaged through the previous two days. I mentioned that the weather was bad, and to do such a thing would surely dampen clothes and muddy his expensive looking shoes. I hovered behind two tall grave stones, watching and waiting. Ten minutes later he re-emerged and brushed off the foliage from his coat. At this point I hadn't really considered how good my eyesight was from such a distance, but I could make out the contours on his face and the dark circles beneath his eyes when he looked around to check if he had been seen.

Rather than confront him alone in a graveyard, I thought I'd be clever and remain one step ahead; I predicted that he would be leaving the cemetery soon and make his way to the main high street. I was confident I knew where he would catch the bus from.

I waited in the doorway of a shop for over thirty minutes to try and catch a glimpse of him. My efforts eventually paid off when he made an appearance walking up the hill towards the stop. I sprinted to the previous stop so that I could already be on the bus without him knowing.

I sat at the back, the newspaper shielding most of my face. He stepped on to the bus purposefully and showed his freedom pass to the driver. At least I was correct about his age; I was stalking a pensioner albeit a tall and powerfully built one. He sat near the doors with his back to me. I noticed a fine streak of white running through his grey hair; his neck was thick and he had broad shoulders; he kept his gloves on, and given his poise, his dress, and his metal staff, I deduced that he may have been ex-military.

For the whole journey I barely took my eyes off him. When I realised that we were heading towards the West End, I knew that there was a good chance I might lose him amongst the lunch-time crowds.

The bus stopped at the start of New Oxford Street and he was one of the first to get off. When I alighted, I let him get some distance between us and quickly surveyed my surroundings. Although I understood the basic geography of central London, the backstreets and alleyways were still relatively unchartered territory. I looked up at Centre Point, my virtual map reference; its concrete skeleton and perfect symmetry reminded me of a microchip, a giant reactor powering the city streets. I turned my gaze back towards the man and cursed my luck, for I had already lost him down one of the capillary streets.

Weaving under Centre Point, I caught sight of him marching towards Covent Garden. I tried to give myself a minimum of 20 metres distance as I spun myself between the lunchtime crowds. He seemed to zig zag, and at times I wondered if it was because he knew that I was tracking his every move, but not once did he look behind him.

Eventually the pursuit led me past the Drury Lane Theatre, and then he took a sharp left onto Macklin Street. I was only seconds behind him when I turned the corner, but it was as if he'd suddenly vanished. I looked up and down the road, checking that I hadn't mistaken it for a different, smaller road, but there were no others. The street was practically empty. I strode up and down, checking café windows and peering through restaurant doors. Nothing. I was more annoyed with myself that I'd wasted three days of amateur surveillance trying to trace his steps, knowing that I'd have to wait until the next full moon to get a new lead – just to have a conversation!

There were a few doors further up the street, but too far for him to have run ahead in time for a man of his age. On reflection I was too stubborn; I should have just approached him in broad daylight at the cemetery, shook his hand and asked him politely what he was up to, but I had grown obsessed with the idea of stalking him and playing the intimidator. And I had failed at that also.

I crossed to the other side of the road to check for any other clues and drew a sigh as I began to accept that I had lost him. I walked past a communal entrance to some council flats, stepped up into the porch and peered through the glass in a last ditch attempt to search for movement. Using my hands as a visor to block out the glare, I could see nothing but a scruffy looking hallway littered with takeaway menus, a doorway to the stairwell and the entrance to the lift. When I stepped back I noticed a new reflection in the glass.

The man stood about ten inches above me, his silhouette shrouding me in darkness. I turned around to face him but before I could get a clear look at his face I noticed something pushing into my chest - six inches of glimmering, cold steel, poised to strike.

'Say a word and I'll kill you here and now,' he snarled, eyes fixed into mine.

I couldn't breathe. Here I was for the second time in as many months, face to face with death.

Play along, I thought to myself, don't be the hero.

He removed a key fob from his pocket and pressed it against the buzzer. The door clicked and a gust of wind seemed to suck the door open.

'Move,' he muttered, his warm breath condensing on my brow.

I did move, slowly through the door. I saw an opportunity to escape, to run for the stairs; I could have easily slammed the door on his arm and kicked wildly to escape, but all I could do was shake with fear – this man knew what he was doing and I would have been an idiot to think otherwise.

He marched me into the lift. There was a strong smell of sanitizer and piss - it hung in the air as our feet clapped against the mottled marble-effect floor. He made me stand facing the corner like some insolent child as he pushed the button - I couldn't see which floor. I could feel the blade scraping against my neck, the goose bumps almost bursting as the steel scratched up and down, then he pulled down my collar. I sensed him examining my scar as the deep growl of the lift pulled the cab upwards.

The lift jolted and then the door opened suddenly. He gave a quick marching order: 'Move.' I was led towards a narrow pale green door, unnumbered, at the end of a dark hallway where the light had deliberately been broken. This is it, I thought, this is the price I pay for my arrogance, all my fuck ups in life, for thinking I could outsmart an old man; for being a child, playing a dangerous game of hide and seek, all for the sake of some answers.

He pushed a key into my hand and told me to use it. His voice was deep, disguised almost, but I could detect the strong accent of hate and fear which did little to settle my nerves.

The door was double locked. On the second click, the door opened and his size twelve boot forcefully kicked me through, propelling me into what looked like a messy living room. I landed against a small pile of plastic ice cream boxes. As I stood and regained my balance, I turned to see him bolt the door shut. He's going to kill me now, I thought, I'm a fucking dead man. It was dark inside, there were no lights on and the curtains were all drawn; only sounds of ticking clocks, and lots of them, echoed off the chipboard wallpaper, counting down the seconds as he turned to address me.

For almost a minute we stood there in silence – watching each other. I could see flecks of white in his heavily bloodshot eyes.

'How did you get that scar?' he asked.

I paused. 'I was stabbed.'

'Doesn't look like a stab wound to me.'

I managed to get some air into my lungs. 'Look, I'm sorry – I think there's been a huge misunderstanding.'

'There's no misunderstanding. You followed me here. Now answer me - how did you get that scar?'

Another minute must have passed. I had told the truth. I could not give him another answer. I just remained fixed within his gaze. In the corners of my eyes I began noticing details, like how the whole room was littered with ice cream tubs, each one filled with old keys, watches and broken jewelry. There were also scrap books, newspapers and books; old types, some original hardbacks with sticky tabs protruding from every other page, others looked hand bound.

'Your scar!' he hissed again. 'Who gave that scar?'

Come clean, I thought. 'There were these two black guys-'

'Did they bite you?'

'What?'

He pulled down a large, heavy looking blade from a shelf next to where he stood and within a heartbeat he had thrown it at me. My whole body shook as I felt it bang against the wall. My legs went to jelly and I began to blabber on about not wanting to die. He stomped over to me, grabbed me by the neck and pinned me to the wall. 'Did-they-bite?'

'No . . .' I gasped for air. 'I wasn't bitten by them.'

'Go on!'

My feet were dangling inches above the ground. 'I don't know what it was. The doctor said-'

'Forget the doctors. What bit you, demon?'

'It was . . . I don't know . . . a fox?' He looked at me like I was lying to him. 'But then I saw its eyes.' The man's eyes, cold, grey and bloodshot, flinched and suddenly I grew more lucid. 'Its eyes . . . they were neither a foxes nor a dogs.' I fought for breath. 'Only in my nightmares do I remember them. The doctors say there's no bite mark, but I see it. You . . . you see it, but it's so hard to see it in the light, but in the dark I notice it, I notice it more. I can see it. And it burns at night. I'm not fucking crazy!'

He let go of me. I slid down the wall into a heap. I watched him turn away, placing the blade he held at my neck on top of a small, square dining table. Nothing was said. I wanted to run for the door but my legs refused and my arms shook.

'What's your name?' he asked, his voice less tense.

I paused for a second. 'My name's John.'

He began to rummage through drawers, sifting through metallic objects. 'Sit down, John.'

I picked myself up from the ground and looked at the doorway again. There was a chance, I thought, that I could escape, but I felt compelled to know more. Gingerly, I sidestepped my way to the table.

'Why were you following me?'

'I'm so sorry, I shouldn't have – I saw you at the cemetery and had this wild idea that . . .' I stopped myself. What was I going to do, divulge my secret to a man who, seconds earlier, would have taken great pleasure in driving a sword through my rib cage, and might still? Was I about to confess that I thought I was becoming a vampire? Oh, and could he be so kind as to recommend a holy specialist. I knew that if I said the wrong thing that I could end up being skewered to the wall.

'What idea?' he said, listening intently.

'That you might know a bit more . . . about its history.'

'Read a book,' was his blunt reply. 'That's not why. You're a liar, John, and I don't like liars. You followed me because you liked the feeling of hunting someone, didn't you?'

'No. Honestly, I would never mug a pensioner.'

He gave a small chuckle. 'Who said anything about mugging?' He filled a kettle with water and placed it on the tea stained Formica. 'Why don't you just tell me the truth? The real reasons, then I'll tell you what you want to know, and if we both get what we want out of the conversation, then you can leave here alive.' With that bold statement he clicked the kettle on. 'You have until it boils.'

I was stunned. At least he was being fair and gave me a choice, and some time, but my judgement was clouded on whether I could trust him. I searched the room for clues, at all the keys; I noticed that some were hung up, and others were stacked in boxes on bookshelves, along with small notepads and audio cassettes. I could hear the deep straining of the kettle trying to heat the water. I didn't have much time.

'I thought you might be an expert,' I began. His eyes beckoned me to continue. 'On vampires.'

His face remained straight. 'Let's say I am. What were you going to ask me?'

The honest answer was, I didn't know. My life hung in the balance and I couldn't even pick a single fabrication out of the sky. I hadn't even thought about what I would really ask him if the day had matched my pre-empted scenario. There was no script for this. If he's mad, I thought, then it doesn't matter; just tell the truth.

'I think I might be one.'

He shifted his weight off his staff and paced back and forth in front of the kitchen work surface, his eyes fluttering towards the kettle.

'When were you bitten?'

'October.'

'And what are your symptoms?'

I shook my head. 'Er, Fever – some nights I lay awake . . . my mind can focus in on every sound. Some days I get headaches, muscular and joint pain and . . . my teeth and gums feel swollen.' I sounded so unconvincing. Pathetic.

'You mentioned doctors, what did they say?'

'To rest and take paracetamol.'

He burst into a fit of laughter. The kettle was nearing the final stage of boiling.

'Anything else?'

I was still afraid to admit my worst doings. 'Sometimes I retch. I'm sick.'

His faced remained expressionless. He's slipped back into character, I thought - I'm going to die.

'The other night I dined with a friend. When I went back to hers I . . . had a dangerous urge to kill.'

Clack. The kettle had boiled and the final plume of steam mushroomed around the room, creating a dangerous haze between us. My eyes kept darting from the kettle to him. He was in deep thought.

'And did you?'

'No!'

He turned his back on me and I heard him open a drawer and tinker around with various metallic items. I immediately thought that he was sharpening knives and other assorted torture devices. I went to make a run for the door when he called out: 'Do you take sugar?' Poised to sprint, I shook my head. 'You should, you know!' he barked. 'It helps alleviate the symptoms.'

I stood there, watching him as he pulled two mugs and one tea bag off a shelf. Alleviate the symptoms?

'So you think I might be turning into one?' I asked, my limbs numb from the adrenaline.

He began to laugh again. 'No. There's no such thing as a vampire.' He poured scalding hot water and lots of sugar into each of the brown mugs, prodding and stabling the one teabag with an old, tarnished fork. 'There are things you've told me that make me believe you're not yourself,' he began. 'And then there's the things that I can see, like that scar of yours – that certainly intrigues me.' I listened to his breathing, air hissing through his nose as he stirred each mug vigorously and added long-life milk to each cup. He turned with almost a half-smile across his face, walked over to the table and beckoned me to sit opposite him.

'There's no nice way of putting this . . .'

I finally sat down. 'What?'

'You've become a member of a very exclusive club.' He took a long sip of his scalding hot tea.

'I don't follow.' Half of me still thought this man was mad; half wanted to believe that he was.

'Vampires are a myth, you see, an erotic

fantasy glorified by the Victorians. But I'm sure you've already looked it up: very entertaining stuff, especially the modern works.' He took another sip of tea and smiled. 'Yes, I'm afraid you're much worse than a blood-sucking, sex-mad vampire.' He slid the mug of grey tea across the table. 'You're the villain no-one's written about.'

I looked at him confused. He had a knowing smile, revelling in private gratification at what I didn't understand. I thought about throwing the tea in his face, but I could tell now that he was only starting to warm up.

'I still don't understand.'

'Why would you?' He looked down at my mug and encouraged me to take a sip. I lifted it to my mouth and drank. It was boiling hot and sickly sweet. 'Drink, it will help with the shock. If it's any conciliation, I know how you're feeling.' He reached for his collar and pulled the scarf away from his shoulders. Clearly I saw a scar on his neck, though it was more of a marking, not too dissimilar from mine and much more pronounced. I was in awe; it didn't resemble a mass of aged scar tissue and sinew but was perfectly symmetrical, almost star shaped as if it had been tattooed on.

'I'm Michael, by the way.' He removed his gloves to reveal pale hands with long, tanned fingers. He sat back and loosened his jacket. Behind him a small chest freezer began to wheeze.

'How did you get that?' I asked. 'I mean, you were obviously bitten too, that means we're the same?'

'Calm down, it's not that straight forward. We are all different but we have the same mother.'

Every time I caught his eye I had to look away, there was something about him that made me shake and lose my concentration.

'I'm not going to kill you,' he whispered.

Hearing him say those very words made my heart gyrate. I took another sip of tea. 'Can you tell me how you got that scar, how it happened to you?'

Michael drummed his fingers on the table and breathed hard through his nose. 'Years ago: April 1974 to be precise. Of course, things were a lot different then.' I watched him rotate the mug in his hands, back and forth as if he were trying to crack a safe. 'I used to be an actor. I was the understudy for the lead at the Drury Lane Theatre.' He spoke with a trace of regret in his voice. 'One night, after a particularly long rehearsal - days before we were about to begin our run - I was one of the last people to leave via the stage door as usual. I still remember it clearly, stepping out into a perfectly still night with a luminous full moon. As I went to leave, I heard an unusual rustling from behind the rubbish bins and I could sense that something was not quite right. Foolishly I approached to investigate. The next thing I know I was hit on the head from behind.'

The more he continued his story, the calmer I became. I could already see the similarities between his experience and mine, almost to the point where I could predict what he would say next.

'I could feel them removing my wallet and watch, whilst my head throbbed from the pain. They left me lying behind the bins with a huge gash above my right eye.' He motioned to the scar with his finger. 'And so that's where I lay, exposed to the brutal winter elements, staring up at the night sky, trying to regain my senses. But the danger had not passed. Something was watching.'

'What was it?' I felt bad for cutting him off from his train of thought; it was out of nerves more than anything, but I knew this was a man whose mind was full of stories and, perhaps, wisdom; but most importantly, I believed that he had answers.

He looked frustrated, exhaled and sat back in his chair. 'I still haven't discovered the source, but I've come close.'

That was it. I had broken his train of thought in the retelling - the climax - of his story, and because of that he had skipped right to the end which, in hindsight, was typical of him. He had denied me a definitive answer.

'So, are we like werewolves?' I asked.

'Wake up lad!' A flash of orange burnt within his eyes as he banged his fist on the table. The whole room seemed to shake and his calm, almost hypnotic, voice now sounded like a snarl. 'If you think I'm full of folklore and sentiment, then you're wrong. I'm full of hate!' His face bubbled with rage. 'Werewolves, vampires; these things are less believable and would be much easier to kill. If you're telling me the truth about your illness - as you so put it - then you and I are very much in the minority. A reject of evil! And your life ended the night you got bitten. Forget a family, a career and whatever aspirations you had in life. You've now only got one serious choice to make: let them find you or find yourself.'

My hands remained fixed to the table, palms down, as I tried not to react to his outburst, even when foamy bits of spittle sprayed out of his mouth in my direction. He stared back down at his cup shaking his head; I could see the vein pumping in his temple beneath the dappled grey skin.

I waited for a moment before I politely drank some more of my tea. I decided it best not to ask any more questions, even though I desperately wanted to know what he meant by 'find yourself'.

'Go,' he said, now much calmer. 'I can't help you.'

I placed my mug back on the table and rose from my seat in slow motion. He instructed me that the door could be unbolted and I backed out of the room, leaving him in the company of forlorn memories.

'Don't come back here ever again,' he called out to me as I left. 'My aim might not be as bad next time.' I looked at the heavy dagger which protruded from the wall, a stark reminder of how lucky I'd been.

I fumbled with the bolt, slipped out of the door and sprinted down the stairs.

I was so relieved to burst out into the open, on to a London street and feel cool air blowing against my skin. I gave a fleeting look back up towards the windows but it was impossible to know which one was his, or even what floor. I saw nothing although I imagined that he could see me. I started running towards Tottenham Court Road where I was intent on catching the first tube train north. All the while I could feel my throat tightening, as though I'd dry swallowed an acidic pill.

The whole experience had been a disaster. My body shook as I sat in the carriage, rocked by the metrical imperfections of the track. An intense feeling of nausea fell over me, accelerated by the stress of cheating death once again - or was it the tea?

I raged at myself for being so stupid, whimpered like a child under the stares of frightened passengers. I'd been a fool for acting so impulsively on such a madcap, unplanned whim – what did I really expect the outcome of that day to be? Any sane person would confirm that stalking an old man who rummaged through graveyards religiously for six days of the month would be a bad idea and unlikely to yield intellectual conversation. I felt cold and my trail had also gone cold. I was back at the start, feeling empty and unfulfilled, seeking answers to my questions about my condition - about my purpose in life.

By the time I got to Highgate station I had been sick twice in the carriage much to the disgust of the other passengers. I remember apologising profusely about the bile coloured liquid that seemed to trickle along the carriages, snapping at the heels of people's feet like a serpent. Many of them moved away, saying that I was a fucking drunk, that I was diseased, and that people like me ruined London.

I shook my head. 'The whole of London is infected,' I called out as I left the carriage.

It wasn't my fault.

SOLACE

My dad was out when I got home. I threw my soiled clothes into the washing machine and ran upstairs to take a long shower. The heat soothed my aching muscles and I soon began to settle. I remembered Michael telling me that sugar helped alleviate the symptoms of sickness, so I raided the kitchen and munched through a whole packet of biscuits. He gave me one good piece of advice at least. I felt contented and fell asleep on the sofa.

It was dark outside when I woke. I prayed that it had been another dream, that my amateur ghost hunt was just a careless meddle with the occult, like a child trying out the Ouija board during a sleepover, and fretting at the way in which the glass moved by itself. I thought back to the experience, that perhaps I had been poisoned by Michael - who drinks tea made by a fucking madman? As I sat there coming to my senses, I began to convince myself that his outbursts were emotive and not specifically directed at me. I concluded that he was what I originally thought: a mad man.

Find yourself or let them find you, those were his words. I had to get out of the house, so I decided to go to the gym.

I was the only person in the club bar eating a steak. I drank some red wine and ordered a sugary desert for good measure, trying to convince myself that being a jobless bachelor was a good thing, that my life was about to take a turn for the better. I told myself that I didn't want to turn out like Michael or my dad; a life of solitude just didn't seem right for me.

I knew nothing about Michael, yet within minutes he had given me a snippet of his whole life story, perhaps more if I hadn't interrupted him. The rest of Michael's life had to be pieced together from the clues I saw, and by looking at the way that he lived. Why were there so many keys? Masses of papers and notepads were stacked in piles along the walls, and I recall a map of central London peppered with thumb tacks. I turned my attention back to the TV in the bar, it was on mute but showed footage of world news from the day: war, famine, economics, and natural disasters – the usual – a dead body lying in the street of a war zone caught my eye. In truth I knew that what was happening halfway across the globe was awful but it didn't affect me, and deep down I didn't really care.

As I watched, I couldn't help but notice one or two other people sitting in the lounge without drinks, their bodies angled towards me. Perhaps they were engrossed in the news, but they irritated me nonetheless, so I headed to the changing rooms for my nightly sauna and Jacuzzi.

I sat, arm to arm, with complete strangers as the bubbles popped all around us. To this day I still find it bizarre that no-one makes real eye contact or starts conversation with strangers in Jacuzzis when you are already half naked and wet through. But that night someone broke that taboo. She was perhaps a couple of years younger than me, with dyed blonde hair and high cheekbones. We had both smiled at each other, as though we were having the same conversation in our heads. I noted that she had a good colour to her skin as I watched her get out of the Jacuzzi, and a beautiful hour-glass figure. I had never seen her before that night. As she left the pool area to go back to the changing rooms, she stopped and stared over at me and gave one last smile. Everyone else around me was at one with themselves, unaware of the connection that had just been made.

Minutes later I made my way to the sauna, where I could only manage 20 minutes. I concluded it was because I had been sick earlier and because I'd drunk some red wine with a heavy steak dinner less than an hour before. It also didn't help that the bald headed man – the one who beat my personal best of 41 minutes - was sat staring at me the whole time.

It was late when I left the gym. I walked briskly to my car which was near the bottom of the overflow car park. By this point I had cleared my head, all but forgotten my harrowing experience with Michael, filing it away as a stupid misadventure to laugh about in days to come. But as I walked I was troubled, hindered by the same feeling I'd had all week - the sense that I was being watched and followed. Imagine then that feeling intensified when I could see nothing but my car and one other left in the darkest corner of the car park. I could hear only my footsteps and those of another. He's followed me, that was my first thought. My muscles began to tense.

I span quickly to confront my pursuer. My arms were spread apart to appear more threatening, but rather than be confronted by some hooded youth with a blade, to my surprise – and delight - it was the same girl from the Jacuzzi.

She smiled nervously and apologised for scaring me, before quickly pointing out that her car was parked right next to mine. I can't really recount what happened next, I apologised myself, we laughed it off and then it was if I had a chat up bible to hand – we exchanged a few pleasantries, walked besides each other to our cars, and then she asked me if I wanted to go for a drink. Things were suddenly looking up.

She recommended a bar called The Village in Muswell Hill. Inside, we got chatting and she told me her name was Sarah. She said she had recently moved down from Lancashire which explained her friendly, down to earth nature and lack of London pretentiousness. But I couldn't have cared either way, because I was still flattered by the fact that a woman had asked me out on a date. All of Michael's spiel suddenly seemed like worthless, bitter rhetoric.

After a large glass of wine my attention was held by her completely. Her backstory was very credible, especially the bit about splitting up from her long term boyfriend; the woes of starting her new job and having a boss she didn't warm to, and renting a flat on her own for the first time away from her mum. Most of the conversation was about her and not me. I preferred it this way and I saw my predicament reflected in much of what she said.

The bar became noisier and we agreed to look for a change of venue. As we walked, she made the mistake of asking me back for coffee. Albeit a cliché, I did not refuse for the night was young and I felt a connection with Sarah.

Sarah led me to a door along one of the roads off Muswell Hill Broadway. Her flat was two floors above shops. She led me through her front door and conversation and jokes soon turned to kissing and caressing. It felt wonderful to feel intimate with another woman, to feel the gentle breathe of an attractive stranger ripple off my face and excite my pores. Hours before we were complete strangers and now we were literally eating each other's faces in her living room. Things heightened and we began stripping off each other's clothes. She led me into her bedroom: a clean, tastefully finished room with modern décor and a small bedside lamp which was already on. She didn't speak once as we kissed and got naked on the bed, which I found a bit strange; I thought that perhaps our bodies were somehow in tune, on autopilot and giving in to a primitive desire. I remember touching her skin and noticing how it was cool, almost waxy in places, and her pubic hair was completely shaved. Before I could enter her, she gripped me by the neck and whispered that I should lie on the bed with my face down, something about completing a course in tantric massage and wanting to activate the meridians to reach inner peace. It sounded good, so I rested with my head on a pillow whilst she went to fetch some essential oils.

The whole flat fell silent. I had so far stayed in control of my darker urges and remained relaxed. I thought about the massive shift in fortune from hours before, from being captive in a council flat, to being picked up by a beautiful stranger in a Jacuzzi. I knew it was the noughties and that this process of causality between consenting adults was not frowned upon anymore, but I was concerned about the fact that I knew nothing about this girl,

Sarah, and that she had not even asked once about my history with other women.

I soon became troubled by the lack of noise. I couldn't hear Sarah rummaging for massage oils or detect the sound of matches being lit. Then I heard her walk back into the room, except from the sound of her footsteps she had put on weight. Before I could turn to see, several mighty blows rained down on my head and I felt two pairs of heavy hands seize me by the arms and legs, binding them together with cable ties. Then, by my hair, I was pulled off the bed and dragged across the floor back into the living room.

The lights were off, and as I managed to flip onto my back, one of the attackers pulled me up and threw me into the corner of the room with such force that I felt my shoulder pop out of it socket as I hit the wall.

Bound and naked I lay there on the floor, breathless, helpless and in shock. I immediately thought that Sarah had also been jumped, and that she was in the process of being raped, but as I turned myself over on to my side I could see all of my attackers watching me. The room had indeed been lit with candles and I could sense the presence of at least three men in the room. Sarah's voice blended calmly into the background, and as I began to focus I noticed that she was walking back and forth behind them in the process of dressing herself again. She shot a look at me with cold, grey eyes and I saw nothing of the bubbly northerner she had been only minutes before.

'Why?' I called out to her, but then a thick pair of hands the size of paddles hoisted me to my feet.

I was manhandled on to an ornately carved oak chair which had a tall, thin back. With my hands tied together, my arms were looped behind it leaving my chest pushing outwards.

'Let me go!' I pleaded.

'So, you're the one she's picked,' a voice said. I focused on the area in front of me and noticed a man sitting on the sofa. In the low light I didn't really see the details of his face until he leant forward. I hate to use stereotypes, but he reminded me of the early Nosferatu by the way in which his head was so oval, and how his arms moved so slowly. Pointing at me, he got up off the sofa and came closer so that I could see his face more clearly; he looked gaunt, almost starved, and his eyes were heavily bloodshot; his lips were two glistening leeches pressed tightly together.

'Been fighting it have we?' he asked.

'I don't know what the fuck you're talking about,' was my honest and frank reply. 'Whatever it is, you've got the wrong guy.'

'No, we have the right man,' he said, sliding closer to inspect my neck.

I looked over at Sarah, a heartless wax figure in the corner of the room. 'I've never met her before tonight.'

'We've been holding out on you for a while - anticipating your emergence,' he continued, ignoring my pleas. 'But you just didn't want to embrace it?'

'Embrace what?'

I could hear the sinew of his muscles twist as his jaw dropped lower. Glaring right at me, his eyes two lumps of onyx set amongst grey mottled skin, he whispered, 'The gift.'

I was sick of people talking in riddles; all I wanted was straight answers. Part of me wanted to yell out for help, but the other half felt consoled in the fact that I was no stranger to the very transformation I had just witnessed – from feeble man to feral savage. My heart began to pump harder as I felt something stir within, and all the while I thought back to the words of Michael from earlier, words I ignored, words I discounted as virulent lies: they will find you. I tried to free myself between involuntary convulsions, but a heavy pair of hands held me tight against the cold wood.

'You feel it, don't you?' Slowly he raised his hand to reveal a perfectly shaped nail that looked as though it had been fashioned into a claw. He held it above me like a shard of mirrored glass. 'The predator racing within you, longing to be set free.' He took his index claw and pressed it against the centre of my chest. 'Here.'

I yelled with pain as he slowly and deliberately cut into my flesh. A long incision from the chest plate about twenty centimetres down below my ribs was made in one slow, downward stroke. I writhed and tried to scream but my mouth was clamped shut. I was helpless, watching the blood as it began trickling down my stomach, soaking into my pubic hair and collecting in a puddle on the wooden seat.

'You know, she's very upset that you haven't come looking for her,' he said, coolly making a horizontal incision like some upside down crucifix.

I begged him to stop. 'Who?!'

'Your mother.' He inspected his finger and licked the tip clean, got up and paced methodically in front of me.

'My mother's dead you sick bastard!' I scowled. The pain was like having two hot iron bars pressed against my chest. My muscles tightened as I tried again to break free again. They stood there laughing at me and all I wanted to do was rip the man's head off.

'I'm afraid that's not quite the case. You see, we all have the same mother. That makes us family.'

I felt so cold. 'I'm nothing like you!'

'In some ways that's true. You have failed to let go of your human shell and instinct, which is why we are going to do it for you.'

Already I knew his intention - no need for riddles. Like a surgeon, the process of making such fine incisions was not a deliberate method of torture: they were going to pull out my heart.

Gaffa tape was fixed around my mouth as he came in close to me again, this time his hand was outstretched, ready to pull apart the epidermis. On a small table that I hadn't noticed before, I could see a selection of small surgical tools. I stared at him but saw nothing but the candle flames flickering in his eyes. The man had no soul. He was what I imagined a demon to be, void of humanity, his sole purpose on earth to inflict misery upon my body.

The front door clicked.

The man froze and the room fell silent. He fired a questioning look at the others. I could tell that they had read each other's thoughts, and that whoever stood on the other side of the door was certainly not expected. Then the lock clicked again, this time slowly, as if to deliberately heighten the tension. I gave a muffled cry. Sarah, if that was really her name, went to investigate. She peered through the spyhole and looked back, shaking her head. Then she inspected the lock.

The door suddenly burst open and she was thrown back inside the apartment. One of the men reacted quickly and charged at the doorway to try and push the door shut. Seconds later he fell back into the room, a handle of a silver letter opener sticking out of his chest. His limbs thrashed about the floor as fluid seemed to spray out of his wound and began oxidising as it hit the surfaces.

A figure strode in, tall and imposing, his frame filling the doorway. He raised a long thin barrel and pointed it at the man stood behind me. I flinched as a succession of metal darts fired out, peppering the man's face and neck. I felt spatters of blood in my hair and across my neck. He fell dead beside me at my feet and I watched as a milky secretion seeped from the exit wounds on his head.

The surgeon stooped down to the floor with the elasticity of a gymnast, then lunged at the figure, covering several feet in seconds, only for the gloved hands to catch him mid-air and redirect his momentum, hurling him towards the edge of a door frame. There was a powerful cracking sound as part of the wall crumbled and I saw the surgeon's head partly split open. He sprung up again and I could see fluid seeping out of his wound like red gelatine. Within seconds he was running at the man again. The figure deftly removed a crescent shaped sword and sliced the surgeon's torso in half. There was an unearthly howl before a hissing fountain of blood decorated the white walls of the apartment.

The figure turned towards me and spoke. 'Are there any more?' My eyes looked over to Sarah who seemed to be getting herself to the floor. He walked over to her, stamped his foot down on her neck and thrust a sword between her shoulder blades. I shook as I heard her scream into the floorboards and watched the blood spill across the floor, this time red blood, human blood. He looked back at me again. 'Any more?' I shook my head, and then I recognised the voice.

Michael pulled back his hood and shot me a troubled glance. Effortlessly he flicked his wrist to reveal a small instrument and used it to free my wrists from the cable ties.

'Grab yourself a towel and get your clothes on,' he said. 'We've got about two minutes before things get dangerous.'

I staggered into the bathroom and tried to soak up the blood. Surprisingly it was already starting to clot. I recovered my clothes from the bedroom where false promises had been made and quickly put them back on.

When I returned to the living room I saw that Michael had laid all the bodies out into the middle of the room. Sarah's body was motionless and her face was turned towards me; her skin had shrivelled up, as if it had become drained of all beauty and mummified in the minutes that had passed; the sticky liquid that gushed from her chest was now replaced by thick black lava which collected in a pool on the floor and was already clotting.

Michael pulled out a small canister of liquid and began dousing the bodies, and then he struck a match and lit them up. The flames took hold rapidly. Michael then used the lighter fluid to create a trail towards the curtains and settee.

'Dangerous things, candles,' he said, sliding the silver dagger back into the top of his staff. It was the same blade he had pressed against my neck only hours earlier. 'Put your clothes on, it's time to go!'

A black cab, coughing out white smoke into

the night air, was parked up when we emerged onto the street. 'Stay calm,' he uttered, pulling open the door.

I got in, still doing up the last of my last buttons.

'Leicester Square,' he bellowed and the cab jolted forward. I took a final glance at the flat above, enough time to see the orange eyes of the apartment window flutter with rage.

I listened to the roar of the engine as the taxi driver accelerated down Archway Road towards the West End. Michael hadn't even said a word or looked at me since we got in; all he had done was toss some baby wipes onto my lap. Eventually I burst. 'What the fuck just happened back there?'

He shot me a stern look, almost disgusted at my choice of words, and I curled back up into the corner of the cab. I had seen his true capabilities and knew that he was not a man to upset. The cab driver was staring at me in his mirror also. I looked back out at the streets but l could only see lights blending into one another.

The cab pulled up outside a small taxi rank near Leicester Square. Michael tipped the driver generously before ushering me out. I looked at him in disbelief; he wanted me to step out into the busy streets on a Friday night when I was still bleeding from an incision in my chest. He grabbed my shoulder and directed me out. I didn't fight him. Instead, I flanked him cautiously as he strode purposefully towards the main square, weaving between late night revelers, hawkers and drifters.

'What's happening?' I asked.

We stopped outside the Häagen-Dazs café and he turned towards me. I stared at him in bewilderment and gripped my shoulder in agony; I should have been taken to a hospital, not an ice cream parlour.

'Trust me,' he said, leading me inside. A waitress gave him a smile and led us to a booth by the window in clear sight of everyone. I could tell I looked awful by the stare that she gave me. The atmosphere couldn't have juxtaposed further from the way that I felt. Beneath the bright lights, colourfully dressed teenagers and adults were chatting and laughing in several languages, which all varied in their pitch and tone but seemed to hover at one continuous volume. I felt as though I'd been placed on display in a fluorescent zoo tank, slumped against the glass for all to see. I grimaced at my reflection in the window, defined by the shimmer of grease and sweat on my face.

'What can I get you?' the waitress asked.

I didn't acknowledge her; my mind was still in Muswell Hill. I couldn't even read the menu which, somehow, I had managed to open. Michael ordered for me and she left, giving me chance to reason as to why he'd brought me here of all places, a fucking ice cream tourist trap in the heart of London's West End.

Michael removed his gloves and got comfortable in the pod shaped chair. How he could be so relaxed was a mystery to me, I'd just watched him butcher people - or what I thought were people - with knives, swords and projectile darts. And if that wasn't enough, I watched them slowly decompress into putrefactive matter before being set alight like tinder wood.

'It's a relief,' he said, brushing some fluff off from his shoulders.

'What is?'

'When you realise you've hit rock bottom.'

His placid reaction to the whole situation began to agitate me. My mouth felt dry like I was about to be sick. He continued. 'You know then what it feels like, and can prepare yourself for better things.'

'Okay, that's beautiful.' I said, grinding my teeth. 'Now, do you mind explaining to me what the fuck is going on, and how whatever happened this evening can help me prepare for better things?'

'Because now you realise the truth. Nothing more will shock you so much, because you'll know what to expect.'

The waitress returned with two glasses of iced water which Michael must have ordered without me knowing. I drank it and gasped at how wonderful it felt, how soothing it was on my gullet. It took me a minute or two to register what he had just said.

'I don't know what to expect.'

He leant forward, stared deep into my eyes and lowered his voice. 'I can tell you, if you'll let me.'

I felt a warm crackling in my sinuses. Michael reacted quickly and passed me a napkin. I brought it up to my nose to stem the flow of blood. 'Am I safe?'

'For now you are. That was a scouting party. When word gets back to the nest that you're gone and four of them are dead, they'll think twice about finding you again so quickly.'

'But eventually they will?' I asked.

'Eventually.' Michael looked around the cafe. 'I found you easily enough, didn't I?'

I paused. I hadn't even given it a second thought about how he knew where I was or had even managed to find and save me. I hadn't even thanked him, just followed him obediently into the cab - no questions – whilst buildings burnt.

'The first day I saw you at the cemetery, I followed you home,' he said.

'You followed me?'

'Yes. You've a nice house.'

I jolted upright. 'My dad, will he be okay?'

'If he has lots of connections then he's not such an attractive target. But you, you're transient – no fixed abode, no job, no financial or social commitments. To them you're ripe for taking; young and impressionable.'

I took a moment to consider his words, reflecting on my current predicament and the twists and turns my life had taken in the past two months.

'So who are they?'

'They're the same as you and me.'

'Vampires?'

The waitress brought over the ice creams. Two Belgian Chocolate Heaven's; rich ice cream balanced on top of a waffle and laden with chocolate sauce, freshly fanned strawberries and whipped cream. Two steaming hot chocolates were also added for good measure. I could feel the waitress staring at the cut on my head as she placed them in front of us; sweat seeped into the wound and made it sting even more.

She walked away and I looked back at Michael. He shook his head.

'None of what you're saying makes any sense.'

'You keep saying that,' he said, freeing the waffle from the weight of the ice cream. 'You came looking for answers. You wanted to know what you were becoming. Back in Muswell Hill is a pretty good example of how you could be in years to come.'

'I'm not like them.'

'Yes, you are.'

I watched him begin to eat. Glimmers of delight flashed across his face with each mouthful. 'Eat. You'll feel much better.'

The cool sensation of the ice cream soothed my aching, dry throat. It was certainly comforting, and the rush of sugar settled my nerves and my hands steadied slightly as I drank the hot chocolate.

'What were they going to do to me?'

'They would have tortured you some more. Played with your skin, cut off tiny pieces of flesh and chewed it in front of you.' I held a piece of soggy waffle in my mouth. 'To them, you're a lab rat – an experiment that went wrong.'

'An experiment?'

'Apart from our age, you and I *are* both alike. We were bitten with the expectation that we would turn and slowly evolve into them; become members of their dark, elitist organisation and share their thirst for killing in the name of sport, all in the justification of natural selection. Instead, you're fighting what's inside. And you don't want to embrace what's lying dormant, wanting to emerge, and that worries them, because you might expose them, attract the wrong type of attention from the people we originally belong to.'

'The man who cut me – he said that she'd picked me.'

Michael arranged the strawberries neatly across his plate and rolled the ice-cream towards the center. 'He was referring to the queen.'

I shook my head. 'Now you've lost me completely. Is this some kind of royal conspiracy theory?'

He gave a gentle laugh, and I laughed with him. It felt good to laugh, to release some endorphins rather than more adrenaline, to ease the tension and anxiety that held my body rigid to the point where my limbs felt weak. Then my laughter suddenly turned into tears and I sat weeping at the table, unable to restrain my burst of emotion. It felt horrible to feel so deflated; emotionally and physically drained. I just wanted to curl up into a ball and howl, but he had dragged me to one of the busiest cafes in London for reasons that would only make sense the next day. I could feel the stares of people in the café, stopping themselves from indulging in the luxury ice cream to stare at this piteous being by the window, a man that must have looked like he had been dragged away from a street brawl, taken pity on by an elderly gent in a scene reminiscent from a Dickensian novel.

Michael reached across the table and gripped my arm firmly. 'Perhaps we're doing this too soon,' he said. I looked up at him, at the hint of sincerity lurking behind thick, bloodshot eyes. 'I'm sorry for scaring you earlier today in my flat; I thought you were one of them.'

'I don't know what I am.'

'When I said your life had changed, I meant it. If you want a more satisfying remedy to the pain you feel, then meet me here tomorrow at 3pm. But, if you decide that a quick ending is what you want, then this will be our last ever meeting.'

'What's the quick ending?' I asked.

There was a hint of sadness in his face, as if asking him that question had quelled his anticipation for an ally.

'Finish your ice cream,' he said.

I bowed my head and finished eating. I had

offended him again. I couldn't harbour any more questions or dialogue, the atmosphere was now too subdued. All I wanted to do was close my eyes and wait for the experience to end. I still knew nothing about this man, except that beneath his disheveled exterior was someone who commanded an array of blades with tactical prowess, and had the strength and ferocity of a knight defending the realm. And he liked ice cream.

We sat in silence for about five minutes. I began to understand his logic about meeting again – whatever he was going to tell me would be big. My mind couldn't handle information, theories, and technical explanations, not after two incidents in one day. All I could do was satisfy a primeval instinct: eat.

I watched Michael scrape every morsel of food from his plate and finish his drink. He reached into his wallet and pulled out a crisp twenty pound note from a bundle of about thirty. For a man who lived in a small high-rise studio flat in central London he didn't seem hard up.

He passed two crisp notes in my direction. 'Go home: take the first available cab that you can see. Clean yourself up and get a good night's rest. Stay away from empty spaces and think about what you want to do.' He got up and tightened a scarf around his neck.

'3pm tomorrow?' I asked.

'I'll be here.' Michael turned and left.

'Thank you,' I called after him, although not

loud enough to rise above the hum of noise. I felt like my voice was lost, swallowed up. He turned to face me one last time and raised a smile, as if he'd acknowledged my appreciation. Soon he turned a corner and disappeared amongst the late night partygoers.

I gazed out at Leicester Square; days before it had been the focus of so much global attention and appeal because of the glitz and glamour of celebrities launching their latest film, then I contemplated the disturbing thought, that beneath the pretense of fun and success, wealth and infrastructure, that we weren't as safe as we thought we were.

***

"God grant me the serenity to accept the things I cannot change, the courage to change the things I can, and the wisdom to know the difference."

Reinhold Niebuhr

ACCEPTANCE

The cab ride home was the longest journey I had ever taken. Not only was I still in pain, but I was incredibly frustrated by the ease at which Sarah - if that was even her real name - had led me to the flat with the intention of killing me. It was cold blooded to say the least, and scary to think that such a normal girl could suddenly switch personalities, but I only had myself to blame.

As the cab approached Archway, I began to wonder whether the incident had even happened. I was in denial again. It was impossible, what had happened to me, but the burning feeling across my chest was real; I ran my fingers along it and felt the crust of a scab forming. I opened up my jacket further and could still see patches of blood that had soaked into my shirt.

'I need you to take a detour,' I said to the driver.

The cabbie half turned his head, awaiting

instructions. 'The meter's still running,' he said chirpily.

'I need you to swing by Muswell Hill.'

He changed lanes. I knew that if that night really did happen then there would be a flat on fire and ambulances and police vehicles dealing with a crime scene. If there wasn't, I'd know that I was going mad.

On the approach to the Broadway there was no shortage of activity. I could see the flashing blue lights and could still sense the danger. Sure enough, the flat I was held captive in was easily identifiable because of its smoldering window amongst a row of flats. Even the cab driver stopped to have a look.

A police officer stood waving cars through a single lane as firefighters walked to and fro having brought the fire under control. I couldn't see any ambulances. I asked the cabbie to wind down the window so that I could speak to the officer.

'What happened?'

'There's been a fire,' he replied with a hint of sarcasm in his voice. I asked if anyone was hurt. He told me that he was not at liberty to say.

'My friend lives in the flat next door. I really need to know that she's okay so that I can put my mind at rest.'

The officer leant forward and looked at me. I pulled my jacket tightly around me.

''There are no reported casualties,' he said, and with that he gave me a subtle wink and seemed to scoop the cab along with his hands.

'Where to in Muswell Hill?' the cabbie called.

I told him to return back to Highgate. The fire was under control. This was real.

The shower was a welcome relief. My body ached so much from being thrown across the room and I already had deep red marks to show for it. In the mirror, I looked at the part of my chest where the surgeon had sliced at me with his nail. The wound had already begun to heal but still wept slightly.

Later on, I lay in bed wide awake, staring through the skylight at the night sky, reflecting on the events of that evening. Michael had concluded that I was firmly at rock bottom. I had planned to do so much in life but never got round to doing it, always putting it off for another day, and at the time I felt even further from achieving my dreams with this 'gift' I had been given.

I could hear my dad watching the TV News when he got up in the morning. When I came down for some breakfast, walking a little stiffer than usual, he told me that a body had been discovered in woodland near Alexandra Park, not too far from Muswell Hill.

I didn't say anything. I had seen enough bodies of late to care. Each time I saw or read about a murder I began to believe that these people were somehow behind the attacks. For that reason, I made sure that I would be on time to meet Michael later that day.

The weather had deteriorated by the afternoon. The sun had faded behind heavy rain clouds and a cold, northerly wind blustered through the streets of Soho as I walked to Leicester Square. I was early. I hovered around the café, looking for signs of Michael. And then, staring at the menu through the glass, his reflection suddenly appeared. I turned to greet him but he didn't say a word, instead he strode straight in to the café. I followed after him.

'Two of my usual, please,' Michael said to the waitress. .

'So this is like a routine for you?' I asked. 'Picking up lost souls and taking them for an ice cream.'

'No. I just like ice cream.'

I looked at him, noting how invigorated he seemed. It was if the events of the previous night had lifted his spirits.

'You got here too early today,' Michael began. 'You stick out like a sore thumb, the way you hover around entrances. You need to learn to be a bit more discreet.'

I felt embarrassed. 'I'd like to discuss this remedy of yours.'

Michael smiled. 'That's more like it, why don't you just come out with it.'

'I've got some questions, though.' He said nothing, just looked at me and nodded. 'In the taxi ride back home last night I asked the driver to go via Muswell Hill.'

'A waste of petrol, but enlightening I hope!'

'I spoke to a policeman.' Michael looked wary. 'I asked him if anyone was hurt.'

'And he told you there were no bodies.'

'How is that possible?' I asked.

'We're jumping the gun a little,' he replied. 'I think that before we talk about their tactics and support network, I need to tell you a little bit more about them.'

'They're vampires aren't they?'

'Vampires don't exist. I told you that yesterday in my apartment. Weren't you listening? They're just a convenient folklore used to describe things that cannot be rationally explained.'

'So who are they?'

'Do you have an interest in nature?'

I raised my hands to my head in despair. 'A simple answer, please . . . I'm going crazy trying to get some kind of identity together.'

'If I'm going to help you then you'll extend me the courtesy of listening. Patience is a dying virtue in today's society.'

'Okay, I'm sorry.' I thought back to what he had said. 'Nature, yes, I love nature – who doesn't?'

'It's fascinating, especially when you look at the many different species of this world, each one uniquely designed, and each one given a purpose on this earth, designed to live in a state of symbiosis with others. Marvellous, don't you think? I mean, it's only when you stop and regard certain intelligently designed specimens that you inherit a real appreciation and understanding about the natural world, and can conclude that there must be beings other than humans who share a complex nature and superior intelligence.'

'So are you saying they're a different type of man – like a new race?'

'I don't technically like to class them as human. Humans don't eat other humans, at least not in today's culture. They're predators, a step up the hierarchy.'

The ice creams arrived but this time Michael didn't tuck straight in like before.

'What about cannibalism?' I asked

'It's all linked,' he continued, 'but for us humans it's hard to fathom, the idea that something that looks human can behave so differently and be so dangerous, yet can co-exist amongst us.'

I took a spoonful of ice-cream as I thought about what he said. 'What you're saying is nothing new, there are those who already argue that the human race is arrogant to assume that we're the top of the food chain.'

'Look at insects,' he said, leaning closer. 'Masters of camouflage, well organised, sometimes invasive, just some of the characteristics that they exhibit.'

'Six legs though,' I added.

'Yes, six legs. But what's to say six legs didn't evolve into two.'

'That's impossible.'

'As impossible as a small micro-organism evolving into a man? Yes, impossible you say, but still a largely believed theory by millions of people all over the world. So daft, in fact, that this is taught to children around the world and is a view adopted by governments internationally: evolution over intelligent design.'

I contemplated his theory. I knew nothing about religion yet I understood the basis of Darwin's theory. 'But you don't believe they evolved separately?' I asked.

'I believe we were designed. Created using the same building blocks of life as everything else on this planet.'

'But you and I were both born human.'

'And still are, just about . . . I'm afraid you won't find this in any text book, and what I'm about to tell you is based on over thirty years of me studying their behaviours whilst trying to avoid them. At first I thought I was mad.' Michael stared right into me. 'I thought that everyone was trying to kill me, but then I realised that they were trying to protect something far deeper than their identities: their origins.'

I had to take a natural break. Already he was confusing me. Was he saying we were all the same but that one evolved into something more deadly? Or was he saying that we were designed to co-exist, two very different beings? I felt he was trying to steer me away from the events, to deny me the logic that I needed. I had had real encounters with these people and I needed to understand them before I bought into his theories.

'What about the ones from yesterday?'

'The people I killed?" he said coolly.

'Yes, there was something about the way in which they behaved, and how they died. I didn't think people died like that. It was almost like something burst inside of them.'

'Are you a chemist, John?'

I shook my head.

'Have you ever heard about what happens when phosphorous reacts with air?'

'It burns?'

'It explodes!' he said gleefully. 'The human body has about 800 grams of the stuff, assimilated in your bloodstream and your bones, regulating tissue growth and repair. For some reason, they have a little bit more than everyone else.'

'But the police said there were no bodies. They don't just totally vaporize.'

'There are usually workers nearby who are on standby to clean up any mess. If we'd been any longer getting out, we might not be here now.'

'Clever.'

'Extremely. They're highly organised, and very calculating.'

'But if I'm infected, then why am I still me?'

'You haven't given me a chance to explain. It's not that we're massively different, it's just that they are carriers and humans are not.'

'You mean like a disease?'

'A parasite to be more precise. Ultimately it will consume you and your thoughts unless your body is strong enough to fight it off or you figure out a way to remove it. I was friends with a biologist once. She told me that during the initial stages of infection, it takes time for the parasite to take full control of the body. But it will eventually. Sometimes all it takes is a serious drop in the immune system to overcome the body's natural defences.'

'Like a serious illness, stress or hospitalisation?' As I asked the question I nodded my head, it made sense. I thought back to the events of October. 'Okay, I get it. Then what?'

'Then it grows. And did you notice the third heart beat? It's quite amazing really, you hear it now and then, like a foetus, it wants to be born and carries on growing, a placenta to your heart, hence the body needs more phosphorous.'

'That's not possible.'

'And of course, you would know. One day you'll discover for yourself the insides of their heart. Look at how nature operates, at the Phorid fly for example, how it lays an egg inside its fire ant host which then slowly gets eaten alive by the larvae until it is ready to hatch. You've seen the science fiction, but this is science fact. A mother grows a totally new organ to support the baby in her womb. Yet you question me like I am mad,' he countered.

'So the fire, the spraying blood . . . it's a self

defence mechanism, the last defence?'

'Don't think I'm trying to mislead you, for I will confess that I do not have a biology degree, but to a large extent yes, the parasite will do what it can to ensure its survival, even when the host dies.'

'But what if they were to remove the parasite from me? What then?'

'Normally it would signify death, especially without proper surgery. But to go to all that trouble, you must signify great importance.' He leant forward. 'But understand this: there have been others like you, people who have tried to fight their resurrected instincts.'

I looked at him with hope but I could tell by his facial expression that this wasn't a story he wanted to tell. 'What happened to them?'

'Another time,' he said dismissively. 'The outcomes are generally the same. Some turn and they end up embracing the collective, others defect and end up killing themselves because they cannot accept the changes they are going through, and others are caught and killed by their own.'

'So, what you're saying is that the outlook is good.'

He managed a half smile. 'I'm still alive and I was bitten years ago.' With that he ate his ice cream. An uncomfortably long amount of time passed, so I started to spoon some of the praline flavoured ice cream into my mouth.

'How many of them are there?'

'Worldwide, I couldn't say. There might only be

a pandemic in London, but that's doubtful given air travel. London has a population of over seven million people. I've identified pockets of activity here and there across the capital, anything from a few drones and workers to larger gatherings. It's hard to give you accurate figures.'

I ate more ice cream. 'How did they find me?'

'They foraged, most likely, unless you were deliberately infected. I'd like to show you proof, that the parasite triggers a release of pheromones perhaps, or to say that there was a dramatic shift in your magnetic field, but most likely it was good old fashioned detective work.'

I looked at him, this old man who came across as an expert on just about anything. 'How do you know all of this exactly?'

'Let's just say I saved someone once and he's been eternally grateful to me ever since. He knows about the fight I'm up against and he's helped me investigate ways in which I can dispose of them.'

'Interesting friend to have,' I remarked.

'If you're lucky, you might meet him one day. I refer to him as the Donor.' He brought a napkin up to his face and rested his hands to the side, as if to have a break. 'I've tried to map them to something in the insect world and there's one species that fits the bill.'

I pondered what it could be, but my mind was already overloaded with information and conspiracies. 'Spiders?' I said, forgetting that they had eight legs.

'Ants. They're some of the most complex, well organised and invasive insects around.'

'I know a bit about them and their caste system. They communicate by chemical signals and by touch, which would back up your idea about foragers sniffing around for newly changed people like me?'

'They don't sniff, they investigate. Do your senses not feel heightened?'

This I knew to be true; nights lying awake and developing a different type of hunger as my tastes and senses changed. 'How did you find me?'

'Straight after you left my flat I was already down the stairs by the time the elevator door opened. I knew your instinct would be to head back the way you came, and since the quickest route back to Highgate was the tube, I had no problem keeping up with you. I was about three carriages down from where you got on. Slowly I worked my way along until I could keep an eye on you. When I saw the mess you made in the carriage, that's when I realised you were at the crucial stages of development. I simply followed the trail.'

'Was it you that put the note through my door a week or two back?'

Michael shook his head. 'What did it say?'

'Finish the job.'

He brushed the side of his hair. 'Interesting, did you notice anyone?'

'I saw a figure loitering outside beneath a

flickering streetlight – and he waved at me before disappearing.'

'You're adamant it was a he?'

I shook my head.

'So, the plot thickens,' he continued. 'It seems like they may have had their eye on your for longer than I thought. How curious . . .' He finished the last mouthfuls of his dessert and seemed to reflect in his own private moment. 'Did you feel anything else on the night you received the note?'

'Shooting pains in my head, and sometimes flashing images.'

'Get used to it,' Michael placed his spoon down as if he was about to declare something great.

A couple across the café turned to look at us with smiles across their faces; perhaps they had overheard our conversation or were amused by Michael's extroverted moments. Michael, unaware of his passionate rhetoric, lowered his voice. 'Each of us omits an electrical field. Some ants, not all, but a few of them are able to manipulate this field to confuse their prey and to send messages. If you've ever been hit by an EMP, you would feel something similar, but you would not get hurt. I tell you: they're the human equivalent to ants.'

I couldn't help but laugh – EMPs I understood, they were a high-tech weapon used by the likes of Tom Cruise in action films, now they were being fired by vampires just by thought alone. 'I can't help but think that some of this is all wrong – nonsense even.' I began to doubt everything. The sugary ice cream had made me feel better but Michael continued feeding me with theories, too many bits of information which I didn't know to be true or not. My mind was at capacity, ready to burst and expel most of his rich conspiracy. Yet despite this, everything sounded feasible in some way, and because of his age and the way he acted so serious about it, I couldn't help but want to fully believe.

'Why is there no science behind this?' I asked.

'Everything I have told you is based upon the theory of science. You will find evidence in nature, and understand that all scientific principles support what I have told you. Remember, all science is based on theory, a collection of facts that is understood and helps us make predictions.'

I focused in on a stain on his shirt beneath his jacket. I couldn't tell whether it was tea, coffee or dried blood. I couldn't imagine myself being in his shoes, living with this curse for over thirty years. I grew sceptical about some of the things he said. Perhaps he found comfort in some of these theories to keep him sane given the huge physical stress he was under; beneath the cold blue eyes, I could sense his agony, a deadly catalyst for his explosive temper.

'You have a theory about me, don't you?' I asked.

He nodded. 'She bit you.'

'She?'

'The queen.'

THEORIES

We continued to debate and discuss his ideas over a hot chocolate. By the end of it all, I felt like I had been given an unedited copy of the book of Genesis according to Michael. He also discussed his theory of their evolution right up to the point when they became the hidden master race. He talked about the Egyptians, the Incas, and even threw in some Chinese as frontrunners in early hierarchical rule. It all got a bit much and I spoke bluntly with him.

He concluded that once man had founded religion that many of them (us) learnt and understood the concept of free will, and then used the skills against the elite (them), which explained why so many of the wonders of this world lay abandoned. It was feasible to a layman like myself, but it challenged every historian's perspective that there was. And despite there being bits of it which I believed - it was a concept too far. He threw more at me. Michael sighted particular events in history, from the Great Fire of London, The Black Death, even events such as 9/11 – all acting as catalysts which forced them deeper under the earth; to regroup, reassemble, and consider ways to regain control again once equilibrium was restored.

I suggested that to do this meant there must still be a high number of them and that they must rank highly in society, which I then declared, was like every other conspiracy theory out there. He agreed with me to some extent, saying that people like myself (a bum) were common and not elite, but that for an organisation to remain funded and be kept secret that it only needed a few at the top.

Michael stated that there was a network of underground tunnels beneath the capital which connected them to several hotspots. He promised to show me one day.

The most intriguing aspect of Michael's lecture to me, however, was that many of them lived normal lives and worked within various service industries, including the public sector, which gave them greater coverage and links. He said that if I joined him in trying to defeat them that, in their eyes, I would become the equivalent to a terrorist, a threat to their way of life and a barrier to their operations within London's seedy underworld. He said that things would get hairy, worse than in Muswell Hill, and that I would see things that I would not be able to block out of my mind.

I was pretty much taken in by everything he

said and I grew excited at the prospect of fighting for his cause. I didn't give a second thought about his real motives, the fact that he was driven by anger and what they had taken away from him. Perhaps it was because I felt the same; my simple, non-descript life was under threat.

Michael steered conversation back towards the events in October. 'You say you weren't alone when you got bitten.'

'No, there was me and one other guy.'

'This character, Ed.'

I couldn't recall telling Michael the full story before, or even mentioning his name. 'Yeah, although he remains adamant that nothing else other than the mugging happened.'

'We must assume that Ed has also become like them.'

I felt cold. I nodded slowly. In my heart I knew he had changed and that something wasn't right – it all suddenly started to make sense and confirmed my suspicions: the visits to members clubs, sleeping at the office, and increased vigour. But Ed had thrived. 'Is he like me?'

'He's as bad, if not worse. I've seen men I've tried to help before become so consumed by their power that it ultimately leads to their death. Have you been watching the news lately?'

'On and off,' I said.

'Some very horrific attacks have been going on against women, more than is reported. You need to follow Ed and suss him out, make sure he's not in too deep.'

'Surveillance?' I felt like the rookie detective being given my first assignment – to tail an old work colleague and dig up the dirt on him.

'You did well to follow me,' Michael remarked. 'A few careless mistakes here and there gave yourself away, but there are other skills available at your disposal. Sadly, I can't teach them to you - you'll have to learn them for yourself.'

'Okay, so I find Ed and follow him around for a bit, but then what do you want me to do exactly?'

'Make notes, take pictures, monitor his behaviour, and talk to his friends: gather evidence.'

'Evidence?'

'The incriminating kind – to prove that he's a killer.'

I shook my head to try and slow things down a little. 'Look, I'm not living out an episode of CSI, this could take weeks, months even. If I find evidence, what do you want me to do, ring the police?'

'No, once you've confirmed what we suspect, I want you to kill Ed.'

I felt nauseous at the word. Whilst I was indebted to Michael for saving my life and roused by his rhetoric about Ants, I wasn't naïve, and I knew that I was being groomed to kill. Find yourself or let them find you. Kill or be killed. Those were his words.

'You want me to kill him?'

'He's as good as dead - you'd be doing him a

favour.'

'What if he's innocent, have you considered that?'

'Unlikely. If he's embraced them then there's little left of him. Use this.'

Michael rested a long object, about 18 inches in length and wrapped in thick black cloth, on the table. I had a peek inside and saw the edge of a blade.

'What is this?'

'Aim for the heart, anywhere else is just a flesh wound.'

'I thought you said we weren't vampires. Yet here you are, giving me silver stakes and telling me to aim for the heart. What next, fucking garlic capsules?'

Michael started laughing out loud. 'We're not vampires, were infected hybrids. Take the heart out of any living thing and it stops working. No scientific degree needed to figure that one out.'

'And what if he's not infected?'

'If what you believe you saw is true, then he will be. You said you've had visions, of murders and attacks. We must therefore assume that a link between you both has been created, that they are shared memories. His memories. Eventually, he will grow strong and influence you to do the same as him – kill.'

Michael was entering psychic territory again, dabbling with the occult, theorising about mediums; I didn't believe any of that type of stuff.

Ed was a work colleague I grew suspicious of. Thinking I'd have to kill him made the danger seem real.

'When you kill him, you'll break the link, then we'll see the real you.'

I assumed that 'real me' he was referring to was about getting my life back to some degree of normality. If I was going to kill Ed it would have to be in the context of insects and him being an ant. Michael kept the insect metaphor going, telling me that some breeds of caterpillar can trick ants into offering them shelter by sending out false pheromones. Effectively I would have to do the same, infiltrate the nest, make them believe that I was one of them, and feast on their secrets before returning to transform myself.

'You have no idea how preposterous this all sounds – using insects allegorically to justify all that you have asked me to do.'

'What you do,' Michael whispered, 'will control your fate. Control it before someone else does. You're still a newcomer, a novice to this sick world I live in. There have been others before you, others I've had to kill because the thirst took hold.' His whole mood had suddenly switched and the colour seemed to wash out from his face. 'You won't see me again after today until the job is done. And please, don't try and find me - I'll find you.'

Whilst we didn't know each other intimately, I was hurt by his rash decision, again brought about by my flippancy. I pondered whether he was bipolar or whether it was a reaction to my ignorance, which would have been perceived as arrogance to a man of his age. He was not simply asking a stranger for a favour, but it felt like I was being asked to complete one of the labours of Hercules. Secretly, however, I was seeking redemption for the trance induced murder of the prostitute in the brothel, the deed I dared not to mention to him. I may not have had the whole world on my shoulders, but I was conscious that I would eventually have to do battle with mythical beasts.

I accepted the challenge, for I owed Michael my life. How could I forget that?

He finished his drink, rose from his seat and simply said, 'good luck.'

I didn't rush to leave the café, and I didn't bother to see which direction Michael left. In some ways, I was glad he had left for I was able to collect my thoughts.

I was tempted to trail home but I decided to walk to East London instead. It would give me time to rediscover some of London's architectural gems.

I remember marveling at the size and shape of certain buildings that led away from Trafalgar square, all the while new foundations were being laid and built upon. How did we build such structures? I suppose ants were no different - and using just their mouth. And then there was the spider, building its own web without a blueprint, just an instinctive desire to snare its prey. If the secret collective that Michael talked about actually existed, then where would they live? And why had we never seen them before? The suggestion that man had learnt the foundations of knowledge from a master race and then broke free was plausible - after all, who abandons a load of pyramids in the desert?

My phone blipped as I walked. It was a text message from Claudia:

What the fuck are you playing at?

I felt sick – the move, the handover, my stuff was still in the flat.

The phone blipped again:

I ask for one fucking favour and you do this to me!

I sent a text to apologise. I said that I'd be at the flat within the hour to tidy up; that I'd drop the key off with the agent afterwards. She texted back some obscenities and that really was the last time I heard from her.

I arrived at the flat to find my belongings had been tossed randomly into boxes. I loaded them into my car and drove over to the agent's office, explaining that the place needed to be cleaned. They told me that half of the deposit would have to go on cleaning bills. I shrugged my shoulders and asked that any remaining balance go back to Claudia.

MICHAELSON PI

It had only been a couple of weeks since I left work, but as I walked through the doors of the agency I felt like there had already been big changes. The office was nearly empty except for Grace, who stood up and came running over to me wearing her beautiful smile. I was so glad I left her untouched; killing her would have given me a good reason to commit suicide.

'Just you?' I asked.

She told me that everyone was out on appointments. I saw that my desk had already been colonised and that Ed's looked very different also.

'It's all kicked off since you left,' she began. I asked her to elaborate. 'Well, Ed's gone for a start.'

I felt sick, my one solid lead, and my first step towards cleansing myself of murderous thoughts dissolved there and then. Ed had vanished into

London's workforce of millions.

'That's unexpected.'

'Tell me about it, Julian had a fit!'

That I could believe, I almost felt like laughing. I asked her if she was busy. She shook her head and said she had 20 minutes to kill.

I took Grace to the best coffee shop within a two minute walk from the office and treated her to a vanilla latte. I still hoped for there to be a connection between us, although I felt that she had already moved on from that night.

'I'm sorry I never rang,' I said sincerely.

'Don't, I feel awful about what happened,' she replied.

'Why? It's nothing about what you did.'

'I know that, I mean, in a way I'm glad we didn't go any further.'

That hurt. I tried to look into her eyes for answers, but she was putting up a brave front and I didn't feel like prying. She had rehearsed it. Her hands were wrapped tightly around her latte.

I nodded my head and smiled. 'So, tell me more about Ed, I was sure he was going to be the next office manager.'

'He just came into work one day and said that he'd been offered another job in the city, and that they wanted him to start straight away. And you know how it is in this business, once you're off they want you straight out.'

I shook my head in disbelief. 'Did he say where he was going?'

'No, he said nothing, just hinted that some property management company in London had offered him a better deal, and that he'd be mad not to take it.'

'That's a shame,' I said. 'I really needed to see him. Do you know which agency?' She shook her head. 'What about where he lives?'

'I'm sure I can find that out for you when I get back to the office.'

I thanked her. I was glad that Ed was no longer involved in Grace's life.

Graces' phone rang. It was her two o'clock appointment. 'I've got to go,' she said.

I stood up and kissed her on the cheek goodbye. Things felt a bit awkward between us as she left, the affection offered so freely weeks ago had disappeared and I was to blame; I left her that night and didn't so much as visit her for a couple of weeks after that evening except for a piteous phonecall the next day. What did I expect apart from a cold shoulder?

'Pop in and see me again soon,' she said. I smiled at her as she left. That was the last time I would see Grace alive.

I didn't want to visit the office again; I needed to move on with my life. After leaving the coffee shop I chose to visit the car park where it all began for one last time. Michael had explained to me all that he could – or wanted to - and had left me like some apprentice to try and figure the rest out for myself. I was in the pupae stage, according to him, ready to punch through false walls and evolve, but into what?

The car park attendant recognised me as I popped my head into the cabin. He stopped playing darts and made random small talk about the weather and how kids were still breaking in. I explained my motives for being there and he let me go straight through.

I stood scouring the perimeter for clues, trying to discover where the carrier of the parasite might have come from. I found nothing new. There were just dark corners and wire fences. I decided to head back home.

I stopped at the confluence of small roads and traffic lights. At about fifty yards, audaciously in broad daylight, a black youth peddled drugs to two women who looked dressed for a 'fun night out'. I continued to stare at them until I caught one of the girls' attention and got a glimpse of her face. Her hair was back-combed and set in large curls, and she wore fake gold earrings and a nose stud, but this did not disguise the tired hollow eyes and the onset of scabies around her mouth which had been disguised by heavy brown lip liner. The man ushered them both round the corner into an alleyway. She turned and looked at me before I walked away; some spy I would be, standing in the middle of the road with my mouth wide open. Rookie, Michael had said.

I wanted to follow them and see more, but I'd already concluded that the women were street prostitutes and that he was their pimp; there were no leads there, only misery. I had to focus back on the task: find Ed.

Michael's best piece of advice was to strike in daylight if I could, that at night they were twice as hard to kill because the urge grew stronger. Even I could not fault his logic, for at night I felt that my senses were heightened and my long term memory failed me.

It was night when I arrived back home at Highgate. I'd received a voicemail from Grace, she had managed to find Ed's home address for me and read it out aloud on the message for me twice, perhaps so that I wouldn't ring her back. I memorised it, replaying the message and listening to the soft accents of her voice again and again.

I drank black coffee, strong and sugary, and sat in the conservatory for an hour trying to make sense of the world I was living in. I was so naive to think that finding Ed would be easy; and I could not overlook the fact that others might still be looking for me and may have already got to him. I needed to stay sharp in every sense.

I thought back to my conversations with Ed, recognising the clues that pointed to a change in his behaviour, assuring myself that they were not a result of my paranoia but of gut instinct. The biggest giveaway was the night he kipped at the office. But my evidence was still a very thin, not justifiable for me to kill him, and if I was truly going to, I needed to find more proof. I desperately hoped that Michael had been wrong about everything, that if I got within a few feet of Ed that he would appear and tell me that it was just a test, to see if I'd actually go through with the act of premeditated murder.

I got out my London A-Z and checked the locations of theatres where Michael was attacked and where most of the private members clubs were located in and around The Strand.

I put on my large winter overcoat and found a place to store the blade that Michael had given to me. The sword was surprisingly lightweight and sharp; I rested it lightly upon an apple and watched it slice clean through without making a sound.

I knew that what I was doing was morally wrong, and that I didn't fit the stereotype of a knife carrier; to get caught with a sword in London would land me with a prison sentence. To avoid drawing unnecessary attention to myself, I dressed smart like a trader in the city; no-one would give me a second look if I entered a bar or a club or any other kind of establishment in that area. The police certainly wouldn't have had any grounds for stop and search.

As I went to leave I caught a glimpse of my dad in the office. He gave me a bemused look and checked his watch. 'Got a new job?' he asked.

'Not quite.'

'Got a date?'

'No, I'm going to a private club.'

'One that I would know?'

'I hope not,' I said, smiling to myself as I walked out of the front door.

PARTY CAPITAL

Ed's address yielded nothing. When I knocked on his door, my heart was beating uncontrollably in my chest. A bearded man, the philosophical student type, told me that he had just moved in and that the previous tenant, Ed, had moved out two weeks prior. I asked for a forwarding address but he had nothing. In desperation I rang Ed's old work mobile, but that was also disconnected. My leads had all gone cold and, to cut a long story short, I had to consider plan B: scouting the private members clubs of London.

December nights in the city buzzed with office parties, late night Christmas shoppers and tourists who somehow saw a reason to visit the dark, cold capital at that time of year. Most of the bars and clubs were relatively full and traffic on the streets was constant.

I travelled down Great Queen Street, thinking

that there was something in the name as I entertained Michael's Ant metaphor. My feet felt like cold anvils banging on the stone pavement as I took in my surroundings. Sometimes a gust of wind would bring me to my senses and I would pull my coat tighter around me and stare down at the depths of city basements; only then did I start to realise the scope of what Michael was trying to tell me: there was another city below the street level, beneath what we saw and understood. I recalled seeing the remains of Roman walls built in and around London Wall, many of the remains could be seen from street level, but many were hidden several feet under. I remembered reading a news article about a Roman amphitheatre being unearthed beneath the Guildhall and I started thinking about the barbaric spectacle that Londoners would have seen there.

I passed the Freemason's hall, a great hulk of a building with large, cast-iron torches strapped to the wall like sentinels. I used to believe the folklore that the masons were a mysterious, secret organisation up to no good, but walking past their HQ they seemed far from shadowy. There was a big advert outside inviting people to visit their museum and get a tour of the building. Nothing to hide there, I thought. Churchill, Edward VII, to name but a few, had all been masons and part of a society that fought so hard to protect the morals of the British and prevent it from falling into the hands of an evil organisation hell bent on destroying the fabric of society. What was wrong with that? If anything, I could have argued that the world needed more Masons, and to vilify them was throwing people off the real scent of the deep rooted problems gnawing away at London.

I was tracking a secret society that didn't want to announce its existence and grandeur, one that held its own mysticism and desire for power.

To satisfy my interest I popped my head in through the main door and a security guard was quick to greet me. I made polite conversation and asked if he had any leaflets.

'There are two tours every day,' he said, handing over some nicely presented literature to read through. 'Admission is free, and here are our opening times.' He pointed to the sign as if to highlight that I was too late. Before leaving, I gave the foyer a quick glance, noting the lifts and stairs leading to the basement. I imagined that such a building must have had all sorts of chambers, and I wanted to see if it was connected by a network of secret tunnels that piped through the capital. I left with the intention of visiting soon.

I had circled two possible Locations where I figured a nest could be built – purely based on how I read the map. Michael had given me nothing at this point, and at the end of Great Queen Street and Long Acre there was a large building that had excellent links heading in all directions. From my research and the aerial images of the building it was structured like a fortress; turrets and rails enveloped the tough exterior and I imagined there to be heavy security. The main entrance had an imposing bright foyer and a number of respectable businesses had opted to set up there. The road was served by one way streets which no doubt gave access to feeding grounds and tactical defence.

As I walked the perimeter I could feel the heat coming from the basement and hear the deep whining of fans circulating the air; huge vents ejected steam from various access points. I felt like I was close, but it was all a bit too obvious. Nonetheless, I finished my inspection of the exterior and noted down the location of all CCTV cameras.

I stopped outside the main entrance and it slowly dawned on me that the prospect of finding Ed seemed so remote in such a large city. It was a daunting task, too - within minutes hundreds of people walked by me in every direction. I contemplated how I was going to be able to identify who was who in the ant world. Michael taught me little, and what he did teach me seemed hard to believe. I felt like giving up already. Mission: impossible.

I checked back over my map to decide where a good place to have a private members club would be. Given the wealth of the area, I should have just stabbed a pin onto any part of the page.

Walking towards the Strand, London's concrete concourse towards Trafalgar Square, the roads were dotted with plush offices, doorways to cobbled forecourts and law firms. My instincts led me down Maiden Lane where I saw some plausible bars that would make good pick up joints. I saw private doors leading to grand residences – maybe even clubs. I sensed that I was close to something, that there was a connection somewhere amongst it all, that the nest was near, but I was equally cautious and sceptical. I cut through alleyways and investigated Adam Street. As I did so I kept thinking about Michael and how he had attacked the ants so brutally, making light work of my captors. Michael had since armed me with a sword, but in truth I was a coward, and if I were put in a similar situation again I feared that I might not be able to handle myself; I didn't want to fight.

For ten minutes I walked up and down the road, looking for clues. Eventually, a large black door opened and two tall, heavily built men emerged, dressed in black suits. They walked towards me. Michael's theory about ants and their caste system suddenly struck me as particularly ingenious. I stopped walking and held my spot and their gaze. The two of them marched in unison, never exchanging a word; both looked right through me. They passed in a blur and I became confused. I recalled how ants knew each other through an exchange in chemical signals and by touch. If the principle was true, and they walked past me and I hadn't caused alarm, then it was likely that I was bitten by the same queen - assuming that they were part of this secret collective. The whole concept gave me a migraine. Everyone was treated like a suspect unless I knew otherwise, and that was how I was starting to behave: like a paranoid schizophrenic. Yet I had seen, first hand, the ruthlessness of these beings, and I was plagued by terrifying images of Ed's brutality, if that were even him, if he was even infected. To say I had doubts was an understatement.

I felt like calling it a night but I found myself stood outside the door that both men had emerged from. It was like staring at a Victorian photograph. At both sides of the wonderfully ornate, glossy door stood two mighty grey pillars, and beneath them I caught a small glimpse of a basement, perhaps twenty feet beneath street level, and air vents, lots of air vents. My heart began to stir, the three beat murmurs had returned, fading in and out. This is it, I thought. I'm standing at death's door. I would have thought it bigger or more heavily guarded if it were. But this, I soon realised, was just one of many private clubs in the vicinity. There was not even a plaque to say what the building housed.

A black car pulled up directly outside and two attractive models were escorted out of the vehicle by a gaunt looking man in a black suit. The women muttered something in Czech and pulled away from his grip only to be tugged back again. The door suddenly opened and a doorman wearing a similar suit, black glasses and an earpiece greeted them all. He watched the car pull away and then he gave me a questioning look as he saw me loitering. He shut the door and I cursed myself for staring so obviously rather than taking cover.

The door was now shut again and there were no other obvious entrances. I scanned the building to see what other properties it was attached to. I went to see if there was a back entrance, when the two men who had passed me only minutes earlier reappeared. I thought at first that it was by coincidence. I stepped back onto the road and walked away from the building in the opposite direction to them. I was however reassured by the feel of the blade tucked neatly in my jacket but I didn't want to look like an amateur if they were to reappear again. I carried on down a path and took a right turn until I was out of sight. Then I sprinted down one of the many alleyways in that vicinity. I dipped into the first bar I came across and peered out through the window.

I could feel my core temperature surge from the adrenaline. Moments later I saw the two bald headed men half jogging. I breathed a sigh of relief when they went past. Surely I was safe in a pub? I was wrong, a couple of minutes later they both strode in and were scanning the premises. I made my way to the bar and kept my head facing away, watching their reflection in the mirror behind the counter. My instincts were telling me to run out of the pub and find somewhere else. I was adamant I would be faster than them, but I had to learn to show no fear. As long as there were people around me, I believed that I was safe. That was Michael's survival tip.

I ordered an ice cold beer from the barman and propped myself up at the bar. I was sweating and I could feel my t-shirt clinging to my skin underneath several layers. To the left of me were a group of post-graduate American uni students, all of them ordering rounds of flaming Sambuca. I glanced to my right to see where the men had gone, only to find that they had disappeared. I didn't like it when people just disappeared. I took a few sips of the beer and hoped that I had imagined the whole incident. A man ordered some wine to the left of me and then walked away. When he did, I caught sight of the one of the men. Then, as if rehearsed, the other man appeared to my right and I found myself sandwiched at the bar. They didn't say a word but I could feel the malice off each of them. I couldn't look them in the eyes so I pulled out a twenty pound note and waved it frantically to grab the barman's attention once more.

'Three flaming Sambuca's,' I said. The bartender smiled. Bam-bum-bum, there it was again, the same physical anomaly I felt when in danger. Bam-bum-bum. My muscles tightened in my arms and my vision sharpened. My gums felt puffy and my temples throbbed, like I had ingested spoonfuls of MSG and could not stop the pulse at the roof of my mouth from pounding. I looked at the ant to my right; his eyes were clearly fixed on me, and the man on the left did the same. His jaw seemed to quiver; I imagined it shaking itself loose and dislocating at any moment.

Not here, I thought, not in a public bar. All I could think about was how Michael was right - how there was something far more sinister lurking under the city's streets, and now that I was part of this game, the danger suddenly felt all too real, and came all too quickly.

My drinks arrived. I paid for them and then watched the barman light each one for me. Then I became transfixed by the flames - they were blue, lethargic even, as the alcohol burned slowly around the rim of each shot glass. But I knew that the sugar would warm up and the liquid would reach a good enough temperature, as long as it kept burning. I forgot for a moment that I was flanked either side by soldier ants. I could feel them trying to read my mind, doing what they could to unnerve me. And I just stood there, drinking my beer, watching the Sambuca's burn. I began plotting my exit, but I had a theory I was eager to test.

'Cheers!' I said, raising the glasses to my two adversaries, and before they could react I tipped the contents of each shot onto their chests and watched the flames spread across their shirts. They reacted wildly, trying to pat out the flames as I ran for the exit. Michael's theory was right: one of them was soon in flames, his clothes and skin burning rapidly like he was doused in accelerant. I heard a woman scream as I ran out of the door. I gave one final fleeting glance and saw the other soldier ant hurtling in my direction, his shirt smoldering from the attack.

I made it out of the door and back into the street where I headed for the most open of spaces. As I ran, I began questioning whether I had made the right choice or just inflicted a serious injury on two bald headed men who took a funny liking to me, after all, the majority of revellers in theses bars were all men and dressed similarly.

I felt like I was running on air. I saw police ahead on the street and quickly darted down a side alley before they could see me. A call to the police might not have been made, but I couldn't afford to be stopped carrying a weapon; and if the soldier ant continued to give chase, it would show to them that something was definitely up. Police intervention would be inevitable.

I stood there, in an alleyway, listening for footsteps with my heart in my throat when I realised that I had taken a dead end. I looked for a way out. I turned back only to see my path blocked by one of the men. He streamed towards me, his shoulders arched like some metal plate had risen out of nowhere and I could see his eyes were bloody.

I had no choice but to stay and fight. I fumbled within my jacket and withdrew Michael's sword. It felt light and sensitive to every movement as my limbs shook. He stopped a few feet in front of me and didn't make a sound. His arms were outstretched like he were about to grapple with a bear, goading me to lunge at him. One untimed swoop, a clear miss, and he would have me; but a speedy, accurate blow would give me enough time to escape and fight another day. Perhaps.

He suddenly lunged at me, hands outstretched, trying to take hold of my arm, and he made a low unearthly grunt as he did so. I pushed off against the wall so that I could strike a blow down upon him but he saw this and reached up, hitting me in the chest and throwing me off balance. We both fell to the ground. I looked down at where his hands had caught me and could see blood straight away. He had scraped my ribs so quickly that I barely felt the sting of his nails ripping into my skin. Somehow he was back on his feet and charging towards me again with his arms outstretched. I sprung up off the ground and swung the sword at him, purely in a defensive manoeuvre. And with complete shock, the sword cut clean into the join of his right arm.

He staggered backwards, his face void of emotion as he looked at me, yet he remained eerily silent. His arm hung limp to one side, badly severed, attached by sinew and the tendons that did not get sliced, and a mixture of thick red blood and clear fluid began to seep out, down and along the ridges of his hand. He came at me again without warning, grabbed my sword wielding arm with his good hand and pinned me against the wall. I went to yell for help but had no voice because he was pushing all of his weight into me to trying and crush the life out of my lungs. I held him back as best I could. He managed to raise his bad arm and point it at me, flapping it in my direction until I could feel the hot blood splatter on my face. It was warm and sticky, and it stung. We locked eyes and I could see that he was void of any emotion, like he had died years ago and I was peering into an empty vessel. He tightened his grip with his other arm and I felt his nails pierce through my clothes and into my skin, then I realised that he was trying to split my veins apart, push deeper into my pressure points until I grew faint.

I kicked him. Nothing happened. So I kicked him again and again and again – sometimes using my knees - each time harder until the point of exhaustion, and each time I found it harder to see as his blood sprayed across my face; and the pain of feeling sharp needles push into my arm became unbearable. I kicked again and tried shaking my body. Out of sheer effort and frustration I eventually found my voice and began screaming in a low, guttural moan. I summoned one last kick and I managed to throw him off balance. He fell back momentarily and then I stuck him across the face with my fist. I took the sword from the other hand and with my free arm I swiped it across his shoulder. Then I swung it again until his grip slowly loosened. Each blow rained down on him faster and more frantically than before, until a perfectly angled hack struck him directly in the neck, severing his main vein and bringing his life to an end.

He sunk to the floor on one knee, mute, and then slumped into a twitching wreck of blood, limbs and plasma. Perhaps it was the cold air, but I could have sworn that steam came from his body. I wiped the blood from my face and found that it had already clotted into some darker looking substance. I frantically began rubbing it and picking it off as it began to set like gelatine. My breathing slowly returned to normal as I watched thick black liquid ooze onto the floor.

I remember what Michael had said to me, that if you make a kill you need to be quick and evacuate the area, for others will sense the distress call. I pulled the body away from the wall and rolled it next to a set of industrial bins, and then I replaced the sword into my jacket and jogged back up the alleyway towards the main road. But I didn't want to face the world, not caked in blood.

I passed the back entrance to a pub kitchen and noticed that the door was open. Without thinking I surreptitiously gained access and scrabbled my way towards the gent's toilets without detection. There I was able to rinse the last of the gunk away from my hair and face and wash my hands thoroughly. Wearing a dark jacket and top had helped disguise the blood but it would not disguise the fact that I was still bleeding from the wound on my arm. I stuffed a handful of tissue around the wound and decided to leave.

I exited the bar without drawing attention to myself and, once outside, ran towards Covent Garden, and then cut through to Tottenham Court Road. From there I hopped on the first northbound bus I could find.

I sat away from people on the top deck at the very front so nobody could see my face and stretched out my limbs. They ached, and I could feel the wetness from the blood underneath my arm pits. Yet despite this I couldn't help but feel jubilant, that I had passed my first task set by Michael, and survived a night in London on my own. Perhaps this was how Michael had started out, all those years ago. Then I reflected on how I couldn't have blundered it any better. As the bus crept northbound, I realised that I would be on camera, that there would be endless CCTV footage of me: in the bar dousing two strangers with flaming Sambuca's, running frantically down main roads, slipping up alleyways where a body was later found, and then weaving back to catch a bus. I did consider that if there was no complaint or grievance made by these ants, and they dealt with everything in-house like Michael said they did, then there would be no reason to investigate. I reflected on how many acts of violence must have been caught on London's CCTV cameras on a daily basis, and how many of them would not always result in a conviction or a complaint unless the crime was severe; like assault against a bus driver, rape or even murder.

I decided to get off sooner than Highgate, so as the bus passed through Camden I saw an opportunity to slip along the canals and work through the market where I could blend in and then carry on with my journey to Highgate by foot.

As I walked, I reflected on my kill. I thought about the soldier ant, the bald headed monster laying in an alley, and how the ant network would deal with such a thing in a busy area. There must have been a hive nearby.

My hands had blisters from where I had gripped the sword so tightly and then swung it wildly at my adversary. I knew the skin would heal, grow back and become tougher; I hoped that my spirit would harden with it. Michael told me that, if left untamed, I could become a savage hunter. That made me uncomfortable.

Dad was still awake when I walked through the door.

'How was it?' he called.

'How was what?' I replied, lingering close enough to the doorway so that he didn't need to get up.

'Your evening.'

It was unlike him to take such an interest in my life. 'Pretty uneventful,' I replied. 'You're up late.'

'I'm doing some work for an old friend.'

I half believed him, knowing that he had probably been connected to some private webcam show in Estonia. He asked me if I'd like a cup of tea. I said that I needed a shower first, but if he wouldn't mind bringing one up - lots of sugar - that I'd appreciate the gesture.

In the bathroom I undressed myself and looked at the damage. There were bruises along my neck and shoulder from where we had struggled against the wall, and scabs were already covering the puncture wounds from where his nails had dug into my arms – he had narrowly missed the cephalic vein. Surprisingly, my ribs seemed the worst; he had slashed me across my stomach and peeled off lots of the skin in the process. Both the wounds wept slightly when pushed but the fluid was clear. I decided that it was a possible weak spot and thought about ways to give myself extra protection in the future.

As I stood in the shower, I realised just how much of a near miss it had been. One false move on my behalf and I would have been the one killed in that alleyway, and it would have been my body they would have taken away and buried somewhere. I thought about the man's eyes: black, lifeless and bloodshot with almost an orange tinge to his whites as he stared at me when I dealt the fatal blow. I tried desperately to disconnect the idea that the man might once have had a life, like me and Ed, and how he had now served his purpose, a pawn in the greater scheme of things.

How many hundreds more were there like him?

And how many of London's missing stayed gone at the mercy of their handiwork?

WHITECHAPEL

Gale force winds and heavy rain kept December barely above freezing. My wounds from my night excursion in London's theatre land were all healed and I was in the process of deciding whether to venture back in for more exploration based on some research I had done into buildings in the vicinity. The venue I had suspected of being a hive was one you could hire out privately, and they didn't give out client information. Another dead end.

Each morning, my dad would say, 'There's fresh coffee in the machine.'

I would fetch myself a cup and add plenty of sugar, and then I would swamp several slices of toast with jam. A high sugar diet seemed to be working and I felt less nauseous than I had before meeting Michael.

'He's struck again,' Dad said one morning,

referring to a local news article. I read the story about an attack on a student from Birckbeck University. How my dad seemed to know that I took an interest in such stories was beyond me.

'He's going to get a taste of his own medicine one day,' I said, without really thinking.

I sat in my bedroom and contemplated my next move. I couldn't just sit at home and waste another day hiding from the world. I had to focus all my efforts into finding Ed. I had printed off a large map of the city and stuck all the pages together to form a mural of sorts. A black marker in hand, I noted down all the attack spots that had occurred since October based on all the research I had collected from news articles and the police reports. I couldn't see an obvious pattern, but it did give me places to investigate.

I dressed in a suit and my large jacket which I'd had repaired and dry-cleaned, and specially tailored to conceal an 18 inch object in the lining; I had told the seamstress that I was an architect and that it was for carrying a spirit level.

During daylight I concluded that I could take photos and look for any evidence of safehouses. I purchased a digital camera especially

Rain came at me from all angles, slicing at my face. As I waited at the bus stop I read a feature article a newspaper had run on Jack the Ripper and the psychology behind the attacks. Whenever a spate of brutal murders happened or violent attacks took place against women - London especially – the world-famous misogynist's name always came up. Why women were the prime victims still remained a mystery, I had always figured that it had been because of a sexual motive, but of course there was no evidence of intercourse with any of his victims.

Interestingly, the other half of the news article had a map of old London and where Jack the Ripper killed his victims. I began thinking about what Michael had said about the ants; about cohabiting with man, the great fire of London which, according to his theory, could be attributed as an attempt by early hunters to smoke the ants out of old Roman colonies and tunnel networks buried beneath the city. But in retaliation the ants torched many of London's streets. I know what the history books say, about cinders from a bakery on Pudding Lane, but I can't help but find some plausibility in Michael's motives, no matter how far-fetched they seemed at times.

Jack the Ripper, who was never found (supposedly), was a perfect archetype for Ed – a viscous, out of control beast who was unable to control his rage. Certainly, the psyche of Jack the Ripper matched the feelings I had felt at my lowest point through my visions and dreams. Some ripperologists believed he committed suicide by jumping off Tower Bridge; others believed that he was caught elsewhere by a vigilante group or racketeers and justly killed; Michael believed that he merely became assimilated - or rather reeled in -

by the ants who grew concerned at his sloppy behaviour which conflicted against their interests.

Michael claimed that hunters back then, made up of masons, philanthropists and priests, were just as bad as the collective; butchers who were a little too impulsive and killed in retribution, often in a foolhardy manner. It was his explanation as to why there were several copycat murders at the time. Of the hunters that prevailed, only a few were able to pass on their knowledge to the next generation, those that didn't end up being hanged for their crimes or admitted into a lunatic's asylum.

I had my own theory about Jack, of course, and it was all about geography. By committing a string of brutal attacks against women, the unions eventually came together and demanded action. Thus, the most deprived area in the country benefitted from a massive restructure and development which continues to this very day. Handy if your organization is hell bent on improving links between the city and east London, whilst at the same time satisfying the thirst and letting the anti-Semitic Londoners blame a trail of deaths on the influx of migrants from Europe. Nothing much has changed in today's society.

I choose to visit the first scene of Jack's crime that evening. I considered that visiting the locations of attacks might give me clues about where a killer could strike again in London.

Even though I was the most unlikely cockney you'd find, I'd acclimatised myself to the atmosphere of a sprawling city and become inured to the hostility sometimes felt whilst treading the capital's hectic streets. And stranger still, I felt at home in East London. I watched one of the many Jack the Ripper tours filter away from the scene of Jack's first crime and began taking pictures with my camera.

'Any luck?' a voice asked.

I nearly leapt out of my skin at the sound of Michael's voice. He was leaning against the wall of a shop in the shadows.

'How did do you do that?' I asked.

'It's all about technique, and experience.'

'Sadly I'm without the luxury of either.'

He beckoned me to follow him. 'You need to be careful around these parts at night – you've still got that smell of fear about you.'

'I think that's fair considering my predicament.'

Michael nodded. 'It's understandable, but it's your biggest weakness.'

'So what do you suggest?'

'We'll deal with that nearer the time; right now you've a killer to catch.'

'Well, if you've come to check up on me then I'm afraid you're going to be disappointed. It's a complete lottery – what makes you think that I can trace him down?'

'You need to have a little faith, boy,' he uttered. I didn't like the way he called me boy. 'Faith is one of the pillars of humanity – use it if you want to stay human.'

'I have been trying – he's the only reason I'm out here looking.'

'Had any trouble?'

I nodded. 'Soldier ants - two of them.'

'Really?' He had a look on his face as though he already knew. 'You like the ant metaphor then?'

I ignored him, focusing on recounting my story. 'They tracked me to a bar when I was snooping around the Strand.'

'And did you dispatch them?'

'Sort of.' He looked at me like a teacher about to grade a student's performance. 'It got a bit messy, but I'm here am I not?'

Michael pulled out a photograph and passed it over to me. It was grainy and dark, but I soon made out that it was me on the night that I killed one of the ants.

'How the hell did you get this?'

"How is not the problem, what' important to know is that we've got you covered.'

I didn't like it, not one bit. 'You knew?'

'I got second hand information. We can work on your technique at a later date.'

'Have there been others?' I asked.

'Others?'

I'd tried to have this conversation with him before but Michael had stalled, sidestepped my question. 'Others like me.'

'Yes, there have been some.'

'What happened to them?'

He didn't say anything straight away, but when

he did speak it was in a cold voice: 'Well, I killed some of them.'

I stopped in my tracks, squaring up to him. 'Tell me you're kidding.'

'I said some, not all. Some of them killed themselves, and some I never saw again.' He turned and carried on walking.

I caught up with him. 'And you're going to dispatch me if I get messy, is that what you're hinting at?'

Michael began to laugh. 'Let's sit and talk, I want to take you somewhere.' Michael beckoned me towards Aldgate tube station and I followed.

EDGWARE ROAD

'He's going to strike again,' Michael said morosely as we exited the station.

'I know. I can feel it coming.' I was relieved to hear him speak again. During the entire tube journey, Michael did not make eye contact with me once. It was if we were strangers again, silently staring at the rows of commuters.

'Be careful how far you go, the press will be all over it. You might need to start acting like a journalist if you want to make progress, that's how the ants get to people.'

The pavements got busier as we passed juice bars and restaurants.

'Will you help me find him?' I asked.

'My boy, look at me.' He stopped and held himself regally in his thick navy cloak. I was unsure as to whether I should revere him, but his face and eyes were sad. 'I'm old and you are young. You can enter their world far more successfully than I can. Over the years I have merely become an observer, an opportunist should the right intervention be required. This is your fight for your generation. I will tell you what I can, but you need to find him on your own if you are to discover who you really are.'

'Stop being so bloody melodramatic,' I scorned. 'I hate all this mystery - why can't I get straight answers?' I looked around at the crowd of revellers streaming up and down Edgware Road. It was a hive of activity: lights, shisha pipes and an abundance of hot shawarma and fresh juices were being carried about and devoured in front of our eyes.

Michael beckoned me over to the late night juice and ice cream bar behind him. 'Shall we?'

We managed to get a seat in the corner at the back. I had a mint tea and took satisfaction in dissolving several cubes of sugar into the hot liquid, watching each one liquefy. Michael ordered a house special which consisted of a fruit platter and three scoops of chocolate and hazelnut ice-cream.

'Have you've been reading in detail about recent attacks?' he asked.

'Yes, but maybe too much. Sometimes I'm not even sure there's a link. People attack people, it's nothing new. I feel my mind is saturated with theories and ideas, almost as if I'm being deliberately steered off course, like I should be focusing my efforts elsewhere.'

Michael nodded. 'You need to go with your instincts - try and think like him. After all, you've shared his fantasy, which makes you a silent accomplice. He's going to strike again – you've seen it in your head.'

I shook my head. Yes, I had gruesome visions, but they were not the same women whose faces appeared in the papers. Perhaps they were the missing, the forgotten.

'You said that we're anomalies, living with this infection but still conscious of our humanity. But I just don't buy it!'

'In over thirty years I still don't know the answers to the deepest questions,' he said in between mouthfuls of chocolate ice cream, which left a glossy brown finish on his pursed lips. 'Look at the stories of old: biblical stories, Cain and Abel are a good example – you're no different to Cain. One of you must become the righteous one and die for the good of mankind, and one of you must remain cursed. But understand this – there's a link going back through time. Sometimes you need to embrace the darkness to lead you along the path; that in turn will put you in contact with them. Think like a killer, decide where hot spots are, where opportunities to smite your own real life victim would be, and there you might just find someone with answers.'

I was shaking my head at this point. 'This is London we're talking about – close to 8 million people in a city the same size as Luxembourg. I'm going to fail. And for the record, Cain was cursed for the rest of his life. Tell me more about the others, others like me.'

He settled down his spoon for a moment and drank half a glass of water. 'Well, none of them had a case exactly like yours. For example, most were all bitten whilst out on their own.'

'How many?'

'In over thirty years there have only been four that I've come across. You're the fourth.'

He was lying – he had to be. I prayed that he was being modest. 'So, number one, tell me about him?' I took a sip of the tea and held it in my mouth before swallowing it slowly.

'Actually it was a she. They don't just prey on men. Deborah was her name – a very beautiful lady, late twenties, and ambitious, which was ultimately her downfall. I got to her too late. We met and I tried to support her, to show her the ways to survive, but one day she never came back to me.'

'Why?'

'I guess they got to her first. That's why I learnt to follow any potential converters later, to see who was watching them.'

'Like you did with me?'

He nodded. 'Several years later there was a man like you, a successful city trader. I found him trailing Soho's brothels and girly bars.' He stopped and began eating some more ice cream.

'And . . . '

'He was too far gone. When you live a comfortable way of life, sometimes the thought of living in the darkness is just too much. He took his own life, threw himself off London Bridge and drowned.

He polished off the ice cream and stabbed the last remaining bits of chocolate and banana with his fork. 'The last one, nearly ten years ago now, found me. He was nearly as experienced as me, but when he saw that I was no closer to finding the source . . . well, he figured that if you can't beat them, join them.'

'What happened?'

Michael wiped his mouth clean with the napkin and finished his water. 'We met again under different circumstances.'

'You mean you killed him?'

'Self-defence, actually. I remember the moment I drove a knife into his heart and looked him in the eyes. I could see that there was no humanity left inside of him, only darkness. He made the wrong choice. I didn't kill a man that night, just another drone.'

'Will you kill me?'

Michael didn't react to my question, almost ignored it completely. 'No, because I think you're different from them.'

'But not different from you.'

'Yes, much different. These are hard times we're living in. I live alone, sheltered from the technology and media that saturates us. I'm out-dated and can't get inside places like I used to. This is a secret war I'm fighting - and losing. People in society today have become so self-centred and driven by the desire to succeed. So when the ants come along and offer them greatness, there is no moral fibre left in them to offer resistance since they are already conditioned to make such a choice. They already embrace their dark side willingly and it feeds off of them.' Michael palmed his hands upwards and lowered his voice. 'You need to defeat Ed and send out a message that there is still a fight going on, no matter how small. And when you figure out how, you will need to show the world the truth.'

I wanted to tell him that he couldn't make generalisations about everyone, that there were plenty of good people in London, but I needed to keep the conversation flowing and not upset the flow of rhetoric. 'How am I going to show the world the truth when I haven't even discovered it myself?'

He didn't answer.

I finished my tea. Everything I heard had frustrated me even more. Yet again, more questions planted in my mind. More doubts about Michael and his sanity. I'd been told about countless others, only to discover about four in nearly 30 years – it didn't fill me with hope. I felt empty.

'Where do you suggest I start looking?' I

asked.

'Go back to the source of where it all began.'

'I've tried that – twice! There's nothing! No clues, no hints of activity, just grey spaces and black holes.'

'You're missing something – they got to Ed before you, through some sort of guise, somehow. I suggest you try once more, try people you wouldn't expect to help you.'

Michael began putting on his gloves.

'I suppose you'll be watching me,' I said dejectedly.

'No, I could get in the way. Come find me when you're done.' With that he stood and left me again, this time with the bill to pay. I remained in my seat, not even bothering to turn my head. I wanted him to leave. Deep down, I wanted to believe that he was a figment of my imagination, that I had somehow created him to deal with my situation; this world I lived in which I was yet to fully uncover, a world that merely highlighted my feeling of insignificance. But as the waiter came and carried both glasses and bowls away, I knew that this was no make-believe world. Knowing about the previous people that failed made me understand how hard it must have been for Michael - to pray for light once you've lived in darkness for over thirty years.

Go with your instincts and think like them. That was probably the best piece of advice Michael gave me.

OLD HAUNTS

I woke at 7am, no images, no revelations, just sleep, although I would define it more as junk sleep because of the amount of time I had spent researching on the internet the night before.

I got into my car and drove towards my old workplace, loathing every minute I spent queuing in traffic.

A whole array of new faces sat at their desks as I strode in purposefully. Julian rose from his seat at the back of the office, came forward and shook my hand. He was wearing a bright pink shirt by Jaeger and a chequered yellow tie by Armani, both of which I found offensive. He asked how I was and we made small talk. I mentioned that I'd heard about Ed leaving and Julian added that Gary had also been given his marching orders having lost his battle with alcoholism.

Grace's desk was empty. I asked where she

was and he told me that she had gone back to visit a sick relative in Ireland and wouldn't be back for some time. Small talk over, Julian looked at me and I could tell from his body language that he had things to be getting on with.

'You know when Ed and I were in hospital,' I began, 'and some woman paid you a visit?' Julian nodded. 'I don't suppose she gave you her number did she?'

I watched the clogs of his brain turn as he thought about whether to help me or not. He nodded and went downstairs to have a look. I said hello to the new faces at their desks, avoided eye contact with Martina and Diana, and looked at the flats for rent on the wall – the same ones as always. Michael had told me to search for clues, for anything beyond the ordinary. I noticed the road running parallel to DLR line, and saw that there were many warehouses and businesses occupying the arches. I hadn't even given it any thought that they might link to the car park in some way. My biggest lead, however, was brought about when I realised what Michael had said about the ants acting like journalists.

Julian returned looking sheepish. He held a business card in his hands. 'You're lucky I still have it,' he said. 'She came in the day after the attack and left her name. Said she worked for The Sun just down the road in Wapping, but I can't see how that's the case.'

I took the card and looked at the name: Veronica

Miles.

'What do you need it for?' he asked.

'I'm dying to get hold of Ed,' I replied, thanking him. We shook hands for the last time and I turned to leave the office, mildly euphoric that I had a new lead.

Michael talked about how a group of foragers would gather new recruits once they had been bitten, but I had been so preoccupied trying to find Ed that I neglected turning my attention to look for these groups. I crossed over to the opposite side of the road and took a discrete alleyway which led me under the arches to the car park entrance. I noticed straight away that part of the wall was not fenced off and anyone could easily climb or jump over it. I felt stupid at this point, annoyed that I had missed the obvious, just like Michael had suggested. There was no parking attendant so I felt obliged to investigate the spot where I became infected. A large Jaguar was guarding the archway. I could see the strip light above and the black cables trailing away from it down the brick walls. I followed them into the next archway and then the next before they disappeared into the other side of the wall, a side I could not see. I felt such a fool, discounting the building just behind it because there was no obvious access point; several networks could have been running under my feet and I was only focused on one obvious entry or exit.

I ran back onto the street, imagining I had a

giant LCD clock strapped to my back, counting down the amount of time until Ed became assimilated forever. The small side road was a popular cut through for cab drivers to avoid the one-way system and miss the lights. It was occupied by car washes, garages, timber merchants, and other units protected by locked doors, each one hammered shut, their corrugated doors scraping against the ground so that I could not even peer underneath. I imagined that the source was there, somewhere, or an entrance at least, lurking behind a fucking wall I couldn't get through. And then I remembered that I had the card in my hand, an even stronger lead.

I ducked into a payphone on Prescott Street, rooted for some coins and dialed the number. It was a mobile number and above it was just a name: Veronica Miles. I instantly had an image of a sharp looking, red headed woman with long legs in my mind. I had no idea what I was going to say, I just wanted to hear her voice, and then I would know if there was anything untoward. Go with my instincts. Surely I needed a back-story? I certainly wasn't going to tell her my real name so I decided that I would pretend to be Ed, and it made sense, after all, if they had already found him then they would know I was lying, but if not then they would pass me along the chain, arrange a meeting and I would have a chance at finding my way in. I had to know just how far up the chain this person was.

I remember feeding 20 pence coins into the

machine until it started spitting them back out, then I dialed the number and pressed the receiver tight against my ear, listening to my heart pound in my head.

The phone crackled in protest and then connected.

'Hello?' a voice answered.

'Veronica?' I asked, my voice strained.

'Who is this?' She said assertively. I could hear her brain ticking away.

'We need to talk.'

There was a pause. 'I think you have the wrong number,' she responded.

'It's Ed.'

Silence. My heart sank, I felt like she was about to hang up, but I could just about hear her breathing on the other end, crossing those long legs and lighting up a Marlboro red cigarette. Her card mentioned nothing about being a journalist; it was ivory in colour and crisp with her name embossed along the middle of it.

Thirty seconds passed. I watched the timer count upwards and still nothing was said. I realised this wasn't going to work. 'Hang up and I give the police your number.'

'Hello John,' she said coolly. 'Don't do anything reckless.'

'We need to talk about Ed.'

'Not on the phone,' she replied.

'Where?'

'My office.'

I laughed. 'You must think I'm a fool.'

'So where?' she said bluntly.

I had to think of somewhere busy. At this point I wish I had planned things out a bit more, accounted for this scenario. I needed it to be somewhere I could easily disappear if things went wrong.

'Charing Cross Station. Bring your phone.'

'When?'

'One hour.'

The line went dead.

One hour! What the hell was I thinking? I found myself listening to my own breath, the phone still pressed into my ear. When I moved it away I felt the blood rush back to my temples. Whilst I was pleased to have held on to my nerves, mostly, Julian would have described my negotiating skills as piss poor. Nonetheless, it was a step closer. I didn't even want to consider what Michael would have thought, suicide probably.

I checked my watch and thought about the logistics of getting to Charing Cross in one hour, and how I was going to meet Veronica; I didn't even know what she looked like apart from Julian's shit description.

I caught a bus. Once I arrived I did a quick recce and decided where to call her from. In my pocket I had packed an old analogue phone I kept for emergencies. It would come in use once more and if I needed to ditch it I wouldn't lose any sleep.

I made my way out of the station and looked up

at all the glass offices and multinational HQs within a stone's throw away. With twenty minutes left I thought back to everything that Michael said about them, their level of intelligence and ability to work together collectively, and it dawned on me that she would not be alone. If what he said was true, then I knew that they would want to do more than just meet for a chat – I couldn't afford to be naïve this time. I had to prepare for the worst. If she were the queen, or one of the queens, she would bring others: soldier ants. And they would track me down; follow me like they had a week earlier with a view to disposing of me discretely.

It had been an hour. I found a good vantage point from behind a fast food outlet in the main part of the station and then rang her number. Using Julian's description, I scoured the crowds and picked out two red haired girls, but they both looked far too young to be involved in anything ant-like. Then I thought back to Sarah and how she had tricked me so easily in Muswell Hill weeks before - there was no way I would have suspected her. No-one, it seemed, could be trusted.

The phone rang several times before she answered.

'I'm at Charing Cross, where are you?' she said.

'Close enough,' I said, lying. 'Move towards the information sign by the main escalator.'

I could hear movement, the sound of heels clacking on marble floor, and I believed that she had kept her side of the deal. 'You haven't told me what this is about' said Veronica, sounding pissed off.

'It's about Ed,' I said, scanning for figures amongst the crowds.

'I know lots of Eds, you need to be specific.'

'The Ed you're grooming into a killer.'

There was a pause and I could sense that she had stopped walking. I waited and watched, and in the centre of the station I saw a well dressed woman with straight red hair hovering about twenty yards from the information sign. Her hair contrasted beautifully with her aqua coloured winter coat and she looked every bit the powerful city woman you'd expect to find on the top floor of any corporate office. She had a delicate upturned nose and porcelain white skin and didn't seem like the threatening type, but trailing behind her, searching the crowds, were two stocky, bald-headed men – one of them I recognised.

'So, it really is you,' she said coldly, a creepy change in her tone. It was chilling to watch her scan the crowds, even though I had deep satisfaction that I couldn't be seen.

'You need to give me Ed,' I said.

'It's you we want, John. Why don't you come down over here and join us? We can talk face to face.'

'Join what?' I could tell that she was buying herself time so that they could find me.

'You've been given a gift,' Veronica said.

'That's what the last group said.'

'Yes, and you didn't take them up on their offer. That was neat work by the way.'

'There was nothing up for offer. They tried to kill me. You'll do the same.'

'They were ill prepared, obviously not realising how powerful you are or great you can be.'

I watched one of the soldiers disappear through the arches towards the trains. 'You're animals,' I said.

'No, we're leaders.' She looked up and acknowledged one of the other soldiers who had reached the other end of the station.

'Ed's become reckless. He'll expose your world before I do.'

'With what evidence? It's not as simple as that, John. You really underestimate how many there are of us, and how long we've been operating in London.'

I saw one of the soldiers approaching.

'We should have taken you sooner. We found your flat easily enough, and your ex-girlfriend. Who knows what we'll find next when we come looking again.'

I went cold when she mentioned Claudia. Then I thought about Grace and her sudden decision to leave London back to Ireland. How much of that was real or just coincidence? I could see the soldier ahead of me, checking all the booths, inspecting the faces of commuters who passed his way.

My head began to buzz, like I had the onset of a severe migraine, and I could sense that he was doing something as he looked at people, giving off some type of signal that only I would react to. I needed Michael. I thought I could comprehend this world, this new way of life, but I felt trapped already – I was in too deep and my attempt to snare them was about to massively backfire. I hung up and began to move away casually in the opposite direction. My only advantage now was that I was in a busy station – nothing bad would happen to me if I stayed within sight of ordinary people. Veronica wasn't going to tell me anything, just keep me talking whilst they searched for me. I pulled out my old mobile and dialed her number again.

'You enjoy this, don't you?' I said as the call connected. 'What were you before they got to you, a real reporter? Did they catch you chasing their tail, and now you run errands for them?'

She laughed. 'I was grateful for what they gave me. Now I know what it feels like to be a part of a community . . . ' I pulled the phone down into my hands whilst she gave me her spiel about how good it was to be like them. I didn't want to know. I stopped at a vending machine and fed some coins into it to look busy as a soldier walked past me. The phone was now in my pocket. I made my selection and waited for the drink to drop, grabbed it and then made for the stairs that led away from the station foyer. It meant that I was going to make a pass of Veronica. If I wasn't going to get answers, at least I could get a good look at her face. I grabbed a Metro in my hand to go with my Coke and walked directly at her trying to look like an ordinary commuter. I could see her looking into her mobile and around at the soldiers patrolling the station. I stared boldly at the exit as I approached her, trying to make myself feel totally relaxed, like this was any other day at the office. A group of tourists passed in front of me and helped diffuse my isolation. I used them as cover, closing in on her. She looked back to her phone and began dialing a number. I could see her features more clearly now; her skin was marbled in appearance, like dusted cellophane and she had high cheekbones. She was deadly attractive.

I passed within a couple of feet of her and could sense her shift in mood, even smell her scent, a rich, sweet perfume that seemed to cling to my clothes as I powered over to the exit. I wanted to exhale, look back and glance at her, to stare deep into her eyes, but I had seen enough. No make-up could disguise her hideous intent.

I walked out of the station and had clarity again. I hadn't come any closer to finding Ed, but I had seen her, and I knew that it was real.

I took up my position by a phone box outside and waited to see if she would come out of the station. If I was lucky I had a chance to find their safe house, if I remained patient and didn't lose my nerve. There was a biting wind and I had to pull my collar tight around my neck, then it began to rain and it felt like pin pricks against my skin. I could feel the monster within me rattling against my chest plate in anticipation. The hunt was on.

Five minutes passed. Then I saw one of them emerge into the open – a soldier. He ran across the boardwalk towards an underground exit. My immediate thought might have been that Veronica had taken a train or left from another exit. I was unsure whether or not to follow. A minute later, which seemed much longer, Veronica exited the station flanked by the other man, the one I had encountered weeks before in Covent Garden. They headed towards the Strand, also by foot. I was unsure of my success, wondering whether they were setting a trap for me to walk into. The third man had disappeared.

I followed Veronica, hard not to given the vibrancy of her jacket; she looked like a giant spearmint leaf being dragged through grey crowds. I stalked her like I had Michael, only he had effectively led me to his lair that day, he knew it was what I would do. I imagined that they were about to do the same, luring me to their den of despair. I used the newspaper as cover from the rain as it started to volley down and disperse the crowd. I was able to trail Veronica with ease. It was becoming too easy.

They crossed the road opposite a theatre and I watched as the two of them slipped into a small side alley. I hesitated, anticipating this being the trap I feared. I was in no doubt that if I followed them up that same alley that they would appear somewhere else with backup – the third man waiting for me. My instinct told me to run ahead, up to another alley to try and cut them off. If they emerged, I'd follow again, and if they didn't then I had something to go on at least, an area to document, an alleyway to investigate on another day.

I emerged by one of the filter roads leading to Covent Garden, my paper wavering above my head as I searched the street. Taxis sloshed through puddles and people ran with their umbrellas in hand.

Nothing happened. For minutes I stood there, my irregular heart beat drumming slowly as it settled back down. A few figures emerged from the alleyway, but none wearing a turquoise green jacket so I started walking closer to get a better look when suddenly they reappeared – the three of them again. I quickly ducked into the first coffee bar I could see and sat myself at a table by the window to watch them. I watched her speak to the two men who had been guarding her and then they left in opposite directions.

'Can I take your order?' A waitress asked. She stood over me, a notepad in hand.

'Coke, in a bottle please,' I replied, watching in disbelief as Veronica opened the door of the bar and walked straight to the counter. The barista greeted her like she was a regular and I heard her order a hot chocolate.

'Anything to eat?' the girl asked me. I snapped

out of my trance, realising that I was staring again. I shook my head and looked down at the wet paper I had kept in my hands. The headline was about scientists making a breakthrough, something about the god particle.

Veronica stood at the edge of the counter and waited for her drink. She began dialing numbers on her phone. I tried to listen to the conversations but she was too far away and subtle in her cold, commanding voice.

Across the road, the men reconvened and waited on either side of the road. That or they were guarding the coffee shop. I had underestimated Veronica, maybe she was one of the queens Michael had theorised about.

The waitress returned and placed two pathetic blue napkins on my table along with a glass of ice and lemon and my bottle of Coke. I reached for my wallet and looked up at Veronica to see that she had her eyes firmly fixed on me. I could feel a shooting pain in my temples, like she was trying to intrude my personal space, so I fired a wild, wide eyed look straight back at her. She smirked. My cover was blown. I looked down at my bottle, poured the Coke into the glass and watched the caramel coloured bubbles lift the lemon from the bottom.

Veronica collected her drink and walked over to my table, placed it on top of the napkin and sat opposite me. Her eyes were a watery green, her lips brilliant red. I stared at her, almost in fascination for a minute before we spoke.

'Sugar?' I said, sliding the bowl in her direction.

'It doesn't make the urge go away,' she said, taking one and ripping off the paper with her finely manicured nails.

'What does then?'

'A nice clean kill.' She gave a sigh of pleasure as she stirred the granules into her drink. Her teeth looked like they had been veneered.

'I wouldn't know about that,' I said.

She laughed again, disbelieving. 'I see you're still in denial about what you've become. I was surprised to get your call - most of those who fight it lose the battle with themselves.'

'That's a very poetic way of describing suicide.'

'It's just a condition, an adverse side effect. Only the strong survive.'

'What are you?'

She didn't say anything, merely picked up a spoon and stirred the drink. She didn't sit down to give me answers. 'We'll find you eventually, or should I say, you'll come looking for us.'

'If I do find you, it won't be to join you.'

I tried to sound threatening but she was unnerved by my little jibe. The two soldiers had crossed the road and now glared at me through the window as the rain continued to fall. 'Protection,' she whispered, referring to them both. 'Just in case.'

'Where do we go from here?' I asked.

She took a long sip of her drink and licked the

froth from her lips. There was something definitely alluring about her, my body was charged with hormones and the pheromones she was giving off made me want to ravage her then and then. I was confused, the muscles in my eye twitched. 'Are you the one who groomed Ed?'

'We'd have got to you, too, if we'd known how strong you'd become.' She glared at the men by the window and they backed away to the other side of the road again. 'Why waste your gift?' she asked.

'I think of it more as a curse, a disease rather than a gift. And I'm not the only one living with it. You know there are others like me who'll fight it.'

She ignored me. 'I really like you,' she said, 'but why do you want Ed so bad?'

'Just tell me where he is and I'll disappear.'

She laughed in my face, yet beneath the laughter I could tell that she was getting angry with me.

'I know how you work - he told me. You're a collective, you work together. But at the end of the day it's the colonies survival that counts above all else. Ed's been reckless, I can feel it, and I think the police are getting close to finding him. One sloppy kill that goes wrong, a girl who gets away, and the press will be all over this, not to mention how deep the investigation will go. Sooner or later people will start digging, and you're going to have smaller rocks to hide under.'

'You seem very righteous for a man who's been wicked himself.'

'Meaning?'

She shook her head. 'I think you're still in denial. I'll let Ed remind you.'

'So, he's with you?'

She slowly shook her head. 'You sound like you've had help from the old man. Is he pumping you with propaganda about what we do?'

'I've seen what you do. You're animals . . . savages.' I faltered. She knew about Michael and was trying to make me question what he had told me. He had warned that they could manipulate, even confuse their prey. In truth: I was so fucking confused! 'I don't need to be fed anything else. Even now, just looking at you, I can tell that there's no one left inside.'

'How would you like to get inside?' she said, lowering her voice to a whisper. 'How would you like to get inside my wet cunt? Because if you want to, you can fuck me, and then when we're done I will kill you.'

I couldn't help but shake. I had never heard a woman talk so crudely, yet at the same time I became instantly hard. Something told me she'd done this many times before. She began laughing, her eyes almost darkening as she watched my poker face crumble. The more I stared at her, the more I could see evil beneath the movie star persona.

'I'll give you Ed,' she said, 'and I'll make it a fair contest. But my advice to you is to give it up, John. It would be much easier if you just came with us now. Come with me, it'll be less painful that way, and I'll make it quick.' She ran her tongue along her lips and made a gentle moan that seemed to resonate right through me.

'I'll take my chances.' I reached into my jacket and checked that the blade was still there.

She saw this and her eyes flicked back to me. 'Give me your number.'

'Never,' I replied.

Suddenly I felt my phone vibrate in my pocket – out of coincidence I thought. I looked at it and as I did so she held up her mobile to show that she was dialing my number. 'We have been watching you, John. And your little stunt here has just taken it up to the next level.'

'Arrange a time in a public place,' I demanded, sweat pouring down my spine.

'He'll kill you, you know. He's a real hunter, born with a natural talent.'

'We'll see.'

'You should've taken me up on my offer. Came home with me, it would have been fun. I don't bite too hard.' She drew her lips back and gave me a pearly white smile. My heart was racing, the murmuring uncontrollable. Part of me wanted her, yearned for her, was taken in by the promise of safety and warmth of being thrust inside her, but I had seen enough to realise that it was part of a game, a viscous lie, a promise of protection that would lead only to death. I pictured Michael, his cold, grey face staring at me in the ice-cream shop on the first night, laying the truth bare. Find yourself.

'Tell me where he can be found.'

'If you're still alive by this evening then you'll find him booked in for a meal at the Langham, eight pm.'

'Where's that?'

'Come now, John, I'm not going to give you everything you ask for. Stop being so fucking pathetic!' I watched the veins on her throat pulsate as she drank and that's when I noticed her scar; it was tiny but perfectly formed, symmetrical and barely visible to the naked eye.

She stood, buttoned up her coat and then said: 'I hope he rips your fucking head off.' Not saying another word, she exited the café without giving me a second glance. I watched her approach the men outside and mouth instructions to them both, then she turned to me and blew a kiss. A blue Mercedes pulled up seconds later and she got inside with one of the soldiers; the other ant stayed behind, staring at me through the window. As I watched her drive off, I wished I had taken my chance to kill her there and then. It would have been messy, but I would have at least got some satisfaction from doing so. Instead I was left feeling shit scared about seeing Ed and what he had become, and left with the ant to deal with, one who had a score to settle with me.

The soldier ant had heavy brown eyes buried deep within a thick skull. The black jacket he wore made his bulk seem thicker and he would not have been out of place at some National Front march through the capital in the 80s. I wanted to humour him, blow him a kiss, even try and outstare him through the safety of a pane of glass, but my mind kept recounting the conversation of moments ago: The Langham, eight pm. I looked back at her cup, the lipstick mark like congealed blood across the white china rim. I checked my watch, it was midday and I had eight hours to find The Langham and lose a soldier in London. Daylight was on my side at least, for now, and I had the blade tucked safely in my jacket. The soldier must have known this for I had dispatched his companion only weeks earlier.

I tried to stand but my legs felt like jelly. Veronica had explicitly warmed me that more trouble was heading my way and had successfully struck fear into me.

I paid the bill and gathered my belongings, walked over to the bar and asked where the toilets were. I followed a long corridor and saw the fire escape. I didn't think twice, just powered forward and into a small courtyard. There was a metal ladder up to the roof and this led to the back of some offices. Somehow I found my way in and emerged onto Henrietta Street and began jogging to the tube station. That was when I noticed the soldier following me at speed. He said nothing but I could hear air blasting through his nostrils as I broke into a sprint towards Covent Garden Market. I ducked into the mezzanines, past a myriad of shops and cafes, and weaved myself amongst crowds. I was adamant I could lose him, even though his footsteps were only an echo behind. I glanced in his direction and saw that his expression was unchanged, and I sensed the malice in his eyes; if the opportunity came he was going to kill me, public place or deserted alleyway, it didn't matter.

I ducked into a shop and slipped though the exit on the opposite side, then took some winding stairs down to a courtyard where musicians were gathering. I slipped into a bar and left through yet another exit, then ran up some stairs. It was effortless. I looked back and watched him emerge in the wrong courtyard and I caught a glimpse of his frustrated expression. I had given myself a one minute lead. I ran to the underground and caught the first train to Leicester Square. He was gone - for now.

I was paranoid. Every person who looked at me was a potential suspect. When the bus dropped me off at Highgate, the walk felt like the longest I had ever taken.

Back home, my sword drawn, I did a quick sweep of the house, just in case. It was empty. I went straight to the PC and typed in 'Langham London'. A few eateries came up but I knew which one it had to be – The Langham Hotel by Oxford Circus. Who he was going to be with I didn't know - I considered that it would be Veronica in one of her twisted games, asking for a threesome.

I rang to book a table for 8pm but they were fully booked for that evening. The maître-de recommended that I eat in the Brasserie, so I mentioned that I'd drop by on the off-chance of a cancellation.

It was time to dress for death. I had tried to lie down and rest but my mind was too active, imagining scenarios that I knew would never happen, and those that I feared would.

Veronica had indirectly admitted that Ed was a killer and I had no additional evidence other than a gut feeling, all because of the way he had acted towards me during our final conversation at work. The rational side left in me warned that I was on the verge of madness, preparing to kill without justifiable cause. I had been best friends - in a work sense - with the guy at one point.

For hours, days even, I had battled with the idea that Ed was still human; dehumanising him and comparing him to what I had already encountered made it easier, like I was cleansing London of something evil and would limit its progress, but morally I was still planning to commit murder.

THE LANGHAM

I thought about the others before me again - the ones who Michael tried to help. I knew how they must have felt, to disregard a core set of morals engraved in you from birth, to unwillingly succumb to new instincts; to be presented with a mortal choice: join them or run and fight; kill yourself or kill to stay alive. Either way, providing a body was found, you would have police investigators and forensic teams working hard to dig up your history to reveal the person you once knew. It certainly seemed appealing; the thought of just vanishing and being remembered for whom I was not what I had become. The rules no longer seemed fair.

I tucked the sword nearly into the lining of my suit jacket. I knew that Ed, if he were to show, would not be alone and that it could be yet another trap, but I refused to let fear dictate all of my decisions. If I was going to get long term support, I had to prove to Michael that I could look after myself.

I waited in the hallway for the taxi to arrive outside. For a whole fifteen minutes I stood in silence, enjoying the winding and groaning of my dad's antique clocks, ever faithful. The sound helped sooth the ticking of my heart and gave me time to compose myself. My dad was out and I found myself saying goodbye to him, imagining him standing in front of me as I heard the familiar sound of a black cab turning in the road.

The cab raced down Highgate Hill. I sat in the back eating chocolate bars, envisaging the encounter. My limbs tingled with the anticipation of engaging in conflict once more. I understood that to survive meant that I would earn more credibility from the collective and perhaps buy me a few months longer for survival; to fail would mean certain death.

A police car came whizzing past in the opposite direction, its lights flashing but with no sirens blaring – I guess to give the criminal the element of surprise. As I returned to my thoughts of premeditated murder, I concluded that I needed the same tactic.

The taxi made its final turn into Langham Place, past the Embassies which were a luminous blue from all the powerful halogens, completed a U-turn and then pulled up outside the reception of the Langham Hotel. An elderly doorman opened the cab for me. I thanked him and climbed the steps leading to the reception area, later reflecting that my arrival was hardly subtle or covert. I began to sweat.

I shuttled through the reception, scouring the area for any signs of trouble, but there was only the scent of decadence and the hum of aristocracy. Staff and guests criss-crossed in front of me like extras cued on a film set, silent and proud. I watched them disappear through doors and into elevators, and then the scene was empty again. I followed the signs to the main restaurant.

The maître d' greeted me and asked for my name. 'You have a reservation, sir?' his silver pen gripped in one hand ready to score a name off his list.

'No, a table for one if you can?' He didn't respond, instead he bit his lip and checked for availability. 'I'm sorry, sir, I have nothing until eight forty-five.'

'I can wait,' I said, leaving my name. 'I'll be in the bar.' He feigned a smile and looked down at my shoes. Before I did, I asked if I could have a quick look inside the restaurant. He agreed and I walked past an elaborate wine store with black hexagonal racks, the wine bottles stacked like pupae waiting to hatch. To my left a private dining room sat empty, but was set for a party of sixteen. I glanced into the main restaurant and scanned the room for any sign of Ed, but all I saw was London's high society, scoffing their Michelin starred morsels, exchanging superlatives about how marvelous it was to be them.

I swore under my breath. I thought the worst - that I'd been coaxed into a trap. Looking outside the windows, I could see that the streets looked black. And as I walked to the bar I began to pray - deep down - that Michael was surreptitiously looking out for me. Something was in the air, something kept me constantly in a state of agitation, something made me aware about the falseness of the whole place.

I sat at the bar and dabbed my brow with a napkin. The barman was finishing off a cocktail for a client and seemed to take forever. I kept checking the clock, now ten minutes to eight, and found myself thinking about what it was like for death row prisoners at the eleventh hour. At least I would eat well.

The bar was as decadent as the restaurant: huge cast iron candelabras hung from the ceiling and stood in front of 10ft high antique brass mirrors. Lukas - who informed me that he would be my barman for the evening – said he was ready to take my order after signing off his daiquiri masterpiece for the young city couple at the bar. I asked for something extra sweet and tangy. His recommendation was a mojito: limes muddled with brown sugar, rum and finished with a handful of crisp mint leaves.

I retired to a booth by the window to reconsider my plan of action. I checked my phone – there were no messages. From the window I gazed at a hotel opposite, the St George's with a matching flag that rippled lightly in the wind. I kept telling myself that if I kept within sight of people then the threat of danger would remain relatively low. The mojito started to ease my nerves. I took out my notepad and made observations of the area, details of layout, staff names and numbers, and how many windows and doors there were, should I ever need to return; I even wrote a review of the cocktail.

I was gazing at the mirrors, trying to work out the angle of each one when I heard a couple enter the bar. I froze instantly as I recognized one of the voices, a woman's voice, one I'd grown so tired of hearing but now sounded so alluring that I could not help but tune in to it.

Claudia was accompanied by a tall, handsome man with thick brown hair. I wondered if it was her internet lover 'Blue_eyes' but I turned my head to hide my face; the last thing I wanted was one of those embarrassing 'how are you?' conversations. The night had all the makings of a disaster. I didn't want her to see me like this, a disheveled loner hanging out at bars I couldn't afford. I listened to her converse. The mirrors gave me the opportunity to watch them both. She laughed at the man's jokes and in the reflection I watched her clench his hand and sidle up to him with amorous affection. It was like watching a ghost. I remembered how we were together; happier times before the ants fucked it all up. I was jealous that Claudia had moved on so easily.

Their moment passed and I listened to them, or rather Claudia, talk about her friends at work, the friends I once knew. It was like catching up on old news, and ironically nothing had changed, she still bitched about her best friend and insulted the others within her 'tight circle' in an attempt to raise her own self esteem. I dreaded that I would be next, that she'd talk about how badly our relationship ended or how quickly I'd cum. My mojito had expired and it felt like a good time to move on and continue my recce down in the basement. There was allegedly a dried up well beneath the hotel, and if there was a well then there were tunnels. I stood up, keeping my head turned, and casually walked out of the bar towards the foyer and down to the gents' lavatory.

I racked my brains to think of other places called Langham in London, that I may have chosen the most obvious one and that I'd been too hasty in deciding it had to be the hotel. It was nearly eight fifteen and there was no sign of Ed. I considered that there was a safe house nearby like there was in Muswell Hill, a labyrinth of feeding rooms and tunnels where a different type of food was on the menu; that was my interpretation of a grazing menu. I was sat in a cubicle, hot and sweaty, anxious and annoyed, counting down each minute until my table would be ready. I washed my hands in the marble sinks and seasoned them with Molton Brown. Looking in the mirror, I could clearly see the agitation in my face – I had to pull it together.

I returned back to the foyer and was informed that my table was ready. I was led to a small corner of the restaurant. My heart pumped wildly as I hunted for signs of Ed. Still nothing. The waiter did some sleight of hand magic with a napkin and a wine glass before leaving me to decipher the menu. It made me even angrier and I grew more agitated thinking that I was in the wrong place, wasting time whilst Ed was probably courting his next victim, lacing her with fine wine and deciding which part of her body he would savage first. I wished that Julian had never found that business card with Veronica's number on it, that he'd accidentally lost it, or even lie like he usually did, then I wouldn't have felt so exposed.

It was 8:40pm. I knew that something was definitely wrong. I could sense two pairs of eyes staring at me so I turned towards them. An elderly couple reacted embarrassedly when I held their gaze and sized them both up: busy bodies or lookouts?

I told myself that perhaps Langham was an anagram or code for something else. The waiter brought over a small white plate and placed it in front of me, on it was a porcelain spoon filled with some frothy white substance called a 'chef's welcome' or amuse-bouche. I looked at him glumly then back at the afterbirth of a cappuccino in front of me.

'I've lost my appetite.' I got up and left without looking back or apologising. I came to find Ed, not to eat like a ponce. As I traversed back through the lobby, I made the chilling realisation that Claudia drinking in the bar was no coincidence at all. She was a South London girl; she despised the West End and hated me even more for making her move to North London. I wavered by the entrance to the bar, deciding whether I should I go in and say hello, but then wondered whether that was part of the trap, the set up. Beads of sweat suddenly began running down the side of my face and I became desperate for air.

Standing in the cool air revived my senses, and as I breathed in I could feel my heart working hard. All Souls Church stood opposite the hotel, a beacon of salvation I thought, but my eyes were continually drawn to the hotel beside it.

The St Georges Hotel had a small entrance in comparison to The Langham. Looking upwards, I could tell that there was a bar on the top floor, probably with stunning views across London. I stood contemplating the idea that I should have been resuming my search around Soho, but I'd developed a taste for sweet cocktails and I needed to stay within sight of The Langham, just in case.

It was a modest lobby compared to the luxuriance of the Langham, but there were three elevators, the one I wanted said 'Express Elevator to The Heights Bar and Restaurant'. I could see behind the receptionist that everything was being recorded on CCTV. I was reassured.

The doors opened on the fifteenth floor to reveal a more exclusive setting; suede box lamps hung from the ceiling, and eight by twenty foot panes of glass were the picture frames of living London landscapes. I sat on one of the neatly arranged brown leather sofas and gazed at the view. Below I had a clear view of the street, even from the 15th floor at night I noticed the most finite of details, right down to the expressions of people's faces as cabs and buses drove past. I realised immediately that it was the perfect lookout for anyone wanting to spy on the street, especially as it overlooked The Langham. And as quickly as the thought crossed my mind, a wave of anxiety washed over me. My heart began its cycle of freakish palpitations as the warm blood in my veins surged into my neck and caused my throat to tighten.

I looked over towards the bar and before I could acclimatise myself properly I saw Ed walking towards me. I felt rooted to the spot, wedged firmly into the sofa. All I could do was watch him stride, in slow motion, towards me carrying a bottle of red wine and two glasses. The menace of his swagger was complimented by a dark crease which I think was a smile etched neatly across his jaw line. He was dressed in a fine Italian suit and looked physically stronger from when I had last seen him months ago.

He sat opposite me and held my gaze. All I could do was stare and control the shaking of my hands by clenching them into fists. The adrenaline, the by-product of months of metamorphosis, crashed around inside of me like some volatile poison I needed to eject.

'Hello, John, I hear you've been looking for me?' he said, sliding an empty glass towards me. 'I'm flattered. So how are you?'

I didn't speak.

'It's a nice bar. Do you like the view?' He gestured down below. 'Did you eat? The food's good, but a bit poncy for my liking.'

'You prefer eating young women,' I said, my voice cold.

He burst into laughter as he began pouring the wine. It was a ridiculous comment to make, even said in such a morose tone, but it was all I could say at the time.

'You really need to lighten up.'

'It's hard to lighten up when you live in the shadow of a killer.'

He placed the bottle down and his charm slowly eased off. 'Let's not get bogged down in all this metaphorical crap. I'll get straight to the point, I'm here to negotiate.'

Whether he was trying to be humorous or nostalgic was questionable. 'Negotiate what? What's to negotiate?'

He took a sip of wine and sat back with an air or assurance about him, like he was about to make me an offer I couldn't refuse. 'Your life.'

'That's funny. For a moment I thought you

were going to negotiate yours.'

A waiter came over to the table and placed down a small bowl of nuts. I could sense something about him and caught his eyes, and then I knew that he was also in on it, he had that same flicker of malice lurking behind soulless black pupils. I stammered, my wits shaken, as I realised that I was already outnumbered two to one. How many more like him lay poised in this establishment? It was an uncomfortable sum to consider, and all I could think about was that I had disturbed a nest – one built so high above the city so that they could marvel at the capital's beauty, its organisation and neatness.

'Veronica was quite taken by you today, which is why I'm here. She thinks you deserve a second chance.'

'No, she gave you up, Ed. And I don't intend on letting you leave here alive.'

He raised his arms and spoke a little louder. 'Fine, let's just do it right here, in front of everyone.' People turned their heads and looked over at us, he was not short of witnesses and he'd rightly called my bluff. I sat there like the gargoyles from the building opposite, fearsome intention but no spine to follow any of it through.

'Don't turn down this opportunity to be something.'

'I am something. I just made the right choice and rejected what you so freely embraced.'

'No, you're still a fucking nobody. And you're

still scared-'

'I'm scared of nothing.'

He laughed. 'You're scared of giving in - I can smell it, you cunt – and I can see it in your face.' I watched his tongue dance about inside his mouth as he spoke, reacting to the tannins. 'You've tasted the life that they can offer you, yet you deny yourself the pleasure of being an elite being. Don't lie and pretend that you would prefer to live life on the run, always looking over your shoulders.'

'I'll never understand, Ed,' I countered. 'I'll never understand how can turn your back on the person you once were. You have to lead a secret double life whilst pushing away all the people closest to you. You're damn right I'm not buying it, and I'm not running anymore.'

I can remember clearly, staring into those shallow brown eyes, that he was too far gone. I could sense him reminiscing about women he had probably raped, stalked and even killed. The visions of women being attacked in my dreams were nothing more but a stark warning, the last remaining moral fibres of my conscience calling out to me, trying to steer me away from the life presented to me. And now in front of me sat a man, spoilt by the luxuriance of the city and the organisation who had handed it to him for an undisclosed price, a man rewarded for his wickedness; a man who had lost sight of what it was to be human.

'It's a real shame,' he said, looking out of the

window but staring at me from the corner of his eye. A subtle smirk had developed across his stubbly jawline. I discretely began to reach for my sword, waiting for a clean opportunity to strike.

'You're not drinking your wine,' he said. 'I could get you another Mojito if you like?'

I stopped what I was doing and concentrated on his words.

'It's a small world,' he continued. 'I mean, what are the chances of bumping into an old work colleague and your ex in the center of London within the same hour on the same night?'

Part of me wanted to play it cool, and in hindsight I wish I had said that I had many lovers and several jobs. But I couldn't and my lack of response said it all. My deep rooted fear about Claudia being there was no coincidence after all, and the Langham was part of the trap - a set up; not only did they want me, but they wanted to show me that they could get to anyone, especially those close to me.

'Whatever choice you make, you can never win.' He gestured to the road again, fifteen floors below.

I followed his gaze and sure enough I saw Claudia emerge with the tall, dark haired stranger. I watched them hail a cab. It pulled over and she got in first, then the man looked up at me, as though he knew I was looking at him, and with my heightened vision I saw the whites of his eyes shimmer as he raised his arm and waved. My heart sank.

I reached inside my jacket, gripped the handle of the sword and went to lash out at Ed, only to find no trace of him except for a half drunken glass of wine, the tears slowly trickling down the side. I scoured the bar with my eyes but there was no sign of Ed, but I noticed that the doors to the elevator lobby were slowly closing. I sprung up and darted between a set of tables, knocking someone's drink to the floor. People stared back at me, alarmed at my anguish, but I didn't care. I should have realized that Ed had no intention of staying - he was mocking me from the moment he sat down. And now I was torn, did I make a run for the cab and try to save Claudia? Or stay and find Ed, knowing that potentially more deaths were at stake if he managed to leave the building and disappear for good?

I ran towards the elevator. An elderly couple were waiting patiently.

'Have you been here long?' I asked.

'Some express lift,' they remarked, half listening. Through the windows I could see Claudia's cab pulling away from the hotel and heading southwards. My decision had been made for me. I punched through a second set of double doors leading to the stairwell. Apart from a ladder leading to a roof terrace, there was a small mezzanine area used as storage: old decrepit chairs, tables, high chairs and loose ends that the management couldn't store in the main bar area.

The stairs leading down to the lobby were badly

carpeted, probably the original from the sixties - a far cry from the decadence of the bar area. I went to run down the stairs when I suddenly had a thought. I listened intently but heard no footsteps or any evidence that I was pursuing Ed down the stairs. Michael's words had been to look beyond the obvious, and I stopped to contemplate whether I should make it to the street in a last ditch attempt to save someone I once loved. I couldn't help think that Ed was still somewhere near. I considered going back into the bar and checking underneath tables, even peering in both toilets, but my gut feeling told me differently. I stared up at the last half flight of stairs where there was no light. It was messy and dirty, and so glaringly obvious. The hatch to the roof was open and only accessible via a small ladder. All that was missing was a sign saying 'danger'.

I climbed each rung, keeping my sword clutched against my chest. It was pitch black up above and I could feel the icy draft from the roof as I lifted my head up and out of the shadows. He was up there, I knew it. Suddenly my mind became clearer, and I knew that to prepare for my life beyond that evening that I had to kill Ed, to save the lives of others – he had now given me a genuine motive for murder. It was the only way.

There was a small terrace and ledge with iron rails. I could hear the cogs and hydraulics of the lift churning from behind a locked door. A small office with a light on was located next to the shaft room, but no-one was at the desk working.

The views of London were magnificent and unfiltered; I had an excellent outlook of the capital's skyline in all its glory. I edged my way along the terrace and round to the roof. There was one final ladder which led even higher, to the very top of the roof, to what I imagined to be a clear, level surface.

My head felt fuzzy from the cold air and noise of the lift shafts and I could sense that there was something large and electrical at the top. Sure enough, several mobile phone masts stood on the roof above a bright yellow warning sign. I ignored it and climbed up further until I could stand and orientate myself.

I walked across, oblivious to the radiation exposure. Suddenly I heard footsteps and turned to feel Ed's fist strike me in the face. I lost my footing and tripped backwards on one of the many cables that snaked across the roof; my leg snagged against a metal clip and it drew blood. The giant metal rods seemed to sway and shake as I fell back and I felt the cool air lick my wound.

Ed towered above me and I could just about make out the whites of his eyes. His jacket had been removed and his arms and hands were poised to strike down on me again. I tried to get to my feet, parrying the blows he rained down on me, but he was so strong and furious that I found it hard to defend myself and regain my balance. He kicked me in the groin so that I doubled over and then in the chest, so hard that - at one point - I felt myself fly through the air until I connected with a small metal cable box. He had broken some of my ribs, of that I was sure, and I had landed awkwardly on my hip. My heart was accelerating as I watched him sidestep the wire obstacles and leap towards me.

I had dropped my sword during the first strike and it would be only my own strength and agility that would protect me from his malicious intent, of which I had none. I felt my hands harden in the cold and the bones in my body were calcifying. I managed to stand as he began throwing wild punches at me again. I felt the blood soak into my clothes as I tried to hold fast and took one deep breath before I saw an opportunity and unleashed a single punch. It connected with him against his shoulder - not the most effective hit - but it did knock him back a foot or two, and given the hazardous terrain, it gave me some breathing space. I knew that if he knocked me off the roof that there was a terrace some ten feet below to catch me - but only on one side. He lunged at me again. This time I was prepared. I held his arm and pulled him forward, shifting his body weight awkwardly across the roof, and followed it through with a limp right hook which somehow sent him to the ground. He sprang back up like a panther out of the blackness, howling at me that he was going to 'rip me apart'.

I can't remember much more of the encounter

other than a deep satisfaction I felt when I smashed one of my fists against his skull, feeling bone crunch against bone. I relished it. And then something inside of me took over. In his rage, however, Ed remained strong, pushing me to the ground at one point and hitting me in the eye to the point where I felt the skin split apart, but I felt no pain. I remember hooking my nails into his neck and pulling hard, and that's when things the odds changed in my favour. I rolled aside, got back to my feet and swung my legs at him. I could hear the wind empty from his lungs and see the stunned look on his face as the shirt he wore, which always looked so crisp and clean, was suddenly spattered with his own blood. But still Ed wouldn't give up. He came back at me again and again, but I soon learnt his pattern of attack and watched him slowly weaken to the point where I regularly struck him back down to the ground with more confidence and greater ferocity.

The city's landscape was a kaleidoscope of colour as I tried to regain my balance and look for my sword. Then I saw it, its sharp edge glimmering on the floor. I remembered how useful it had been in dispatching the soldier ant and ran to grab it. As I bent down to pick it up, Ed kicked me forward into an air conditioning box where I felt my head crack open. I felt him kick me again and again as I struggled to get up, but with the sword finally back in my hand I swung wildly and blindly, catching him in his calf just below the back of the knee. He staggered back and simply fell to the ground, almost like a power chord in his body had been severed. The wound must have been deep because a pool of black liquid seemed to spill across the roof. Knowing that Ed was not going to get up quickly, I took deep breaths and tried to compose myself.

I eventually stood up and walked over to him. He lay on the ground, silently writhing in pain. The monster inside of me wanted to butcher him there and then, to slice off every limb and see how long it would take for him to bleed out, but I soon regained my senses and remembered the human side that I was fighting for. I did not want to be like them.

'It's over Ed.'

I remember the way that he looked up at me. He was a being in limbo, torn between man and monster. His eyes were watery pools of blackness as he spoke to me. 'Killing me won't stop what's already in motion.'

I knew he was right. Claudia was surely going to die at the hands of the ants, but I still had to put my demons to rest. I raised the sword. 'It's a shame,' I said. 'Last year you and I were both living our part of the dream, we had good jobs and good wages . . .'

Ed began to chuckle. 'You could have been great,' he said cynically. 'Don't look at what you lost; look at what you could've had.'

I stood there for a moment, warm blood running

down my chest and soaking into my pants and trousers. My body was cooling and I felt like I might freeze to the spot. Even the blade, which I knew was lightweight, felt heavy, as though I were holding an axe over his head.

'We live like gods. Nothing is out of reach. We're a community, John, one that keeps balance,' he said wheezing.

'You're a pest - you're no different to ants – invasive, hostile and destructive.'

He began to laugh at my analogy, and then his voice deepened a little. 'Do you miss your dad?'

My eyes widened. 'What are you talking about?'

'Don't you find it odd that he hasn't been home these past few days?'

I felt like striking him dead there and then. A man I had hardly cared for was suddenly the only thing I had left of a normal life. 'Nice try,' I said.

'You think we're animals but you're no different. This Michael guy you've got involved with - he's trained you like a dog, to go fetch, hunt down and kill. You take orders from an old man without even questioning why, or even if you're on the right side. You're answer: to avoid death. Did you really think we could kill you without seeing what you could do? You're a fool, John – an ignorant fool,' he scathed. 'We could've made you into something amazing, a thriving leader, especially with your gift to procreate so perfectly. That's your hidden potential.'

I stood over Ed and saw the man I worked with in the office, negotiating for his life. 'The day I embrace it is the day I truly die. I'm going to work twice as hard to make sure that I undo the misery you've inflicted upon the vulnerable. That's my choice – no-one else's. The collar's off.'

'And what about your secret? You think I don't know, John?'

'It's not a secret anymore,'

'I'm talking about her.' He grimaced, one final smirk in my direction. 'That night while I went out and hunted in the city, you crept into a brothel and killed a whore.'

I shook my head in denial not saying a word. How did he know? 'I didn't kill her.'

'No, even better, you turned her into one of us.'

The skyline began to spin. I was so naïve to think that I had not killed, to believe that I was on some sort of trip induced by food poisoning. Yet I knew this day would come, a day of reckoning, and a chance to reach atonement. I had to be held accountable for my actions. He wasn't lying.

'Good choice,' he added, 'and a very clean bite for your first. She'd like to meet you and thank you for your gift.'

'Don't joke, Ed, I've lost my sense of humour. It died that night in October.'

'She's embraced her power, John, strengthened the links in our chain. You gave her the gift. You're a carrier, and you can do the same again and again.'

'There's not a moment goes by that I don't regret what I did. If I could bring her back I would.'

'But you still don't understand,' he said. 'You just don't fucking get it, do you? You're weak, that's why. What I do, it's addictive - I've never felt more alive and I don't want to share it with anyone. And I can't - but you can. That's why they tried to take it from you in Muswell Hill, the gift you don't want. The reason I agreed to meet you was so I could take it from you also.'

I wanted him to stop. I had to follow through. 'You had a choice,' I said. 'You're not insane, Ed, you could still reason. You didn't have to go through with the things you did. You could have been man enough to say no.'

He didn't answer. His eyes were rolling and I feared he was going to pass out. I stood there above him, my hand gripping the blade ready to impale him. 'What did they tell you about death?' I asked.

He looked at me. 'We don't talk about it,' he said.

'The women you've killed, what did you tell them about death, that it was expected?' That you didn't have a choice about what you were doing, that you needed to satisfy your hunger?'

'You can't judge me,' he whispered. 'Only God can judge, and for you, there's . . .'

His breathing slowed. I bent over him and whispered 'I'm going to give you a chance to meet him, but not before you repent. Are you really sorry for the things that you've done in life?'

He spat out some blood and began to laugh. 'There are only two kinds of men: the righteous who think they are sinners and the sinners who think they are righteous. Which are you?'

'I'm just trying to help you make the right choice.'

'Go to hell!' he cursed. Ed leapt to his feet with a knife in his hands. I reacted the only way I could, by ramming the blade through his heart as he continued moving towards me. I could feel the sword scrape against bone as I steadied myself and looked into his soulless eyes. It was a quick death.

I cannot explain fully what happened next, or why I did it. I can only assume it was a type of inherent instinct, a behaviour necessary due to my infection, and perhaps the same reason why the ants lured me into the flat at Muswell Hill. I needed to see Ed's heart. I am not a biologist, and I do not know accurately where the heart sits in the body or how it works fully - or even how to take one out - but I do know that it should look and behave in a certain way.

I bent down on my knees and pulled Ed's shirt apart. Blood seemed to be trickling out slowly from the wound like overflow from a groundwater standpipe. Using my hands, which felt like crowbars, I pulled at an area of skin around his chest. Blood clots seeped out as I tugged at bits of flesh; my fingers rummaged and pushed deep inside until I pulled at what I believed to be the heart.

With Ed's hunting knife, which he had dropped, I cut it free and examined it. It was smaller than I imagined and looked grey in the light, and still seemed to be twitching. Attached to it was a series of grey sinewy strands, but not the muscle or fat layers you might expect: a parasitic type, off-white and the texture of eyeballs, what I now know to be a golem, what was controlling Ed from the heart. Strands of it suddenly began writhing, searching out, and then I knew that the same thing was inside of me also, and that they wanted to join together. Or that it was looking for another host. I quickly threw it to the floor and stepped on it with my heel, crushing it until I felt something burst, like a foetal sac emptying amniotic fluid across the asphalt.

I watched it break down and disintegrate in its own puddle of liquid, returning slowly back to basic elements. I rolled it across the ground like some aborted foetus, probing it with the blade. All I could think was that the same thing was in my chest.

TIME

Michael had warned that it wouldn't be long before others arrived. Sure enough I felt different; something inside of me was reacting to Ed's death, like a distress signal had been sent. I needed to move but at that point I didn't realise how badly injured I really was; internal injuries are not always that obvious.

I dropped to the terrace and felt my way to the hatch that led to the main stairwell. I ran down the stairs, fourteen painful flights, and could feel myself getting weaker with each step I took. An alarm startled me halfway down and I didn't know whether it was a general alarm set off by someone in the hotel or a proximity type as I passed an office floor. It didn't matter - I still needed to get out.

I reached the emergency exit on street level and burst into a deserted side street. I was thankful that the only thing seeing me leave was an old 70s style CCTV camera which I hoped was not working, or at least was not in HD and capture pictures well at night. I sprinted about fifty metres from the hotel towards the main street when I felt my legs start to give way and my lungs fill with fluid. Only when I walked beneath spotlights did I see how bloodied and torn my skin was. I sunk into a shop doorway and checked my hands. They were caked in blood, some of which had already dried into sticky grains which I rubbed off. My jacket was torn and I could feel cuts and scratches down my neck and face which continued to weep. I realised that it was only a matter of time before someone saw me and called the police.

I tried to control my breathing. Deep down I knew that the danger had not passed and I was vulnerable, even more so now than in Muswell Hill. I felt like I was going to die, I felt so cold. I tried to regain my strength and hail a cab, but I knew in my mind that no cabbie would want a dying man in the back of his Hackney carriage, bleeding over the upholstery.

I looked through Ed's belongings – took out a key, some plain cards and some crisp £50 notes. I held one up to try and catch someone's attention.

Waiting there to die, shivering as the icy wind blew through the streets, I began thinking about Claudia, the one woman whom I had once loved, albeit briefly. I rummaged around in my jacket for my phone. My hands were numb, hardened into knuckled stumps and I had the feeling of pins and needles all across my arms and legs. But I managed to find her number and dialled. It rang and rang and rang. No-one picked up - it didn't even go to voicemail, which it always used to. Then I thought of my dad and Ed's cowardly words; I tried his mobile, then the landline; both times there was nothing, no-one picked up, no one heard my plea.

I had the urge to lie down on the floor and curl into a ball for comfort. Across the road, nocturnal pedestrians were glancing over in my direction, and then carrying about their lives with haste. They were oblivious to the horrors beneath their feet, but because the dark truth did not directly affect them they did not care, they did not even need to know. I felt my efforts, a small personal accomplishment to kill a man I once worked with, had been in vain.

As I waited, I imagined that a soldier ant would appear and finish the job so coldly like I had done in a back alley in Covent Garden.

I watched a black cab drive past, stop suddenly and then turn in the road. It passed again and parked on the road near me. I tried to find the fifty pound note with one hand and gripped the sword beneath my coat with the other. It was them, I thought, a clean-up crew, perhaps even Claudia and Blue_eyes themselves were going to finish me off. The cab had a wide silver grill for a mouth and a glistening black body. All I could think about was insects and the way in which the cab resembled a beetle.

The diesel engine ticked over and I figured that someone was either paying the fare inside, that or waiting for the streets to be empty before they moved in on me. Finally the door clicked open and a tall, imposing figure walked over to me. I breathed a sigh of relief at the grand silhouette, and when the figure bent I heard Michael's voice whisper to me, 'We don't have much time.' He helped me to my feet and walked me over to the cab. 'They're looking for you.'

Inside the cab was a pile of blankets, towels and provisions. I tried to see the driver's face but he wore a cap and kept his eyes on the road. Michael got in and shut the door.

'Hagen Dazes café?' I murmured.

Michael gave a muted laugh. He nodded at the driver and the cab pulled away.

'Where are we going?'

'Home.'

I tried to sit up. 'We can't!' I had a moment of clarity. 'Michael, they've got my dad and I think they've got to Claudia, too.'

'You need to rest,' he said, placing a chocolate bar on my lap.

I snapped. 'I don't want a fucking snack, Michael. I need you to listen to me – they know where I live.'

'Then we've got some squatters to evict,' he said coolly. He picked up the chocolate bar and kept it in his hand.

We travelled for a few minutes, starting and

stopping at lights. I had to break the silence. 'It's all gone wrong,' I cried.

'Ed is dead?' he asked.

I paused, suddenly aware of the cabbie staring at me in the driver's mirror. I turned to Michael and I saw in his eyes that I could speak. He asked again. 'Is Ed dead?'

I pulled out Ed's wallet and key and tossed it onto the cab floor.

Michael picked it up and searched through it. 'My sword, please.'

I looked at him confusedly before pulling it out, unsure what he was going to do with it. Suddenly I felt extremely defenceless, like I should have eaten the chocolate bar to have avoided upsetting him. Taking the sword, I felt like Michael was stripping me of rank. The blade still had traces of blood, dirt, grime and prints, and the handle felt sticky. He inspected it thoroughly before cleaning it with a handkerchief and then wrapping it up in a strip of black velvet he removed from his coat.

'I think they've got Claudia,' I said again.

'There's been a lot of activity tonight,' he said. 'You need to rest, and then we can work out where you go from here.'

I didn't have the energy to talk anyway. I rested my head against the cab window and tried to keep breathing. My body was shivering. 'Don't fall asleep!' he ordered, tapping me every few seconds. I kept thinking of the bar at the Langham Hotel, me sitting on my own and trying to order a drink but never being noticed, never being heard. I craved red wine, Chilean, spiced blackberries aromas - and then I would drink it in the sauna.

The sound of the handbrake being cranked up sharply roused me from my delirious state. We had arrived back at my house in what seemed like minutes. I sat upright, temporarily revived. Michael turned to me and told me to stay behind him.

He was carrying what looked like a small black wand as we proceeded up the garden path. The moon was out fully and it seemed to make Michael's hair glow. The cab driver suddenly pulled away and disappeared into the night. I turned back and watched in disbelief as Michael opened the front door to my house with his own set of keys. Before I could say anything he stepped inside and switched on the lights, like he had been there on many occasions. I could smell furniture polish as I stepped in. I followed him in to the kitchen, conscious that I was still bleeding out on to the floor, and watched him as he emptied the contents of a small rucksack he had been carrying onto the work surface. He had bandages, lotions, glass bottles filled with ointments and all types of powders and test tubes.

My lungs felt like they were burning. 'What are you doing?' I mustered.

'Go upstairs, get yourself showered, then we'll talk,' he said.

I didn't move, instead I just stood there staring

at him. He was about to repeat the instruction when I lurched forward. 'I'm not going anywhere until I get some answers from you.'

'You're in no state,' he began.

I was resolute. I snapped and threw my wallet across the room at him. He barely flinched as it bounced off his back; instead he looked disappointed that I had acted in such a way.

'You might think years of being infected can give you some authority over me, to tell me what to do,' I said. 'But how the fuck is it that you can just walk into my house with your own set of keys?'

'Go upstairs and get yourself-'

I screamed at him to answer me for once, to not talk in fucking riddles or hypotheses. What was happening to me was slowly killing me, and I needed assurance from him that I wasn't going to die.

He remained calm, his voice metered. 'I'm losing my patience with you, boy.'

With my last ounce of strength I leapt at him, my arms outstretched. It was a futile attempt; Michael saw it coming and gripped me tightly with his hands. Within seconds he had me lying on the counter with my head tipped backwards and his small silver dagger resting against my throat.

'You don't have much time,' he growled. 'Ask all the questions you want later, but right now you're less than an hour away from leaving this world.' He pulled the knife away and dragged me off the counter and onto the floor. Whilst I was lying in a heap, he continued to organise all of his potions and tools on the counter.

'Trust me,' he said.

He carried me up the stairs to the bathroom. I wanted to speak but I no longer had the energy. Bizarrely, I saw everything like I was the third person in the room. I watched him run a bath whilst I was sat propped against the wall, and then he stripped me of the bloody clothes that I was wearing. He used surgical scissors for most of it and bagged up the clothes in a black bin liner. The halogen lights were harsh and I could see his facial expression, and the occasional twitch of his eyes, as he studied my injuries. I found it odd that he kept his gloves on the whole time.

The bath filled, he lifted me up and gently lowered me into the water. The sensation was strange, numb skin against the water; I couldn't even tell if it was hot or cold. The feeling of pins and needles was everywhere. But I felt cocooned and secure, protected momentarily. Then he took my arms and folded them across my chest. And then he pushed me under.

That's all I remember. The rest is history.

CATCHING UP

When I awoke, I believed that it was morning the next day. The light burnt the back of my eyes as I rolled to my side, and then I winced in pain. I reached down and saw that I was covered in bandages and medical dressings. And then I realised that I was sleeping in my dad's bedroom and not dressed in my own clothes. I got out of bed in a panic but collapsed to the floor; my legs were stitched and bandaged in places and were sore to bend.

I rolled myself over and crawled to the bathroom, where I had my last memories. It was spotless - clean and tidy with no signs of blood. I caught a glimpse of myself in the mirror and saw nothing untoward other than small sutures, a Band-Aid over the scar on my neck, and that I needed a shave.

Once I was able to stand again on my legs, I eased myself downstairs towards the kitchen, which again was spotless. Even the blood stains on the carpet had been professionally cleaned.

I was famished. I began raiding the cupboards. I didn't know what for, I just needed fuel: sugar, carbs, and protein – I ate anything I saw that took my fancy. I sat down in the living room with a spread of cereal bars, crisps, cheeses, milk, fruit and water - breakfast like a king. My memories of that night were in fragments: Ed sat opposite me in the bar and then bleeding out across the roof; Claudia laughing and bitching about her friends, and squeezing the hand of Blue Eyes.

The grandfather clock chimed noisily in the hallway. I went to ring Claudia on the phone but the landline was dead. The PC wasn't working either, so I had no internet connection. I went to look for my mobile but there were no traces of my possessions from the previous night. Even the satellite box was dead and there was no coaxial cable to watch the TV. Nothing worked. The only other option was to use a public phone box and go and get the paper, but I didn't feel up to that.

I returned to the bedroom, my father's room, and looked closely at the many pictures in the frames. My dad, the man who began lowering his emotional guard as I spent time with him of late, was gone. I gazed out of the window and had selfish thoughts. If he really was gone, how would payments continue to be made for things like bills? I scoured the road to look for anything out of the ordinary, and that's when I noticed that a black cab was parked some 50 yards away to the right of the house. No-one owned a cab on our road, which got me thinking about who the cab driver was from the night Michael helped me. On two occasions now the same man had been there, not once questioning the motives of Michael as he brought a bleeding stranger into the back of his cab. I watched, mentally preparing myself to get clothed and investigate, when a figure approached the house from the left. I couldn't make out a face under the hood but I recognised the walking stick.

I heard the front door open and listened to the footsteps treading methodically across the wooden floor. Creeping silently to the corner of the stairs, I sat and watched him from the behind the banisters. He was checking through the mail that had arrived that morning.

I called out: 'Make yourself at home, Michael.'

He span round and I saw that his dagger was drawn. 'You're awake.' He looked surprised.

I smiled back at him. 'It was a heavy night.'

He kept his weapon pointed in my direction. The expression on his face told me something was up. 'How is it that you were at death's door moons ago, and yet now you seem right as rain?'

I walked towards him and shook my head. 'You know if I had internet, or my phone, then I might be able to piece together what's happened. Where have you been?'

He spoke with caution. 'As it happens, I was down at the cemetery as usual for this time of the month, then I came back here to check on you.'

Something wasn't right; it had only been a full moon recently. 'Why is my phone line cut off?' I asked, 'and why are there are no newspapers, or anything else in the house for that matter? I was about to get dressed to leave.'

'Don't do that,' he said sternly.

'Will you ease up,' I pleaded, 'and put that fucking knife down before you do me an injury.'

Slowly, Michael lowered the blade. With his other hand he reached inside his jacket pocket and removed my mobile phone. 'I had to take precautions - just in case you did something rash. I mean look at you! I can see more bandages across your body than skin.'

'Enough about me. Dad and Claudia are missing, I need to get help.'

'That's what we need to talk about.'

I took the phone from him and scrolled through my phone to find the numbers of all my contacts had been erased. 'What's going on?'

'They got to you, John. I had to erase your contacts and put a new SIM card in.'

I shook my head. 'How dare you!'

'Forget about them,' he said, beckoning me into the living room.

I was angry and annoyed at being directed around my father's house by a man I still knew nothing about. It felt very wrong, and what made it worse was that he had several knives in his possession and an explosive temper.

'There's something you're not telling me.'

He nodded. Then he gestured for me to sit on the sofa at the other end of the room. 'There is much to learn, John. For you, this really is the start.'

'No more games,' I implored. 'No more fucking riddles. I've proved myself to you, now I need firm answers.'

'Claudia is either dead or has been turned. We can't risk you seeing her again.'

'Why would they do that?'

'Insurance, extra security in case you came after them. '

I thought about what he said; insurance as in I'd be set up for her murder, or that they would kill her if I got too close? 'And what about my dad, is he insurance too?'

Michael shrugged his shoulders coldly. Without thinking, I picked up a coffee table and threw it across the room. We both watched as it splintered against the wall. As it fell to the ground it knocked off some antique china, a Spode trio which smashed into porcelain pieces that looked like broken teeth; they were scattered across the carpet.

'Let's have a cup of tea,' Michael said.

'Why not a get a bowl of fucking ice cream instead?' I shouted. 'You've been lying to me. I need to know how you got hold of a key to my house.'

'I've got a thing about keys, especially big, brass, shiny ones.'

I went to curse him but quickly realised that he was trying to deliberately wind me up, testing me to see what I would do, to anticipate a type of behaviour; I hated being some kind of lab experiment to him. The fact that he was sat so far away from me told me two things; that he didn't trust me, or he was afraid of me.

"No sugar for me,' I said calmly.

Michael nodded and went into the kitchen. He returned a few minutes later with two cups of tea.

'You even disabled the TV,' I mentioned. 'At least give me something to take my mind off everything that has happened.'

He removed the decoder card from his top pocket and took an aerial cable out from underneath the settee. I took it and hooked up the TV box, switched the TV on and waited for everything to re-sync.

'You really should learn to stop rushing into things,' he said.

'Shut up!' I snapped back at him as I shifted through the news channels. I watched the rolling news, waiting for the breaking news about a body found in London, but there was nothing untoward on the TV, just the prospect of another war in the Middle East and plans to regenerate the economy. Only when the newsreader mentioned the time and date did I stop and take note. I looked back at Michael in disbelief.

He looked at me with that same omnipotent face, the one he had shown me whenever I had felt weak and confused, which seemed to be always in his company. 'Quite a lot's happened in seven days,' he said. Michael put down his cup and pulled out some newspaper cuttings from his coat pocket, both local and national, and handed them to me.

I scoured through all of them and confirmed the dates of each one, searching for a story about Ed, a gruesome murder in the capital, but there was nothing. 'I don't understand,' I muttered. 'Surely there must be something: CCTV footage, a report of a missing person?'

Michael shook his head. 'Look at the one from the South London Press.'

I found it and read the story about a man's body being found beside a railway line. Police were treating it as a suicide. It gave no other details, just a rough description of a man in his late twenties. I knew this unidentified man was Ed.

'I thought you said they always bury their own dead, which is why in Muswell Hill there were no bodies.'

Michael had highlighted a few other paragraphs from other papers which mentioned variations on the same story. 'What the hell does this all mean?' I flicked the TV off. All of my efforts, and all hope of leaving a calling card to the capital about the secret fight that was going on - all of it was for nothing. And now there I was, trapped in my dad's house with a man I still barely knew, being treated like some outpatient from a mental hospital.

'Not quite the 15 minutes you were after,' he said. 'But don't for one reason think that it counted for nothing. You will learn that all too quickly.' Michael gave a short, self-deprecatory laugh. 'Even if your work was found and appreciated, the Media prefer pantomime villains rather than vigilantes running around the streets; the police especially - vigilantes make them look incompetent.'

'How do you manage?' I asked him.

His cold grey eyes looked me up and down. 'In thirty years, I still find it hard to live with what I have become. And no matter how many of them I manage to hunt down and kill - which isn't as many as I'd like - I cannot remove what's inside of me.' He pointed to his heart. 'The pain is still there and there's only one way to make the pain go away.'

He fell silent.

'What do you mean?'

'Now's not the time,' he said. He removed some Ethernet cables from his coat and tossed them to the floor. 'These are yours.'

'When is it going to be the right time, Michael? I feel we've been here before many times. We get to the point where you reveal all, and then you abandon me, leave me hanging.'

'I need . . . more time to prepare,' he said. 'You've only just come round from some kind of parasite induced coma. I can't just fill in all the gaps in your mind. Look!' he yelled, pointing at my wounds. 'Look at where it's left you. Digest what's happened during the past seven days, and then we'll talk about where you go with this.' He walked over and pressed my front door key into my hand. 'I'm glad you made it. See you in a few days'

Michael patted me on the shoulder before walking out of the room and exiting the house.

At first I was angry with him, livid at the way I had been manipulated, kept me at arm's length, but in hindsight it was wise of him to do so, to leave and allow me to catch up on almost a week's worth of news.

I needed time to understand what had happened to me.

REVELATIONS

I figured that a couple of days break would be ample time for me to formulate an action plan. I still had Veronica in my sights, but Michael had wiped all the numbers from my phone and because of my haste and reliance on technology, I had not bothered to write any of them down. Some secret agent I would make. Michael was trying to teach me a lesson, to keep me organised.

As I hooked myself up and got online, I reflected on why he would always refer to this journey as 'mine' and not his. I figured that perhaps hunters like Michael didn't always work directly in teams but were often on their own. The internet became my only companion. I searched not just to get the news stories of the week, but to gauge the world's perceptions of events, and to examine how people reacted to it all using social media.

I watched terrible things: people throwing

themselves in front of trains, men committing random attacks on innocent bystanders, failed suicide attempts, horrific crashes – all of them recommendations, cued up one after the other, uploaded by sick bastards and craved by a natural fascination with death. Then I read the comments and realised that society was diseased. It was an unwelcome distraction from what I should have been doing.

I rang the St George's Hotel, enquiring whether the rumours had been true about a body being found on the roof. The receptionist denied any knowledge of such an event, got annoyed with me and quickly hung up, but not before I told them that they should have a look.

By lunchtime I had regained my appetite. The desire to eat sugar had subsided; I craved meat and lots of it. I had been left the basics in the fridge and concluded that a night time visit to the shops might be on the cards. I drank water, litres of it, and it passed through me as quickly as I drank it. By the afternoon I paced aimlessly around my house, listening to every tiny sound.

I regularly checked the street, looking for signs of danger, for the black cab, for an imposter, for my dad. I saw nothing. It was troubling given Ed's warning. I still hoped that Dad had taken a deserved holiday, or gone to visit friends, but as I searched the house for his possessions, I knew that they must have had him. Either they took him whilst he was visiting one the many clubs or societies he was a part of in London, or they got to him at home whilst I was out. Which then led me to question how Michael had obtained a key to the house. He had skirted around the question when I asked, and in such a way to dupe me from pursuing.

My thoughts returned to Claudia, why I didn't know, but after much searching I managed to find her number which I had written down on an old notepad, it was amongst my old possessions from the flat.

I called the number. It didn't connect. The line was dead.

Sitting in the living room, I reflected on my face to face conversation with Veronica during the hours before I despatched Ed. On the outset she was beautiful, stunning one could say, but her malice was unfathomable. Beneath the pretty glaze of porcelain skin was something far more sinister. I tried to comprehend how she had such control over the other soldiers, as if by thought alone, but even with telekinetic abilities aside, her taciturn candour sent shivers down my spine. In my head, I kept replaying the moment she stared through me, the moment time slowed and she stripped me of my voice by inviting me to fuck her. Now I craved her and thought of nothing else. It was wrong, I knew that, but it was all I thought about.

I spent time considering how I would track her – if I would ever find another one of her calling cards, whether Julian had taken two cards or not.

Maybe Michael had already dealt with her? I didn't expect that to be the case, and in my heart I knew that another meeting would be on the table at some point in the future.

Most of my time was spent laying in my dad's room thinking about my childhood. I stared at the pictures of him - old holiday snaps and grainy shots taken from a Christmas party in the eighties - looking for clues as to where he may be. Surely there were address books or call logs of whom he was in contact with? I searched through his administration in the study and began looking for any old phone records. Sure enough there were loads of numbers for banks, clients, other accountancy firms and auditors; typical of anyone who's ever worked in finance. I began running cross checks against any numbers I didn't recognise using Google. Most of them were shops or small businesses, law firms and even laundrettes; that type of thing, but nothing more. I rummaged behind one of the desks and I found an old porn magazine and some flyers taken from one of Soho's many phone boxes. One of them showed a woman dressed in school uniform, she was the blonde goddess type, obviously Photoshopped, and an unlikely representation of her real self. Most likely, a terrified immigrant, a non-English speaking victim of trafficking would greet the punter. The flyer looked old but I dialled the number nevertheless. It didn't connect.

I tried all the numbers but they were all out of

service. They had all moved on.

The most frustrating thing of about being housebound was not being able to contact Michael. I was, deliberately it seemed, at his mercy. By the evening I felt unable to fight the tiredness and drifted off to sleep, but not easily. I kept reflecting on events in more detail and began to recount small details about Michael's behaviour, details I didn't like.

By the next day I felt my health had improved. And sure enough, Michael kept to his word and visited to check up on me. Each time he arrived in a black cab, the same one I believed. He would redress my wounds and rub ointments into my back to help me recover. Occasionally he would leave me some interesting news articles or features to read over, most of which I'd already discovered online, but I didn't have the heart to tell him. But Michael had something which I lacked, which I never had and felt I never really would. Insight. The articles I hadn't seen were about missing people, fires and murders that didn't seem to have similarities to events of other ant attacks or anything that I would take a natural interest in. I would question him about them but he would shrug and say that I needed to be able to see the link for myself. I couldn't help but feel I was being thrown off the real scent.

I told Michael that I was going to keep a journal, write down all my thoughts, experiences and ideas from start to finish, and to plot the journey, with the intention that one day I might share it with the world. He said it was a good idea, but that I should keep it to myself until I was ready to do something good with it. I asked him what he meant. He didn't say anything. I told him about some of my own theories and he seemed impressed with my level of research. He had a smile though, like that of a scholar who had written thousands of papers and books on the subject, who was being told about a new discovery or theory by an eager student who hadn't read all his teacher's previous papers. But I had the time to read around the topic in more detail, to access more materials online and build my own case against the collective.

During his visits, Michael and I often argued fiercely about his methods of raising awareness; I told him that he wasn't doing enough to tell people the truth, that we needed an online presence to protect us and warn others; he said I was insolent, that I lacked the appropriate experience and knowledge, and that I would turn out like all the other conspiracy theorists. To change the subject, I kept pressing him about tactics and how we were going to continue the fight together, but he kept saying that it was not good to talk about it until I'd fully recovered, that an opportunity would come when I was ready.

When was I going to be ready?

A few days later my rapacious appetite had subsided and my sleep patterns were starting to return to normal. My wounds had all scabbed over and I showed signs of a full recovery from such an ordeal for the second time in almost six months. I knew that the body could repair itself, but the severity of my scars seemed minimal compared to others I had seen on the internet within such a timescale.

I still had a sweet tooth from time to time, but overall I craved natural foods like nuts and berries and seeds more than ever. I had a sneaking suspicion that Michael's sugar theory was merely a placebo remedy designed to keep reduce my anxiety.

Michael continued to visit me daily but for less time, usually no longer than an hour, and he seemed more troubled than ever. He would continue to buy me provisions and newspapers, bring lists of references for me to look over, and share old journals he had kept as a young man of my age. We would often start with small talk before getting down to discussion and debate. He still remained steadfast on his own theories about them which I often challenged him about because of what I'd found online. And each time I did contest his ideas he would accuse me of being immature, a heathen with too much pride, an arrogant neophyte. We debated fiercely about the races that had once dominated foreign lands and then disappeared, although the debate always seemed one sided. The next day he would present me with a Latin name for something on a piece of paper, and when I typed it in online it would be a name for an electric eel or some other specific type of insect that he wanted me to consider. In fact, his fascination for nature carried though to everything he did.   Subtly I believed he was giving me answers to the many questions I had but they were always encoded and I got the impression that it was all some kind of mirage to what he was holding back, the real truth. I had hoped that one day he would arrive with a stack of exam papers and I would take a test, or there would be some other formal hurdle to leap over. I believed that there had been some plan behind this level of nurture, and that our discussion and deliberation might lead to some type of qualification or doctorate in how to deal with pests or human parasites.

In the weeks after my encounter with Ed, the world seemed much different than before. Spring had firmly taken hold and the news stories were dominated by recession fears, tensions between countries in the Middle-East and global issues of famine brought about by natural disasters and corporate corruption.   Did it ever change?   I remained house bound, and during that time there had not been one single knock at the door, or a visit from the police, not even a phone call from someone asking to speak to my dad. It was if he had died years ago and no-one remembered who he was or cared to ask after him. It confirmed what I thought all along, that he was a private man but very much unloved – even by his only son. This made it even harder to be vengeful since there was no resolve; he was either alive and well and living in somewhere like Brazil with a young, working class mistress, or buried somewhere in London, never to be found. If I hadn't have been in so deep I would have reported him as missing. This was the leverage the ants had over me, whatever move I made; they would always have the upper hand.

I was fully recovered and, in my eyes, medically fit. Michael was conscious that I was eager to venture back into the capital's infected streets. I spent much of my spare time watching instructional videos and tutorials about various things, including simple bomb making, sword fighting techniques and other potentially illegal pastimes to cure my boredom; and then there was the pornography – the whole web was saturated with it; I realised it was another method of control and I didn't want to see myself turn out like my dad.

In the boredom brought about by my captivity, I started making my own videos about 'vampires' based on what Michael had told me and using all I had, the web. When he found out, Michael scalded me for doing so, branding me impatient and volatile, foretelling that I could risk turning out just like them (referring to all the other false prophets), but I strongly believed that it might make a difference. Even to this day, I believe that his deep rooted fear of the media was what made him keep me under lock and key.

One particular evening, Michael visited me for his regular slot and I noticed that he seemed less agitated than usual, as though he was on the cusp of salvation somehow. He stayed longer than an hour and even treated me to a good meal, from Marks and Spencer he had proudly announced, which included some of my favourites, including wine and steak.

I remember the evening well.

'Tonight we eat to celebrate your recovery,' Michael said, 'and your victory. Tomorrow, you begin a new journey into the unknown.' He raised his glass and we chinked goblets half full of Merlot together.

'That's very profound,' I remember saying. 'But then with this type of build-up, I'm expecting many things from you also.'

'I'll give you whatever I can,' he said. 'But you must first accept a few things.'

Here we go, I thought. 'What?'

'We'll eat first and talk after dessert.'

'Ice cream?' I asked.

He smiled. 'Our first course is figs wrapped in Parma ham on a bed of rocket with a sweet honey and mustard dressing.'

'Is this symbolic?' I asked.

'Everything from this day forward is a symbol of our commitment to seek justice.'

By the time we finished eating I felt more attached to him than ever before. There were moments throughout the meal when he looked relaxed, and he was lucid, sharing with me anecdotes unrelated to ants for the first time. Sometimes he would talk about his days in the theatre, about people he used to hang out with, and the types of meals they had back then. I shared with him moments that I could not even experience with my own father, discussions about growing up, reflections about relationships, even cheating in my exams. I felt cold hearted knowing that my dad was out there whilst I dined with a more interesting replacement in his own house. Yet they were both similar and connected in some way; Michael was a loner, and so was my dad; and now, like them both, I was following in their footsteps, taking steps towards becoming a secret bachelor myself through circumstance rather than choice.

For our main course we enjoyed rib-eye steak, the best cut in my opinion - iron rich and high in protein. Michael had cooked it so well that the meat just seemed to melt in your mouth. The wilted spinach and hand cut chips were divine; the grilled tomato and flat mushroom a fine accompaniment also. We rounded off the main with another bottle of red before he brought out desert, a luxury sweet caramel and chocolate ice-cream, accompanied by an exotic fresh fruit salad.

It was truly a remarkable meal.

We retired to the living room and sat with the last of the wine between us. The grandfather clock kept time noisily in the hallway as we reflected silently, our stomachs full.

'So where do we go from here?' I asked.

'You're fully recovered, not immortal,' he said. 'You will have to go back out there and learn to hunt properly.'

'Together?'

'Not quite.' He shuffled in his seat.

'Michael, I'm still new to this whole change in my lifestyle – we're both fighting for the same cause.'

'A cause, maybe, but what do you really hope to achieve?'

'I want to find the source of all of this.'

'And then do what?'

'Then I'm going to end it.'

He gave me a long smile as though I had answered him correctly. But there was something else he wasn't telling me - I could see it in his eyes. Michael looked uncomfortable suddenly and shuffled in his seat. 'You must remember that in 30 years I have never got close enough.'

'As you keep reminding me, but you never gave up,' I said. 'You wanted revenge and that's what drove you to keep on at them.'

'Yes, but even I have limits. Look at me, John. Without the monster inside of me I am just a fickle old man waiting to die.'

'I don't like your tone.'

'There's nothing wrong with my tone, I'm just telling you the truth. '

'Then tell me some more truths. The cab driver,

who is he?'

'He's an old friend.'

'I thought you couldn't have friends in this game?'

'When I say friend, I meant that loosely. I have people that help me out now and then, but usually there is money involved, or a vendetta of their own – someone they have lost. Those type of friends.'

'Do they know about me? Do they know what we dabble in?'

'Some do, but not all.'

Deep inside I grew optimistic, excited even, knowing that a network of allies was ready to be orchestrated in this great fight.

'Everything will be explained to you truthfully and openly whilst it's all up here,' he said, tapping his finger against his temples. 'I've kept one or two more journals of my own, detailing all of my findings. They're yours to do with what you want. Tomorrow I'll start you off on a new voyage.' He smiled and took a sip of wine, paused and then swilled it in his mouth.

'But we're wasting time sat here – why didn't you want to share with me before. I've been going mad these past few weeks.'

'I needed to be sure,' he said.

'I nearly died, Michael, how sure do you need to be?'

'You don't remember much after Ed, do you?'

I paused and shook my head. I could only remember waking up, assuming I'd been comatose for several days.

'Tell me the last thing you remember.'

'I remember you putting me in the bath.'

Michael topped up my wine. 'And that's all you remember?'

I nodded.

'Well, that's not it,' he said. 'I watched you die that evening, John. I held you under water until you were dead.'

He said nothing after that, just looked at his glass and waited for me to react. There was no smile in his face as he told me, no hint of deception, and no sense of remorse. He really was telling me the truth.

'Then if I died, why am I still here?' It was a daft question, but all I could think of at the time.

'I don't know,' he said. 'You were bleeding and dying in the house, I watched your body convulse and retch. I saw things I've never seen before, not even in myself. If, John, we are to consider our condition as a disease, then you have a terminal case of it – the worst I've seen. Perhaps even a new strain of this virus.'

I watched as his hands started to shake, and for the first time I saw that Michael was scared.

'The John I thought I knew was gone; you were consumed by this wretched thing. I felt I had no option but to show mercy on your soul, and so I drowned you.' He broke off and looked vacantly ahead. 'It seemed like the most humane thing to do. I thought I was being merciful.' I could tell that he was picturing it all again in his head. 'Afterwards, you looked so peaceful . . . I'm sorry.'

I found his story hard to believe initially but my mind shot back to the night in Crouch End, at the sauna when I bit for the first and last time. I began to believe it now, to believe everything what Ed had said - it all came flooding back. I bit Cha-Cha, clamped down on her until she passed out, and then I placed her in the bath . . . and somehow she had survived. My mouth suddenly felt very dry and my throat tightened. If Michael, the man sat opposite me, was telling the truth, then he had confessed to trying to kill me, and because of Ed's revelation about being a carrier, about making her one of them, I began to negotiate his reasons for doing so.

'You were so peaceful in the water, John,' he repeated again. 'I watched you lie motionless in the water, submerged for almost a whole hour. When I decided to get you out, the bleeding had stopped and I felt no pulse. I wrapped you in towels and lay you on the bed in your room before leaving the house to get help cleaning up the mess. A couple of hours later I returned to find your body gone. You were nowhere to be seen.'

I started to shake myself at this point, my insides resonating with fear as he recounted the events of that evening.

'I thought they had taken you, John. I thought that I was too late, that they had found you and buried you away like they do their own. But eventually I found you, outside in the garden, staring up at the moon. I approached you, I knew it was you, but when I looked at you . . . it wasn't you.' He shook his head. 'Your skin was like ash and your eyes were nothing more than soulless black pits. And so I stood there, ready to put an end to your life for good, but you didn't . . . you didn't react, you didn't seem to pose a threat - you just stared at me, looking right through me. I led you back into the house in your trance like state, lay you down and proceeded to dress your wounds. You didn't flinch once, even when I sewed the stitches. When I finished patching you up the next morning, I decided to lock you in your room. And then I locked the whole house as well.

'The next day when I came to visit you, you hadn't moved. You were in a deep, virus-induced coma. I didn't know what to do, so I paid someone to keep an eye on you day and night whilst I tried to find a solution. And if you were to somehow leave or find a way out, I gave them clear orders to kill you.'

'What the fuck, Michael?' I remember shouting.

He barely moved, instead he just sat there looking into his empty wine glass.

I swore at him some more, telling him how wrong he was to tell me this after weeks of recovery, after everything I'd been through. I felt more lost then than I did at the beginning of my journey back in November, disbelieving of everything that had happened between us since.

'There was no other suitable time, John. I've been in turmoil ever since that evening, thinking about whether I did the right thing or not. Watching you grow strong, watching you believe you had survived.' He looked at me and I could see that he was as confused as I was. 'Your mind is in the right place now, I believe that it is, but I was scared to tell you, scared because I thought that you wouldn't be able to control what was inside.'

I stood up and marched towards the front door, opened it and looked out, searching for signs of anything untoward: a person sat in a car twiddling with a revolver, a man lurking in the shadows with a large knife, lights on in the house opposite. There was no-one there and nothing out of the ordinary; all I could feel was the cold air blowing against my skin and filling up my lungs, and as I exhaled I saw wonderful steam clouds hang in the air. Michael had followed me out and stood a couple of meters behind me, watching cautiously. In the moonlight he looked almost completely silver with two dark pools for eyes.

'Don't you see why I'm telling you this,' he said. 'I'm ready to tell you everything – tomorrow everything will begin to make sense.' And with that he stepped past me and left the house without saying another word.

My blood boiled, he was doing it again, leaving me at a time when I needed more. I screamed - as loud as I could - out into the night sky. The sound echoed off the walls and along the peaceful street where I lived, the street I grew up on. I waited, listening for his footsteps to fade away. Then, as the lights at people's windows began to switch on and curtains were pulled back, I disappeared back inside my home to mull over what had been said.

I returned to the conservatory and sat in darkness, looking up at the stars. I could feel my lungs labour as I breathed in deeply and felt my heart pound steadily. It would not sleep, and it seemed it would not die either, even when Michael tried.

Michael had offered me salvation when I reached my lowest point months ago, a time when all hope had faded. Through him he had promised a second chance and I had been excited at being able to fight for such a just cause, and secretly I had enjoyed fighting Ed in my mind before getting the chance to confront him head on. Michael had, up until that night, offered me hope but his revelations left me perplexed. How had I not seen this coming? And why did I not question his motives as odd?

I had a revelation as I thought about his confession. I had lived, despite his best efforts, but he didn't say why, because I don't think he could explain it, but it was slowly starting to make sense to me. I stared at my right hand and held it up in what light there was. I angled my fingers towards my palms and pulled them in like paws, then I pressed them tightly into a fist and then I felt movement and the ridge of my nail cutting into my palm. I did it again and again until I noticed my nails seemed to protrude from the cuticles by about half a centimetre. My hand felt numb, like the nerves had been severed in certain places. I just stared at this strange natural phenomenon looking for logical answers. Science held many, and for nails to grow so fast and to coincide with my other physical symptoms, I considered whether I had developed a rare form of hyperthyroidism. It could well have been aggravated by a toxin in the body, triggered by an infection. It was plausible, but I didn't have the proof. Not yet.

I repeated this step with my left hand until my nails seemed to protrude and my hands looked dehydrated, the way they do when you leave a swimming pool. I noticed myself in the faint reflection of glass – a shadowy blur of darkness. I looked over at the rattan furniture, walked over to it and then slowly scored my nails across the edges, watching as it split outwards like strands of old rope. It felt glorious. And then I thought about the man, the surgeon as I referred to him, who back in Muswell Hill that cut away the flesh from my chest, how he took the same pleasure as he made a deep incision with his nail. I understood now what they meant by the gift: they wanted what was inside me, wrapped around my heart.

I reconsidered Michael's actions, about drowning me. Submerging me in water allowed the conditions for some type of rebirth to take place, like a physical baptism, allowing the false heart, the parasitic one, to take over, to pump life around my body when it seemed fit to do so, when it knew the immune system could not fight back.

I thought about Cha-Cha and what I had done to her, how I had bit hard during my climax and unintentionally took her life (or so I thought). My parting gift, unbeknown to me, was giving her the same new life that I now endured as a curse. Death might have been an easier option.

The brothel could have been nothing more than a breeding ground for them. I thought back to the two men who looked at me as I left. Surely they knew? Perhaps they had anticipated such an attack? Perhaps they had come to clean up? Maybe it wasn't coincidence after all, maybe it was fate. Either way, that place was now dangerous for me and any other man hoping to blow their load.

Then I considered the thousands of immigrants, legal and illegal, arriving in the UK each year and just disappearing. I thought about many of them working in such places, trafficked from one bedroom to another. Fodder, I thought; another piece of meat in the ant food chain, until the debt was paid and the meat became meat, flesh became flesh.

Michael's presence was still felt around the house. There a smell not too dissimilar to mothballs and mints as I cleared away the dishes and retired to bed. I thought about Michael's return the next day and what I would say to him when he finally revealed to me 'the truth'.

ISOLATION

I woke at the normal time, just before sunrise, and began looking on the internet, thinking of a way I could use this medium to share the truth with the world. After breakfast I felt like exercising and did some basic circuits in the garden to see if I was somehow in better shape. I felt energised, that was for sure, but no different to how I used to in terms of strength or stamina. I had lost most of my fat during the weeks spent in a coma, so I felt leaner than before; the weighing scales confirmed this. My balance was slightly better than before, but by no means perfect. You could say I was a little disappointed not to have any extra benefits if I really was what Michael had indicated, but I suppose coming back to life was one benefit - if Michael were telling the truth.

Whilst lifting makeshift weights - earth filled terracotta pots - I accidentally dropped one of them on my foot and howled out in pain. Without thinking I lashed out and punched through it. I didn't think much of it at the time for there had been incidents before where I had hurt myself and hit something in frustration, but this pot was thick and full of earth.

When Michael hadn't arrived by midday I grew suspicious and felt the tension building up inside me. I felt like a jack in the box, being held down by what he said, and I started to believe that he had told me lies to maintain control, or that he had to invent new stories and theories to keep me feeling desperate and weak.

I read sections of books about anthropology that Michael had given me; he had highlighted several pages, mostly about the evolution of man and the differences between cultures across the globe. It didn't offer answers, merely gave me some insight and made me feel like I should have been a bit bolder in my choice of university degree.

By two O'clock I grew more and more agitated. It was already starting to get overcast and I knew it would be dark outside soon.

At three O'clock there was a knock at the door. I answered it with a degree of hesitation, seeing a man I did not recognise through the frosted glass. It was a courier holding a small package in his hands. I eyed him with suspicion, but looking over his shoulder I could see his van and noted that the logo matched his uniform. I looked down at the package held in his hands – it was a cardboard box of about two feet squared and carefully wrapped in layers of packaging tape. My name was clearly written on it. Apart from Michael and my dad, no-one else knew where I was living.

'Who's it from?' I asked.

The man shrugged, asked me to sign for it and then handed it over before leaving. The package didn't feel particularly heavy and there were no clear and identifiable marks on it. I thought about all the videos and tutorials I had watched online about making homemade bombs and other incendiary devices. I put the box aside in the dining room for a while and went to get myself something sharp to undo the tape. I didn't like the feeling one bit.

I wilfully got distracted and made myself a coffee and then sat in the living room, listening to the sound of the grandfather clock from the hallway as I drank it slowly. Eventually I drew enough courage to inspect the package. I gave it a shake. It was definitely full of various items, but I couldn't figure out what. There was no sender and the handwriting was all done in block caps. I wanted to wait for Michael to arrive; I wanted to show him so that he might help me understand what might be inside. As I cut the first strip of tape, I suddenly feared that I might end up unwrapping body parts or something else equally gruesome, or an object goading me about my dark secret. I stopped and decided to eat something, just in case Michael turned up.

Sitting next to the box, I ate my dinner and

found myself reflecting on how I didn't dream much anymore. I put it down to junk sleep: too much time spent using the internet to find key information, or listening to audio files, or watching late night documentaries about conspiracy theories, right up until I went to bed. My mind was restless and always ticking over and my lack of REM sleep meant my brain was a disorganised rack of ideas.

I pushed my plate aside and pulled the box across. My heart was racing. I felt like this box might be one of the most important deliveries of all time, and that somehow my life depended on it. I opened it carefully and saw a handwritten letter on the top. I instantly recognised the handwriting as Michael's and my heart seemed to sink. I already knew what was written inside.

Below is an edited transcript of the letter. I cannot fully explain to you how it left me feeling, but he did answer my questions, and hopefully he will answer some of yours.

John,

If you're reading this, then you are not as reckless as I feared and are still at home contemplating what to do next.

There are many questions you wanted to know the answers to. Well, let me start by answering a few of them in this letter.

You wanted to know what drove me for over 30 years. Bronwyn was her name. She was my fiancée and my first love. I told you that I had someone and that I lost her after my attack; I told you that we agreed to separate, but that was a lie. In truth, I murdered her.

After I was first bitten I found it hard to control my emotions and feelings. I suffered from anxiety and she tried to console me the best way she could, through love and affection, but it was already too late. Something inside of me preyed on her kind-heartedness and I killed her in cold blood like some barbarian. Naturally I panicked, like any adult would, and kept her hidden, preserved the only way I knew how. But I could never forget. Bronwyn was my world.

You'll never understand how hard it is to conceal a lie, John. I can tell you, it only gets harder. Day after day I let the guilt grow inside, rotting my insides away. Day after day I had to walk past the freezer where I kept her body and know that she was in there because of my heinous act.

I understand the pain you are going though and I know that you struggle to understand the new world we live in. I understand how you must feel, having lost your dad and ex-girlfriend, but you did not lose them in this way – you did not have to watch them suffer or see the life crushed out of them. The only thing that stopped me from handing myself in to the police and confessing to the crime was my desire to avenge her. How? You may ask yourself. It was not my fault that I became the monster I am, and I never planned to kill her.

For years I strived for atonement. Every time I killed one of them, and there were many more than I let on, I found out more about their evil manifestation in our glorious city. Focusing my energy and attention on them also helped to control what lies within me. To repeat an old cliché: it doesn't bring her back but it sure as hell helps.

I mentioned that there had been others like you. The truth was they were never like you. I think back to when you first came to my flat that time, and I wish I'd killed you there and then, for your own good. I knew of the dangers you were going to have to face and the painful decisions you would have to make being like me. The path before you is littered with misery; roads often come to dead ends, and there are alleyways that become one way thoroughfares. There can never be any going back. But part of me hoped that you might be able to get close to the source, closer than I have ever been. I watched you develop, flourish into a determined fighter – but deep within I knew that there was something different about you.

When you killed Ed, something occurred within you. You must have felt it – almost like a leash had been removed and a connection between you and them had been severed. You will feel it, of that I am sure.

The revelation came when I nursed your wounds and witnessed your resurrection. I saw what you really are. I said to you that I never got close to the source of evil, but in hindsight I think I did. You are the source of evil – the blueprint, part of the original mystery, and the bastard child of all this pain. This explains why they've taken such an interest in you, remained cautious and not gone in for the kill so quickly like they have with so many others. The group who captured you in Muswell

Hill did so in the hope of taking what you had, fast-tracking themselves to becoming the master race, stepping up in the hierarchy, heading towards the hive. I had followed you that evening, but not with the intention of intervening – I used you as bait to find a way in. But you deserved a chance, John. You deserved an opportunity to make a choice.

I tried to kill you, not because I feared you, but because I feared for every Londoner you may come into contact with. You're a ticking time bomb waiting to go off, but you're also still John - a man.

I beg you, don't let it consume you. Whatever this power is that lurks within, control it. Don't fear it; harness it. Evil can defeat evil. Use your curse to try and undo the misery caused by the ants, and don't be afraid to euthanize those who you think will turn. Control it, my friend; don't let it consume you as it did me. Be disciplined. Find strength in the word and wisdom of gods. Seek out the wisdom of our fathers and our forefathers, the enigmas and the knowledge of civilisations. We live in godless times. You need to be ready.

Be ready. Erebus is coming.

How you do this is up to you. We never talked much about religion, but my moral standing and my creed makes me believe that I can still get redemption for the things I have done. I am a man of faith. Have faith, for even out of Khaos there came light.

I am truly sorry. I am a monster for what I have done to you. I am sorry for leaving you alone like this and for dragging you down this dark path. You think you are ready to fight, and I agree, but I don't have the strength to fight alongside you. Our methods will clash. It is too risky. I must embark on my own journey now.

I have left four keys under your bedside table, no fobs or instructions, just keys. One is for my flat, but don't go there yet. The other is the key to a private lock up in Camden - I've been busy preparing it for you. The two other keys are for you to figure out – your challenge.

It's not much, but I've also left you some money to help you continue the fight, but spend time familiarising yourself with everything else first before you go about your 'hunting'. You'll see what I mean when you get there.

They will probably never let me out from where I am going, so this really is goodbye. I am done with this life.

Your honest friend,
Michael.

Rather than feel angry and ill-tempered, I smiled and took long, steady breaths. In hindsight, I think it was because I largely accepted what Michael had confessed to in his letter, and I genuinely believed that a veil of deceit had been partly lifted. The letter was indeed an unexpected comforter, but too much to take on board in one sitting. I got up and walked out into the garden and read it again.

The grass was still wet from the morning's rain and I could smell the lemon balm; the herb was dedicated to the goddess Diana, which got me thinking about Michael's warning about Erebus, the unknown place where death dwells. The weeds were starting to sprout around the lemon balm and I understood what he meant. Erebus was coming.

When I walked back inside the house I part expected Michael to be there ready to offer more explanation to his revelation. But all that remained was his parting gift: the letter, which I figured was more about absolution for him that a passing gift; the answers lay with the keys and whatever else was in the box.

I went to my bedroom and picked up the keys in my hand, now realising that these weren't just keys, they were symbols that would unlock part of my identity and lead to greater truths that he had promised; two known, two unknown.

I returned back to the living room, keys in hand, and examined the remaining contents of the box. Three of his journals were inside, of which they detailed many things. One was full of diagrams, sketches and architectural drawings, and rubs from various London buildings with written details of access points and passcodes. It seemed there was a whole network located close to Smithfield. But with each page, scribbled in bold, were the words 'Caution'. The remainder of the contents consisted of old maps of London, a fine silk scarf, loyalty cards for coffee shops and ice cream parlours (there were lots), coupons, vouchers and a set of preloaded cash cards with pin numbers scrawled across post its; there was an old telephone directory, some audio tapes, an old 8mm film reel and a wooden box; inside the box were a set of small, beautifully crafted blades. Some were discreet, small enough to be strapped to a wrist, tucked neatly into a wallet or hidden in a shoe, and others looked like small shuriken stars. I had no idea what to do with them.

I wasted no time, however, and packed one of the small blades in my wallet, took a preloaded cash card and one of Michael's journals, before running out of the door.

I tested one of the cash cards in Highgate and found it to work, and it was loaded with a healthy balance. I treated myself to a taxi ride down to Camden.

On arriving, the place was buzzing, and only then did I grasp that it was the weekend. The lockup was located close to the central canal market and, ironically, to where Goths and Emos liked to hang out.

It was a wise location choice, always busy and within striking distance of the West End, and the garage itself was one of several unassuming one-offs located behind the market corridors.

Approaching the lock-up filled me with deep anxiety. I was either going to be mightily astounded with what I found or highly disappointed with another of Michael's red herrings. As I tested the keys, I couldn't help but wonder if he was there watching me from a distance amongst the crowds.

I unclicked the padlock, pulled up the metal garage door and stepped inside. The room was pitch black and smelt of mildew and rat piss, two of my favourite scents. I fumbled around for a light switch, and on finding one I flipped it up and waited for the florescent tubes illuminate; I heard them clink, like a moth was being electrocuted inside and was pinging through the inert gases, looking for a way out. Eventually I had light and it took me a while for my eyes to adjust before I was ready to close the garage door behind me. Then it was just me and Michael's notes.

The room looked like it hadn't been stepped in for years. It was a long, narrow store room with a small rusted iron door at the back. There were rodent droppings across dust sheets and cobwebs layered upon cobwebs, with all manner of insect shells littered about the place. Life had been thriving in the darkness it seemed. I thought about Michael's passionate rhetoric about how wonderful nature was, how adaptive and versatile they were, how man would not be how he was today without the lessons learnt from insects. I kicked an old piece of wood across the floor and watched a thousand woodlice scurry for safety.

It was hardly the high-tech operation I had hoped for, and the pessimist inside of me struggled to perceive anything positive from this great revelation. The money Michael had promised would go some way towards me feeling more in control, but if he had really been preparing this room for me then he must have treaded lightly. Then I thought about the genius of keeping sensitive materials (if there were any) in a decrepit storehouse and how that would ward off any thief. No addict or trained robber would spend their time and effort trying to find money or electronics here. Piles of rotting newspapers were stacked on old sideboards, and old carpet, sheets and gauze were black with mould. There were a couple of pieces of antique furniture, but even they had white mould spores up each and every leg, and any upholstery had been worn down to the springs.

An old wooden park bench had a row of storage boxes placed on them, each one had masking tape across them with a number written in thick black ink. And to the back of the room was a chest, a heavy metal type - possibly late Victorian – which was padlocked. I looked at my two anonymous keys and walked over to it. My feet crunched over some broken glass as I did so and I noted that pieces of mirror, the type consistent with a ladies compact, were scattered across the floor.

I examined the lock and noted that it was clean with no rust. I used one of the keys and I opened the chest to see a whole plethora of old keys layered on the top. I started to laugh, for I genuinely believed that this was Michael's idea of some sick joke, to literally look for a needle in a haystack. I lifted out the tray and placed it on the bench. On closer inspection I could see that each key was colour coded and labelled with its own number and letter. Beneath the tray I saw the same black material that Michael had given me to conceal his sword when he had presented it to me at the cafe. I cautiously pulled it aside to reveal an arsenal of small, razor-sharp ritual daggers (possibly from the far-east) and several other types all neatly laid out. All that was missing was a signed copy of Sun Tzu's Art of War.

Most of the other boxes in the room that I found, which were often carefully hidden beneath old rugs or tucked away in boxes, had locks on. In one open box, however, I noted a pile of journals; one of them looked nearly new. My heart raced slightly. It was like Michael had only just been there.

I stood for a moment and looked for any other clues. In another one of the cupboards lay another blade with hieroglyphics etched across the handle. It was certainly something typical of the Freemasons, given its excellent craftsmanship and symbolic reference G and vertical lines revolving around a circle. Beside the sword was another handwritten letter. I picked it up and saw that it was addressed to me.

John,

You've come this far – now look around you. You might not think that these are the tools of a modern anarchist, but they will bring anarchy. Take the fight to them. Make it your purpose to do so, but understand that a man of great wrath shall suffer punishment: for if thou deliver him, yet thou must do it again.

Every fight I have had with them has been described, every previous hideout of theirs that I discovered has been documented; all the details I know about them have been written down and passed, in confidence, to you.

The unit you are standing in is secure but nature's tears have dampened some of my earlier journals - they have not aged well. These are all originals, I made no copies.

I promised you answers and here you have many, but you will need to look further to find answers of your own, about what you are and who you will become.

Beneath the chest is some more money to help you in your campaign. You will need to remain hidden whenever possible, so I suggest that you rent out a room in central London somewhere, and use cash for everything – never pay on card unless it's pre-loaded! Stay transient. The dust is only just starting to settle, and they will eventually come for you again when they realise that you will not turn. Do not turn. Do not fail. Do not give in.

People have helped me in the past, but they don't know about you yet and they will treat you with hostility should you come across them. Read my notes first. And remember, people change, even those we know and love. People change.

Never give in. Spare good Londoners a similar fate to ours.

Michael

This was my call to adventure, the beginning of my journey. I packed a few of the items from my new hoard and kept the appropriate keys safe. I looked around once more – it would be my base of operations for the coming years.

I would soon learn that there were several more rooms like this dotted around the capital, all with their own particular theme and style.

And so this, reader, is *my* story. You may still have questions, and I may not have given you the answers you were hoping for; I have been there and I know that feeling well. I want to tell you more, and I hope that one day you will see how it all ends.

And Michael, if you are reading this – I am ready.

"Rouse him, and learn the principle of his activity or inactivity. Force him to reveal himself, so as to find out his vulnerable spots."

Sun Tsu, **The Art of War**

ENDNOTE

Any source that I have directly cited is either referenced in the book or highlighted on the London Vampire Website which is as follows:

www.thelondonvampire.co.uk

Here I have transliterated much of my initial research to save you hours of needless investigation.

My fight carries on and I continue to work tirelessly to understand the methods of these monsters. Much of what I uncover will be revealed online.

ABOUT THE AUTHOR

John Michaelson created The London Vampire website in 2009 as a direct response to a personal experience. People were keen to learn more about this intrepid character and, after years of coaxing, John finally agreed to share his version of events.

Michaelson does not classify himself as a vampire or a vampire hunter. John describes himself as a citizen of London striving to challenge the dark forces that pose an unseen yet prevalent threat to everyone who lives in the capital.

Journalists, publicity agents and TV producers alike have all been attracted to John's elusive and cautious persona, which merely adds to the enigma about who he is and where in London John Michaelson carries out his fights against the Ants.

notes

Disclaimer and References:

In light of feedback since first publication in October 2014, John Michaelson would like to stress that he does not condone the carrying of knives or any other vigilante actions across London; neither do Burton Mayers Books or any of its representatives.

If you have been affected by any of the issues in this book, please see the list of charities and organisations below:

www.knifecrimes.org A support website for UK victims of knife crime; full of online resources and links to several charities, useful information and commentary from victims, relatives and experts. Supported by the Home Office.

www.unseenuk.org set up in 2008 as a direct response to the exploitation of vulnerable children and young adults who become enslaved, both in the UK and abroad, and trafficked into gangs, usually for the purposes of prostitution. Unseen raises awareness about the issue and has made positive steps to rehabilitate those whose lives have been ruined through mistreatment by Ants.

www.nationalcrimeagency.gov.uk The NCA (SOCA) responds on a 24/7 basis, targeting the criminals and groups posing the biggest risks to the UK. They build a single comprehensive picture of serious and organised crime affecting the UK, drawing on information and intelligence from a wide range of sources.

www.stopthetraffik.org A global movement of activists around the world who passionately give their time and energy to build resilient communities and prevent human trafficking.